Zoey And The Nice Guy

CARTER ASHBY

DEDICATION

To my husband and children, for their unfailing support.

CONTENTS

CHAPTER ONE

At sixteen, Zoey was considering emancipation from her mother. She already worked thirty hours a week while keeping a perfect grade point average in school. She alone maintained the house, handling her own shopping and cooking. The only reason she could think of to remain a dependent was the wine.

She grabbed a bottle of sweet, red wine from the fridge. Her mom's ex-boyfriend had worked at a local winery and brought them cases of it.

Zoey poured herself a glass. It had been a long day of tests before Thanksgiving break, followed by six hours waiting tables. Now it was ten-thirty and she intended to indulge in some wine and a bar of dark chocolate she'd bought in St. Louis the weekend prior.

She gathered her goodies and sank into the good spot on the couch. Anywhere else on it, she'd get stabbed by a rusty spring and need a tetanus shot. She'd considered buying a new one, but she didn't want to put nice things in her mom's ramshackle, single-wide trailer. No, she would save for her own place and fill it with comfortable furniture and a television that didn't tint the picture green around the edges.

She flipped on Nick At Nite and took a sip of her wine. She grabbed her laptop off the coffee table and opened it to the new social networking website. All of her friends had profiles on it, now, and she figured it was about time she jumped on board. She figured this Facebook thing would be a cool place to just be herself without having to worry about parents or teachers seeing everything.

Her phone rang. "Yeah?" she said, not having checked the caller id.

"Zoey, please get back with me."

"Oh, God," she groaned. Jeremy. She tucked the phone against her shoulder and started filling out her Facebook profile information. "Not interested."

"Please. I didn't mean the things I said. It's just you make me so crazy. But I love that about you. Really."

"I'm not going to be in a relationship where I constantly feel bad about myself. You can't undo what you said. You obviously don't know how to be with a strong, independent woman. We had some fun. Let's just drop it."

"I swear, Zoey, I didn't mean any of it. I just lost my temper."

"I'm done, Jeremy."

"Zoey, please! I think I love you!"

Was he crying? "My God, are you crying?"

"Please, please, give me another chance."

"Ugh. I totally don't go for guys who cry and beg.

2

Grow a pair and move on, buddy." She hung up and started scanning through the list of suggested friends. She found Maya and Addy, the only two people who really meant anything to her.

The phone rang again. "Fuck off, Jeremy," she said, once again not looking at the caller id.

"It's Addy. I see you've broken up with Jeremy."

"You know, actually he broke up with me. Last night we fought and I told him he was a no good sack of shit and he said it was over. But, now, he's been calling me, begging me to get back with him." She sighed. "What a fucking loser."

"Yeah. Okay. Can we come over? Maya needs us."

"You and Maya? Yeah, you know my home is your home. Come on over."

She hung up and closed her laptop. In first grade, Addy had been ganged up on by some mean girls. Zoey had dragged her out of the fight by her pigtails and proceeded to wail on the leader of the bullies. She'd gotten a meeting with the principal out of the deal, but she'd also gotten a best friend.

Maya's entrance into her small, but tight, circle had been a little less dramatic. She'd been a mouse of a thing. Always sitting at the end of the lunch table alone, hunkered over her weird, homemade lunches, and casting fearful glances around her. Zoey had been so annoyed by her timidity that she'd decided she was either going to have to beat Maya up or make friends with her. A toss of the coin decided it, and they'd been best friends since.

Zoey returned to the kitchen for two more wine glasses. She checked the freezer to assess the Ben & Jerry's situation. *Chocolate Therapy for Maya. Cherry Garcia for Addy. And Coffee Coffee BuzzBuzzBuzz for me.* With a satisfied nod, she moved back to her bedroom to put on fresh sheets. Whenever her mom was off on a boyfriend binge, Zoey slept in the big room. She wanted to have the little room ready in case Maya needed a place to crash. Nine times out of ten, she came here to escape her abusive father.

A knock on the door had her hurrying to the living room, bracing herself to see Maya. Zoey exhaled in relief. No bruises or red marks. Just tears. Maya had the face of an angel; wide, innocent green eyes and skin with a perfect, bronzed glow on her cheekbones. Her light brown hair curled in halo-like wisps around her face.

She was leaning on Addy, who wore her usual, care-free jeans and t-shirt; relaxed, maybe even slovenly to the casual observer, except that the jeans were Gucci and the shirt was Ralph Lauren. Her black hair rolled back in a loose bun, her glasses sliding off her nose. They shuffled past Zoey. Addy deposited Maya in the good spot on the couch while Zoey locked up and poured two more glasses of wine. She topped hers off and handed the glasses to her friends.

Addy took the glass and drank, downing half of it.

"Uh, what's up, ladies?" Zoey asked.

Maya burst into tears. She was still in her cheerleading uniform from that night's football game. Zoey knelt on the floor at her feet.

"She's pregnant," Addy said.

Zoey's world skidded to a stop. For a moment there was only silence, barely disturbed by Maya's quiet sobs. This couldn't happen to her friend. This happened to skanks and drug addicts. Not to Maya, who'd never mistreated anyone nor stepped out of line in her life. The only thing Zoey could think to do was reach up and take the wine glass out of Maya's hand. She sat it on the end table.

"Damon?" Zoey asked, looking up at Addy, who was pacing and drinking.

"Who else?"

"Fuck." And then the inevitable rage came. Zoey either loved or hated. There was no in between. She loved Maya and Addy with an unwavering loyalty she'd never felt for anyone else. Damon hadn't even been on her radar, except for the times that his plans took Maya away from her. Now he had a big, red target painted on his face, and hell was about to rain down on him in the form of a nuclear Zoey.

"That motherfucker!" Zoey leapt to her feet and started pacing with Addy. "He's dead. He's beyond fucking dead!"

Maya sobbed harder. Addy sat next to her on the sofa and immediately hopped back up. "Ouch. Goddammit, Zoey, get a new couch!" She knelt on one knee at Maya's side and took her hands.

"First I'm gonna tie him up," Zoey growled. "Then I'm gonna chop off his balls with a dull knife and feed them to his dog while he watches—"

"Zoey! Not helping," Addy said.

Zoey snapped out of her gruesome fantasy. "Does the dipshit know?"

Maya shook her head. "I don't know how I can tell him. This is gonna ruin his life. He's got dreams of joining

5

the military and seeing the world."

"Fucker never had a dream in his life. Don't tell him, Maya. We'll take care of you. Won't we, Addy?"

Addy gave her another warning look. "I think it's important that we all calm down and deal with the here and now. Maya, honey, what can we do for you?"

Maya shook her head, her angelic face twisted in pain.

"*She's All That* and Chocolate Therapy?" Zoey offered.

Maya sniffed like a sick kid and nodded. Zoey loaded the guilty-pleasure movie in her DVD player and then went to the freezer for the ice cream.

Once they got her settled, Addy and Zoey convened in the kitchen for a quiet conference. "I'm serious," Zoey said in a hushed voice. "I'll take care of her here. I'll work two jobs if I have to. I don't want her marrying him."

Addy's lips pursed. "She loves him."

"She'll get over it. He'll hurt her. I mean physically."

"You don't know that."

"He left finger marks on her arm that time, don't you remember?"

Addy winced and blew out a breath. "Will your mom freak?"

"Please, she won't even notice. Unlike your parents." Addy's parents monitored her every activity. And they couldn't stand Maya, which put them on Zoey's hate-list. Anyone who disliked someone as pure and good as Maya didn't deserve her affections.

"We should definitely encourage her to stay with you, then. Her old man's gonna throw a fit. And I agree that Damon isn't…dependable."

"Stable, you mean. He's unstable. You have to admit

he fits the profile of a future wife-beater."

Addy drained the last of her wine and then went to the freezer for ice cream. "Behavior-wise, yes. But background? It just doesn't make sense. His parents are upstanding citizens. They make plenty of money and are the least temperamental people I know. And Kellen—well, you know Kellen. He walks little old ladies across the street. I mean—how can Damon be bad when he comes from that kind of family?"

"Kellen's only eighteen. Maybe he just hasn't grown into his mean streak yet."

Addy shook her head.

Zoey didn't argue. She was right. There was no making sense of Damon's character. But it didn't matter. Maya shouldn't be with him. She lowered her voice to a whisper. "What about an abortion?"

Addy licked the back of her ice cream spoon and shook her head. "Absolute last resort. If that. And we can help her together, if all else fails. We should be able to provide her enough support that she doesn't have to do something like that if she doesn't want to."

Zoey exhaled in relief. She wasn't prepared to go that direction and secretly hoped Maya wasn't either. "Okay, so we murder Damon and dump him in the Missouri River, then we get Maya settled in here. After that, I guess we need to check out her insurance situation. She's still a minor, so if her dad doesn't have anything, he can at least get her on state aid."

Addy gawked. "I never even thought of that."

"That's because you live with competent parental units. Be grateful."

Addy nodded in adamant agreement.

They moved back into the living room to huddle around Maya. Later that night, after she'd calmed, they discussed her options. She called Damon and broke the news to him over the phone. He didn't yell or anything and after she hung up, her eyes closed in relief.

The next day he showed up with a cheap ring he'd bought at the Dollar Store. He got on one knee in front of Maya and proposed. Zoey watched in horror as Maya tearfully accepted. There was nothing to be done. Maya loved him and refused to hear reason.

The next Monday at school, Kellen Bradley came up to Zoey, grinning like a damn fool. "How crazy is it?" he said. "I'm gonna be an uncle."

Zoey cocked her fist and punched him in the face. She got in-school suspension and was more than willing to pay the price.

CHAPTER TWO

8 years later

"I'm going to kill him. He's dead. He's so fucking dead!" At six on a Saturday morning, Zoey paced the living room of Maya's two-bedroom shack in the shitty part of town. In the background, *The Island of Misfit Toys* played, tinny from the bad speakers of a very old television. Zoey glared at the Claymation Rudolph. She picked up the remote and turned it off.

Addy shot her a frustrated look. Maya was in her bedroom packing her things. Maya's kids were in their room, doing the same. "Pull yourself together. This isn't what she needs."

Zoey choked down as much of her rage as she could, but her vision blurred with tears. "As soon as I saw her face…." She couldn't finish the sentence. The words vanished into a place of blind pain and fury.

"I know. But this is it. It's over. And, right now, you and I need to—"

A sharp scream came from the back. Addy hurried away. "I told you not to try and lift that bag yourself," she said as she disappeared down the hall.

Zoey stared after her, lost in her own pain. Eight years of watching a woman she considered a sister trapped in an abusive relationship…and now it was finally over. An ending and a very rough beginning.

She felt a tug at the hem of her sweater. She looked down to see five-year-old Sophie, who shared her mother's wide, green eyes, staring up at her. Zoey smiled and stroked her hair.

"Will Santa be able to find us?" the little girl asked.

"Absolutely. I'm sending him a letter to let him know where you are. It won't be a problem at all."

Sophie smiled softly and then ran back to her bedroom.

There was a knock at the door. Zoey hoped to God it was Damon because she had her legally licensed gun in a holster at her waist and if he so much as laid a hand on her, she was all ready to defend herself with lethal force.

But it wasn't Damon. Instead, she was greeted with the ingenuous smile of Damon's baby brother. Kellen could not be more different from Damon. He was perpetually kind and generous. Just an all-around sweetheart.

Zoey found him disgusting.

He might have the most perfectly sculpted shoulders you ever saw and a smile that could weaken the knees of even the most stalwart man-eater; he might have gorgeous, sun-kissed hair and eyes you could swim in; and maybe his voice resonated in a deep baritone that vibrated down to your toes—but he was related to the wrong guy; an unforgivable sin, in Zoey's mind.

"Hi, Zoey," he said cheerfully, as though she wasn't scowling at him. "What are you doing here?"

She opened her mouth to tell him to fuck off, but the kids came barreling in. "Uncle Kellen!" they squealed, and jumped into his arms. He swung Sophie onto his hip and slung his arm around Matthew. He kicked the door closed behind him.

After Damon and Maya had gotten engaged, Kellen had started hanging around their little group. She'd already hated him for his relationship to Damon. But when he started worming his way into everyone's affections, her hate took a solid hold, becoming a permanent thing.

"Get out of here, Kellen," she said. "She's leaving him, and she's not coming back."

His smile disappeared altogether and the man actually looked perplexed. He sat Sophie on her feet.

"I know they had some problems. Damon crashed at my house and wouldn't stop crying about it. But he loves her. And she loves him. I really think we should stay out of their business."

"God, you're just as bad as he is! Go fuck yourself, Kellen!"

His eyebrows shot up, and he quickly covered the kids' ears, pressing their little heads to his hips. "Look, I don't know what I did to piss you off this time, but this is Maya and Damon's business, not yours. So let's just get out of their way and let them work this out."

"How can you say that? You probably think he was justified in what he did, don't you?"

He shook his head and rolled his eyes. "The fact is, you've only got one side of the story and your own bias. You don't know what he's going through."

She fisted her hands as heat rushed to her cheeks. Was the son-of-a-bitch actually suggesting there was a good reason for Damon's beating his wife nearly to death?

Kellen had the good sense to look nervous. But, he was hiding behind children, so she couldn't hurt him. Yet.

Just then the back bedroom door opened and Maya came out. Addison was rolling her suitcase with one hand and supporting Maya around her back with the other. Maya's left eye was swelled shut and there was bruising along her right cheekbone. Her lips were cut and swollen and her nose broken. Addison had apparently cleaned the blood away.

Kellen's expression changed. His eyes went wide, his mouth hung open, all the color completely drained from his face. And then he closed his mouth and turned a little green. "My God," he whispered.

He hadn't known. He moved past Zoey and scooped Maya into his arms. Maya didn't object, which was annoying, since she'd argued with Zoey and Addy all morning about not needing any help. "I'm happy to take her to the hospital," Kellen said. "If you guys can take care of the kids."

"She won't let us take her to the hospital," Zoey said.

"She's going to the hospital. Aren't you, Sis?"

Maya just buried her face in his chest and sobbed. Zoey couldn't believe it. She decided to hate Kellen just a little more, even though it was awfully nice the way he was taking care of Maya.

"Thank you," Addy said. "She wouldn't listen to us. We'll take the kids over to Zoey's."

He nodded and moved toward the front door, cradling Maya like and infant. Zoey hurried to open it for him.

"Come on," Addy said in her husky, ever-calm voice, "let's get the kids out of here." She turned to them and stroked the backs of their heads. "Aunt Zoey's been DVRing cartoons all morning. Let's go see what there is to watch." She helped them into their coats and boots while Zoey loaded their bags into her car.

They convoyed to Zoey's house with Addy following in the Mercedes that her parents had bought her on her birthday. It always looked so out of place, parked in Zoey's driveway.

Zoey's house wasn't much, but it was hers. She didn't resent Addy her rich parents, but she took pride in her own hard work and self-reliance. She'd graduated a year early and had taken as many tests for college credits as she could. In the end, college only took her two years, after which she'd gotten her CPA. Because she'd already established a relationship with an accounting firm doing internships, there was a job waiting for her. She'd graduated debt free thanks to scholarships and two part-time jobs. After two years as a junior accountant at Haverty Morris Accounting Firm, she'd saved up enough for a down payment and applied for a home loan.

Three bedrooms and two bathrooms with another bathroom in the basement. She'd had the house remodeled and updated, with bamboo floors all the way throughout, a new roof, and new appliances. And the furniture…she'd gone all out for good furniture.

Each bedroom was fully furnished, though she didn't have any family to speak of. She had her friends, though, and she always wanted them to have a comfortable place to stay. In her basement was some gym equipment—an elliptical and some free weights. On the other side was a wrap-around couch facing a huge TV with two game consoles.

The house was located in an older neighborhood with plenty of space between neighbors. In the summer, the trees provided nice privacy barriers. But being December, the landscape stood stark and naked.

Either way, it was her little slice.

They pulled into the driveway and Zoey parked in her garage. She had the kids with her in the back seat. She helped them out of the car and into her house. They hovered in the laundry room, which separated the garage from the kitchen and dining area. Sophie hugged her teddy bear to her chest, and Matthew hugged Sophie to his side.

"Come on in," Zoey said. "Make yourselves at home."

It was a silly thing to say. They were children. And they'd just had their home ripped apart.

Addy came in the front door. She was only a little better with children than Zoey. "Hey, guys," she said, "come on in the living room. Aunt Zoey's got Pop Tarts, and we'll get you hooked up with some cartoons."

"Do you have *Frozen*?" Sophie asked, as Matthew led her to one of the sofas.

"Oh, my God, I do have *Frozen*!" Zoey said, hurrying to her DVD collection. "I love this movie." She set it up and then went to the kitchen for Pop Tarts. After she'd toasted them so they were warm and gooey in the middle, she poured two glasses of milk and took it all into the living room on a tray. She sat the tray on the coffee table, and the kids knelt before it, never taking their eyes off the TV screen.

She and Addy grabbed coffee and then slumped at the dining table. "I'm glad Kellen came by," Addy said. "She really needed to go to the hospital."

"I think she would have once we'd gotten her kids settled."

"It's good she trusts him. Maybe he'll be an asset."

"I doubt it. He's completely dim. Soon as he talks to Damon, he'll be back to siding with him."

Addy huffed and rolled her eyes. "You've had it out for him forever. What's the deal?"

"He's a douche. I don't see why everyone doesn't hate him."

"He is the farthest thing from a douche. He's the nicest guy in town."

Zoey shrugged and sipped her coffee.

Addy sighed. "Those poor kids."

"It's a rough road, but they'll be better for it. This was a long time coming, but I'm proud of her for finally taking this step."

She watched as the kids, covered in crumbs from their Pop Tarts, huddled together on the couch watching the movie.

CHAPTER THREE

"You'll have to wait outside, Sir."

The nurse looked at him like he was the one who'd nearly beaten the life out of Maya. But he was too devastated to be offended. Maya gave him a brave nod. He squeezed her hand and left the exam room. There was a small waiting room just down the hall and around the corner. He sat in an empty chair and pressed his face into his hands.

The world was a different place to him. In the moment he saw Maya and realized that it was his brother's hands that had done this to her, everything had changed. He felt like there was no ground under his feet and he was struggling to find a place to stand before he floated away.

God it was brutal. She'd been brutalized. Kellen couldn't even imagine being anything but gentle with something as delicate as a woman. How could his brother do this?

He jumped when his phone buzzed in his pocket. He

pulled it out and saw Damon's name on the screen. "Shit," he muttered. He just stared until the ringing stopped. He couldn't talk to him. Not yet.

A moment later, he saw a voicemail message pop up. He listened. "Hey, man," Damon said, sounding hungover, "thought you were just going to pick up my clothes. I gotta get to work. Where you at?"

And just like that, Kellen found his place to stand.

He was six and begging his twelve-year-old brother to let him have a turn at bat. "Come on, Damon, you promised!"

"Shut up, Kellen. Christ."

Kellen kicked the dirt back behind home plate, behind the catcher. Damon was at bat. He swung once, twice…out.

"You're out, Damon!" one of the kids shouted.

"You think I don't know that, dipshit!" Then he rounded on Kellen. "You just won't shut up, will you!"

Kellen shrugged. "Not my fault you can't hit."

"You little shithead!" Damon shoved Kellen. Kellen's back hit the fence behind him, but he rebounded forward and shoved his brother back. Damon smacked him upside the head. Kellen charged him and was immediately thrown to the ground.

Damon landed punch after punch until his friends pulled him off. Kellen crawled to the fence. He collapsed on his belly, rallied, and reached one hand above his head, latching onto the chain-link.

"Hey!" Damon shouted.

Kellen looked back, saw that he was coming toward him with a bat in his hand, but couldn't figure out how to react.

"Next time I tell you to shut up, you shut up." And then Damon brought the bat down on Kellen's outstretched arm.

His parents had brought him to this very hospital. The bat had fractured his arm. His parents had grounded

Damon for a month and made him do the chores Kellen couldn't while his arm was in a cast. But in the end, they'd chalked it up to boys-will-be-boys.

There had been other incidents, though none so severe. And now, sitting here waiting for Maya to be examined, listening to his brother's cavalier voicemail, Kellen's eyes were finally opened.

He called Damon, who picked up on the first ring. "Where am I at?" Kellen repeated the question. "I'm at the hospital with your wife."

There was a moment of silence. And then just as calm as could be, Damon said, "You tell her to keep her fucking mouth shut, you hear?"

Kellen would have punched him if he'd been standing there. "How do you do this to a woman, let alone a woman you love? How?"

"You don't know the shit I put up with. You don't know what I'm going through, so don't you fucking judge me."

Kellen closed his eyes and wondered how he could have been so blind. "You came to my house last night, crying. You had just beaten your wife in a house where your children were sleeping and you came to me and I let you stay there."

"What's your problem, Kell?"

"My problem is that I'm beginning to see my role in what's happened to my sister-in-law. Get out of my house, Damon."

"You don't even wanna hear my side of the story? I'm your brother, for fuck's sake."

"I just can't be near you right now. I'll hear you out

when I calm down."

Damon laughed, and Kellen understood why, even as he hung up. Kellen's version of losing his temper involved frowning. That was about it. He hardly ever raised his voice, and he'd never, that he could recall, thrown anything or stomped or slammed doors. When it came to emotions, he was very much an internal person. He didn't like to show when he was hurt or angry or sad or happy…or anything. He just preferred to stay mellow.

The nurse came out of the exam room. "You can go on in, Mr. Bradley."

"Thank you," he said with a polite smile as he walked past her.

Maya was still in the hospital gown, lying down on the exam table with a blanket over her legs. He went to her and put his hand over hers resting on her stomach. He thought she might be smiling, but under the swelling and bruising, he couldn't tell.

"I'm divorcing him," she said.

Kellen nodded.

"They're coming back in to take a bunch of pictures to document this, so that I can get protection. If you need to be with your brother—"

"I need to be with you."

She was quiet for a moment. "Thank you. I could be here a while. They've got some X-rays to take."

"I'm here as long as you need me."

He saw two tears ease out of the corners of her eyes. When she spoke, her voice was high-pitched and weak. "I should have left so long ago."

"You're leaving now, and that's all that matters." How

long had this gone on? How many times had he hurt her?

"My poor babies—"

"Will be better off, now. They really will. And, someday, they'll thank you for getting them to safety and loving them enough to be so brave. You're doing the right thing, Maya. I can't tell you how sorry I am that I never saw any of this before."

The nurse came in with a camera. Kellen waited in the waiting room again. Sometime around lunch, Addy called for an update. Maya had finished having her X-rays taken by then and was waiting on the results.

He brought Maya some lunch from the cafeteria, and shortly after that, the doctor came in. She had a broken rib and a lot of bruising. There was nothing to do but give her pain medication.

Kellen drove her to Zoey's house and walked her inside. Dread weighed heavily upon him as he entered the lair. Perhaps lair was the wrong word. It looked like a perfectly normal house. But maybe there was a dungeon in the basement. Or a secret gate leading to hell.

He eased Maya into a recliner and then took a moment to examine his surroundings. He'd never been in here. Never been invited. If that fact hurt his feelings a little bit, he didn't see the need to acknowledge it. Sure, there'd been a time when he'd hoped to catch Zoey's eye, but then she'd broken his nose and made his football game the next night pure hell, so he figured she wasn't interested. Her actions hadn't lessened his attraction to her, but they had definitely warned him away.

Zoey and Addy came down the hall and into the living room. They hurried to Maya's sides and took over where Kellen had left off, making her comfortable, asking her questions, offering her food and drink.

Kellen could hear his niece and nephew laughing somewhere in the back of the house. Since Zoey's attentions were on Maya, he snuck down the hall and peered into one of the bedrooms. The kids were jumping up and down on the bed, giggling and squealing.

The first to see him, Sophie shouted, "Uncle Kellen!" She climbed off the bed and hugged him, as though she hadn't just seen him that morning. His favorite thing about being an uncle was that no matter how many times he visited, the kids still acted like he was Santa Claus. Matthew was next off the bed, hugging him.

"Wanna jump with us?" he asked.

"Does Aunt Zoey mind you jumping on the bed?"

"She hasn't come back to stop us, yet."

Kellen laughed. "You two go on. I'll watch and make sure you don't injure yourselves."

He looked around the room and wondered how long the kids would be staying here. It was a nicely furnished room, with matching floral curtains and bedspread. It just didn't seem very inviting to children. "Hey, Matthew," he said.

"Yeah?" Matthew stopped jumping to listen.

"You help your sister and make a list of things you want from your rooms—just the really important stuff, okay? And I'll go get it for you."

"Mom said to just pack what we needed."

"Oh, I know. But now that you all are sa—settled, I

can go get some other stuff. Kind of looks like Aunt Zoey doesn't have any toys for you to play with." He'd started to say now that they were safe, but stopped himself. He wanted to make this situation feel like a fun adventure rather than a flight from danger.

Matthew hopped off the bed and led his sister to the dining room. They found a piece of paper and a pen and went to work on a list. Kellen turned back to the living room and came face to face with Zoey, queen of all that was unholy and violent.

"You can go now," she said.

He hadn't known how to mentally prepare for this moment, so he decided just to talk to her like a sane person. "I know. I'm going to the house to get the kids a few things." He looked past Zoey to where Maya was sitting in the living room. "Do you need anything, Sis?" he asked.

"I don't think so," she said weakly. Addy was sitting next to her, murmuring something.

"I mean go and don't come back," Zoey said. "I can get the kids anything they need from their house."

Kellen shook his head. "I don't want you going over there. Damon could be there, and I don't want you getting hurt."

She snorted and lifted up her shirt just over her lower abs. There was a pistol tucked in a holster in the waist of her jeans.

Holy shit, she had a gun. Kellen jumped back. "Jesus, Zoey!"

"I've got my concealed carry license. I'm always packing now. I think I can handle Damon."

He bit his tongue and glanced back at Matthew and Sophie. "Where do you store that thing?"

"In my nightstand."

"Locked?"

She narrowed her eyes at him. "How would I get to it if there was an intruder if I had it locked up?"

"You've got kids here, now, Zoey. You can't just leave it loose, where they can get to it."

"I guess Maya and I will work out what to do. I want you to leave my house."

He purposely ignored her meaning again. "Yeah, I'll be back in a little while with their things."

"And I told you I'd get them myself!"

"No, Zoey," he said calmly.

"I can handle your worthless brother."

"No, Zoey."

"And I don't need you anywhere around me, my friend, or her kids."

"Enough, Zoey!" he shouted. The house went silent and shocked eyes turned his way. He really hadn't shouted that loudly it was just that no one was used to hearing him…put his foot down.

Hell, he was in shock, himself. Kellen stared at her with his eyes wide. She stared back, her eyes equally wide. There was something strange in her expression, too. Something that definitely wasn't hate. He cleared his throat. In a cool and collected voice, he said, "I'm going to get the kids' things. I'll see you in a little while."

This time she didn't argue with him. She did bite her lip and arch her brow at him as she stepped aside.

Matthew ran over and handed him the list. Kellen

took it and walked past Zoey, glancing back at her. He was slightly afraid of her now that he knew she had a gun, and she was looking at him so strangely. But then, he'd never yelled at her. Maybe this was rage. Maybe she was plotting murder.

He was relieved when he climbed into his truck and headed to Damon and Maya's house.

.

CHAPTER FOUR

Zoey dabbed a little drool off the corner of her mouth with the sleeve of her sweater. "Wow. Kellen being assertive is hot." Suddenly he'd seemed bigger. Stronger. More alpha. It was as though she'd seen a blurry version of him all her life and now, suddenly, he was clear. She wondered what would happen if she pushed him even further.

Addy gaped, half shocked, half disgusted. "What is your problem?"

Zoey plopped down in one of her recliners. "He yelled at me."

"And that does it for you?"

"Not usually. Just with him, I guess. He's always so fucking patient."

Addy glanced toward the dining room, where the children were drawing pictures.

"What?" Zoey asked.

"Language."

"Oh, shit, I'm sorry, Maya. I curse like a sailor."

Maya smiled. "I know," she said softly. "Don't worry about it. The kids are used to cursing."

Zoey put her hand on her stomach at the mild wave of nausea that passed. She'd just been compared to Damon. She drew herself up and determined to make more of an effort to keep a civilized tongue.

"You know, Kellen's always liked you," Maya said.

"Bullsh—I mean, bullcrap. He's just too nice-guy to say anything mean about anyone."

"That's not true. He's very honest, even if he is nice. He likes you. He's just confused about why you don't like him."

Zoey smiled at the thought. "Good. Too many women fawn all over him. He needs someone like me hating him irrationally to keep his ego from getting too inflated."

"So you dislike him on principle?" Maya asked.

"Pretty much."

Maya tried to grin, but the attempt was pitiful. Her voice was so weak. She was frail. Too thin, too broken. Not at all the woman she should be. Zoey bit back a pang of grief. "It's not his fault," she said. "It's just hard to like anything related to Damon."

Addy stroked Maya's hair. The kids talked and giggled in the background. Zoey couldn't help thinking how different this was from when they used to gather around Maya after her father had hurt her. Back then, they'd banded together, closer than sisters. Now, with Addy dividing her time between here and her graduate program in St. Louis, and Maya busy with family, they'd lost some of that tightness.

Zoey hated it. She wanted to push everything out of their lives that was keeping them apart. She wanted to go back to the way things were before Maya had gotten pregnant.

Zoey sensed movement and glanced out the window to see Kellen's truck pulling in her driveway. He usually rode a motorcycle, but she supposed it was too cold.

She stood to meet him at the door, thinking she'd take what he'd brought and send him on his way. But he had two, big duffel bags slung over his shoulders and a box in his arms. He smiled at her like he was happy to see her.

She frowned and stepped out of his way, deciding to make him carry everything himself. He delivered the kids' stuff to their room just as cheerful as Santa Claus and helped them unpack and even played with some of their race cars for a while. Zoey found herself leaning in the doorway, mesmerized.

"Wanna play?" Kellen asked.

"Not with you," she said.

His smile faltered briefly before he turned his attention back to the kids. Zoey returned to the living room, shaking her head and wondering who he thought he was.

"Who does he think he is?" she asked, plopping into her chair. She immediately jumped back up and headed to the kitchen for a glass of wine. "Y'all want some of this?"

"Yes, please," Addy said.

"Not supposed to mix it with my pain meds," Maya lamented, so Zoey poured her some juice in a wine glass.

"So what's your problem with him now?" Addy asked as Zoey sat back down.

"My problem is he's such a fake. I'm sorry, but nobody's that nice. I just feel like I'm being lied to whenever I'm face-to-face with him."

"You'd certainly never bother to spare his feelings, would you?" Addy asked the obvious question with a weird smirk on her face.

"Hell, no. I'll tell him straight up what I think of him."

From behind her, Kellen cleared his throat. He was leaning on the wall at the corner of the hallway and the living room. He didn't even look at Zoey, not that she would have cared if he did. She wanted him to know that she hated him. Even if her face was a little red at being caught talking about him.

"Maya, I gotta head home. Is there anything you need?"

"No, thank you, baby," she said, sounding completely drunk.

Kellen grinned. "What have they got you on?"

"Some really good stuff. You have a good night, now."

"I will. Got a date with Celeste. You liked her, right?"

"She's a doll," Maya said. "Your best pick yet."

He grinned and kissed her on top of her head. Then he headed to the door and glanced back. "Zoey, can I talk to you for a sec?"

Zoey considered telling him to fuck off, but then she remembered her resolution to clean up her language. She stood and followed him outside, wondering if he would yell at her again.

He headed down her porch steps, across her lawn, and stopped at his truck. She stopped a few steps behind him, hugging herself to keep warm.

Kellen turned to face her. His hands were in his pockets and he was frowning thoughtfully at the ground. "I guess you got a right to hate me. I can't change that and wouldn't even begin to know how. But you got my family in there. You're going to have to let me be a part of this." He looked up then, his eyes meeting hers.

"Oh, I am?" she challenged. "I'm going to *have* to let you?"

He nodded. "Yeah."

Yeah, well, she guessed he had a point, disappointed as she was to acknowledge it.

"Would it make you feel better to just yell at me or something?" he asked. "You've never given me a point-by-point breakdown of what I did to piss you off. I'm happy to stand here and take it if we could just be done with it."

God, he made her sick. She literally felt like she was gonna puke. She shook her head in disgust. "It's things like that, Kellen. What is that? What the fuck is the matter with you?"

He shrugged, nonplussed. "I'm just trying to make this easier for both of us."

"By inviting me to tear you down? Jesus, it's like early Christmas. I think I'll take you up on it. Where start...okay, I hate your brother and you're related to him, so that makes you suspect. I hate the way you dress."

He looked down at his leather jacket, torn jeans, and boots.

"I hate how you make your hair stick up like that; you're a grown man for God's sake! I wish you'd just act like a normal person once in a while. You're so nice it makes me wanna vomit, and I cannot stand the way you call Maya 'Sis.' She's not your sister. We never wanted you in our little group, but you always came around anyway, like you just had no fucking clue we couldn't stand you."

She skidded to a stop, fully aware that she should have stopped a full sentence ago. His expression was controlled and careful, but it was as close to angry as she'd ever seen him.

The muscles in his jaw twitched, but his voice was just as calm as ever. "I'm sorry you feel that way. I'm sorry I've intruded. Do you feel better getting that off your chest?"

She didn't. "Yeah," she lied defiantly.

"Good. Because now we're going to act like adults—"

"Don't you dare talk down to me like that!"

He held up his hands in surrender. "Okay. I'm sorry."

She wanted to laugh at what a coward he was. Hell, she was grinning just out of sheer awe. Why would he never fight back?

"The thing is, Zoey, like I said, that's my family in there. She *is* my sister. Has been for years. And I love my niece and nephew more than you seem to understand. So…find some way to come to terms with that, okay?"

"You can't come over here anytime you damn well please. It's my house, and I don't want you here."

His fists actually clenched before he forced them to relax.

She sighed. "I guess if you call first or wait until I'm gone—"

"God, Zoey, you're such a bitch!"

There it was. He closed his eyes and took some calming breaths.

"No, don't stop," she said. "What else you got for me?"

He opened his eyes, and, for the first time ever, there was fire in them. He stepped toward her and pointed at her. "Here's how it's going to be. I'm going to visit my sister and her kids whenever. The fuck. I want. And you're going to keep your goddamn mouth shut about how much you hate me, especially around those kids. You've got no right badmouthing me where they can hear. You understand all that?"

She pressed her lips together to keep from grinning. "Yeah, I understand."

He stepped back, the fire in his eyes replaced by stunned confusion. He blew out a breath and rubbed the back of his neck. "I'm sorry to have to talk to you like that, but you've left me no choice."

She did laugh, then. She couldn't help herself. "What's next, Kellen? Are you gonna spank me and send me to bed?"

He actually blushed.

She stopped laughing and arched her brow. "Is that what you want, Kellen? To spank me?" She was possessed of the desire to flirt. Like a warrior who'd finally met her match on the field of battle, she found a kinship with her enemy, and, in her case, a sudden and exciting attraction.

Kellen, however, paled. "I'd never hit a woman."

It was ice water to her spirit. She felt awful for forgetting Maya's situation like that. She straightened her posture and expression. "I'm sorry. I was just teasing you. It was completely inappropriate. I have a problem with my brain-to-mouth filter."

"I've noticed."

She bit back a smile. "I prefer you honest, just so you know."

"I'm not overly concerned with what you prefer right now, Zoey."

She closed her eyes. "Mmm. Just like that." She grinned and winked at him.

At last he relaxed, smiling, blushing, and looking down at his feet. "I'm going home. Just...stay away from the house and from Damon, okay? I'd hate it if you got—"

"Hurt?" She lifted the hem of her shirt, again, flashing her little Ruger.

"Arrested," he finished.

"Psh. Please, I've got a license."

"To carry, not to kill. Be careful, okay?"

She nodded. "I will. But tell your brother," She drew her gun and held it in a grip pointed down in front of her and, in her best Dirty Harry voice said, "'when an adult male is chasing a female with intent to commit rape, I shoot the bastard. That's my policy.'"

"Jesus, Zoey. You're quoting Clint Eastwood now?"

"'Do ya feel lucky? Punk?'"

"You're certifiably insane," he laughed.

She tucked her pistol back in its holster. "I guess that's why Elliot at the gun store wouldn't sell me a .44 Magnum."

"We can all thank God for that. So, I'm thinking it's weird that you've not only seen, but can quote, Dirty Harry."

"They play old movies on television. I've watched everything Clint Eastwood is in. I have this weird mix of feelings. Sometimes I wish he was my father. Sometimes I wish I could marry him. And sometimes I just wish I could be as badass as his characters." She shrugged and holstered her gun.

Zoey looked up and made eye contact. Suddenly there was a long, uncomfortable silence. At last he cocked his head, his smile still in place, but his eyes narrowing a little. "Did we just have a friendly interchange?"

She stiffened. My God, he was right. They'd been friendly with each other. Eww. "No," she said defensively. "Get off my property, Kellen."

He ducked down and looked in her eyes. "You just showed me your soft side, Zoey. I'm not afraid of you anymore." And then the bastard tapped her on the nose, turned, and left.

She stormed inside, and Addy immediately asked, "What did he do this time?"

"Nothing," Zoey said. "I just don't like him."

CHAPTER FIVE

"Is the lamb good?" he asked.

Celeste was quietly nibbling on her dinner across the table from him. He'd wanted to take her some place nice—some place where they wouldn't run into anyone they knew, so he'd driven her into the city to an Italian restaurant on The Hill.

She smiled sweetly. "It's very good."

Everything about her was sweet. She was petite and soft around the edges. She always blushed a little when she smiled, and she smiled a lot. Best of all, she said nice things to him. She didn't curse at him or hate him for no reason at all. "What do you wanna do after this?" he asked, gazing at her. He'd forgotten all about his own dinner.

She shrugged. "I don't know. I haven't been to the city since I was a little girl. What is there?"

"Museums, theaters…hotels."

She reddened and ducked her head so low he couldn't see her expression. He suspected she was grinning and trying to think of something clever to say, until he saw her shoulders shaking. Her hands went to her face and a sob escaped her lips.

Kellen hurried to offer comfort, but when he touched her, she flinched away. "I'm so sorry," he said. "I shouldn't have come on to you like that. I didn't mean it. This is only our sixth date, so—"

"It's just I haven't been with anyone since Chris," she sobbed loudly. Too loudly. Who knew such a little person could cry so hard. He glanced around the room and offered a reassuring smile to the gawkers.

"I completely understand. Just forget I said—"

"I'm still in love with him!" she cried unabated.

"It's okay, Celeste, this is just a date, it's not—"

"I want to have sex. I want it so bad, but I can't get him out of my head!"

Kellen pressed his lips together. He moved to her side of the booth to give her some privacy from the room, and to give himself some. This was one of the more humiliating dates he'd been on in his life. Not *the* most humiliating, unfortunately, but close.

"I'm so sorry!" she bawled at the top of her lungs. She threw her arms around his neck and clung to him, drenching the front of his shirt with her tears.

The waiter came and discreetly handed him the bill. Kellen just as discreetly handed him his credit card and mouthed the words, "Hurry, please."

"I just wish I was attracted to you!"

He was now officially the most pathetic man in the room. "It's okay, Celeste. Please, don't stress over this."

"It's almost like you're too pretty. Like a woman. Chris

35

was rugged and manly."

"Really, it's okay. Let's just wait until we're in the truck—"

"I thought about him when I was making out with you last week! I'm so sorry!"

The waiter brought his card and receipt back. Kellen quickly signed it, leaving a big tip, and then pulled Celeste out of the booth and away from the restaurant he was never going to set foot in again as long as he lived. He then embarked on the longest forty-five minute drive of his life. Fortunately, there were no awkward silences. No, Celeste just went on and on about Chris's virtues as a man and how Kellen just couldn't live up to him.

After he got her home and inside, he drove straight to Harley's, a bar owned by his best friend, Jayce. The place wasn't trashy, really, though the waitresses did dress in Daisy Duke cutoffs and skimpy tank tops. Kellen had always wondered how Jayce, ultimately a pretty decent guy, could make his waitresses dress that way.

The building had potential. The walls were bare brick and the base of the bar was built of brick, too. The floors were rustic wood planks. There was a stage and dance floor off to the left, but Jayce never made use of them. To the right were a few pool tables and dart boards. The majority of the space was tables.

Kellen bellied up to the bar.

"What's up?" Jayce asked, sliding a beer across the counter. Jayce was a big guy, with a square jaw and a perpetually serious expression. In addition to the bar, he also owned a gym where he boxed—for fun, he said. Never professionally, just in practice for the guys who did box professionally.

Most people found Jayce intimidating on first acquaintance. Kellen, however, had once seen him cry in Kindergarten when a group of girls threatened to kiss him. He could never be intimidated after that. "Bad date."

"You need a whiskey with that then?"

Kellen shook his head. He wasn't a hard drinker. He just needed a couple of beers and a few moments of normalcy. A day of managing crying women and shrieking harpies had left him exhausted.

Jayce moved down the bar to refill some drinks and then came back, leaning on his forearms. "So this was Celeste, right? What happened? I figured she'd be perfect for you."

"She might have been, but I was not perfect for her."

Jayce arched a brow, inviting him to elaborate.

Kellen just shook his head. "She's still hung up on her ex. I don't know. She was so sweet. Or, at least, she seemed that way."

"Maybe you need to look for a different quality of woman. Sweet don't seem to be working for you."

A flash of Zoey and her fiery red hair crossed his mind. He shivered. "No. I definitely want sweet."

Jayce twisted his lips in thought. "Rick's got a sister. Hey, Rick!"

Rick was over at the pool tables. He looked back over his shoulder.

"You got a sister, right? She's pretty sweet, ain't she?" Jayce asked.

Rick straightened and faced him. "Now you keep your goddamn hands off my sister, Jayce."

Jayce broke into a devilish grin. "No promises, but I was thinking about for Kellen, here."

"Oh, Kellen? Yeah, man, Kellen's cool. You want her number?"

Kellen wasn't sure how to feel about this. He knew in his mind that it was a good thing to have a reputation of treating women positively, but the guy could have at least pretended to feel threatened. Rick came over and took Kellen's phone, programming his sister's number. Beverly was her name.

"Yeah, I've seen her around," Kellen muttered as Rick went back to his table. "Maybe I'll call her."

"Problem solved, then," Jayce said.

Kellen turned to look at Rick. "Hey! How come you gave me her number, but not Jayce?"

Rick looked like he thought that was a pretty dumb question. "Jayce's a dog. But you're a nice guy, Kellen. Everyone thinks so."

Kellen frowned, then he turned back to his beer. "Is it a problem that I'm a nice guy?"

Jayce shrugged. "Why would it be?"

"I don't know. Maybe women don't really want nice guys. Maybe it's not considered masculine to be nice."

"Nice is okay," Jayce said. "Being a pushover isn't. A woman likes to be challenged. You gotta pick a fight once in a while, just for the hell of it. You know, dominate."

"I don't know why I ask you for advice."

Jayce shrugged and popped some peanuts into his mouth. "I know what the fuck I'm talking about, that's why."

"Well, you're right about not being a pushover. I don't

think I am, it's just I'm willing to compromise most of the time. I just want the woman I'm with to be happy."

"And sweet."

"Yeah."

"Well can I tell you what else a woman wants?"

Kellen laughed. "Sure. I'm always up for some good fiction."

"She wants a guy with a personality."

"Now what the hell do you mean by that?"

"I mean you're so nice, so focused on making that woman happy, that you put your own wants and needs aside. That's real cool of you, but eventually a chick wants to know who you are. What you stand for. What you want. That sort of thing."

Jayce handed him another beer while he let that thought sink in. Was that really the problem? His dates didn't think he was too nice, they were just…bored with him? It fit with the reasoning behind all his past breakups. He could only remember one time being the one to call off a relationship. The rest of the times had been them breaking up with him.

"I think you got one right, Jayce."

"Huh?" It had been a couple of minutes and Jayce had the attention span of a toddler.

"Nothing. Hey, you haven't seen my brother, have you?"

"Saw him last night. He got completely hammered. Maya and the kids came to pick him up."

Kellen ground his teeth together.

"What's wrong?" Jayce asked.

"He went home and…." Kellen couldn't even say it.

Jayce's eyes widened, and then they narrowed. "He hurt Maya?"

"I guess it's been going on a while. I feel so...so guilty for not seeing it and helping sooner."

Jayce's knuckles were turning white as he gripped the counter. His jaw was tight. "He hurt Maya?" he asked, his voice low and dangerous. His dad had beaten his mom nearly to death a long time ago. Domestic abuse was a sensitive subject for him.

"She's leaving him."

Jayce dropped his head forward as he leaned on the counter. "Tell him not to come in here again. Ever."

Kellen was startled by the intensity of Jayce's reaction.

Jayce looked up at him, his brown eyes gone dark. "I'm serious. I'll kill him if I see him."

"Okay. Okay, Jayce, I'll warn him not to come here."

Jayce stood back from the bar, rolled his shoulders a couple of times, and let out a breath. "So, is she okay? Does she need anything?"

"I think she's good. She's staying with Zoey."

Jayce groaned and rolled his eyes. That was the general reaction among most people when Zoey's name was mentioned. Either that or piss-in-their-pants terror.

"Hey, come on, she's not so bad," Kellen said. And then he frowned and wondered why such foreign and untrue words had spilled out of his face. "What did I just say?"

"You know you have a problem, that's the first step to recovery."

Kellen gave himself a shake. "Anyway, yes, she's horrible. But she's opening up her home to Maya, Sophie, and Matthew, so that's a good thing."

"Sure. And if Satan offered you a place to crash, I'm sure God would promote him right back to angel status."

"Jesus, man, she's not that bad." There he'd gone and said it again. What was happening to him?

"We put her face in the center of the dartboard, Kel." Jayce pointed to the wall off to his left where there was, indeed, a picture of Zoey's face in the middle of the dartboard.

"Seriously?"

He shrugged. "She ran over Eddie's foot last week when she was pulling out of the bank and then she flipped him off and threatened to sue him if his boot damaged her tire. So he's been throwing darts at her face. Hasn't improved his aim." The last part he said loudly enough for Eddie to hear.

Eddie glared at him and threw a dart, missing Zoey's face by an inch. Kellen stared in a mixture of shock and disgust.

"Anyway, at least Maya and the kids are safe," Jayce said. "If they need anything, let me know."

"Yeah. Thanks."

Jayce nodded and moved down the bar to a thirsty customer. Kellen finished his beer and went home to sleep off one of the worst days of his life.

CHAPTER SIX

The next morning Kellen woke up and just lay there. He typically swung his legs right out of bed and jumped on into his day. He had a great life. He'd breezed through college, paying his way with his photography, and had a lucrative freelance career by the time he graduated. Things had come easy to him, he supposed. He also wasn't afraid of work, though, and as a result, he was usually full of energy.

But after yesterday, he was just not feeling it. Times like this he was glad he lived out in the woods. He'd inherited this cabin from a favorite uncle a few years back. With a few renovations, it had become a comfortable home. It was close enough to town that he could get good internet, which he needed for his job. And far enough that he couldn't hear any neighbors or highway sounds.

At the moment, there was a stiff wind rattling his rafters. He knew that outside his walls were temperatures in the thirty-degree range, and it made him desperately want to stay buried under his covers. He needed to check on Maya and then locate his brother. He hadn't heard from Damon since yesterday morning. He would also need to go to his parents' house and tell them what was going on, in case they hadn't already heard.

With a groan, he climbed out of bed, cast it a longing glance, and went to the bathroom to shower and get dressed. He bundled up and drove the seven miles into town. He pulled into Zoey's driveway and saw her garage was open. He climbed out of his truck and approached the edge of the garage warily. Her car was there, and she was standing in front of it, her back to him, next to the door that led inside.

She was letting fly a string of curse words. Just standing there. Saying them. To no one.

"Damn, hell, shit, fuck, fuck, fuck…." She camped out on fuck for a while, then the flow of words got more creative and colorful as Kellen watched. Without warning she stopped, knelt to pick up a bag of salt, and turned.

She jumped when she saw him. She pulled her earbuds out with one hand. "The fuck are you doing here?"

He laughed. "What's with the swear-fest?"

She kept her glare hard and angry for a few seconds, until at last she relaxed and rolled her eyes. "I can't cuss in front of the kids, so I come out here to get it out of my system." She scrunched up her nose, like she was uncertain whether she should be embarrassed.

She was cute. He couldn't believe he was thinking that about Zoey of all people, but she was downright cute. Her red hair was wild hanging out of her stocking cap, and she had a band of freckles across the top of her nose. Her eyes

43

sparkled always. And she apparently suffered from excessive build-ups of profanity that she had to purge from her system.

"What?" she said. "Why are you looking at me like that?"

He gave himself a mental shake. "Uh, no reason."

"Okay. Well if you insist on burdening us with your presence, you may as well make yourself useful. Here." She shoved the bag of salt into his chest. "Salt my driveway. It's supposed to snow tonight. And after that, run down to the bakery and get some donuts for us. We're dying for donuts."

She turned to go. Holding the salt with one arm, he reached out and grabbed her by the elbow. She spun and glared at him. He shoved the salt back into her arms. "Say please," he commanded, because damn it, if he was going to be stuck with her, she was going to learn some basic manners.

He couldn't tell whether she was offended or amused. "I beg your pardon?" she said, accompanied by an incredulous laugh.

"You heard me. Ask me nicely." He closed the distance between them and towered over her, fully intending to stare her down, if necessary. No more of this being pushed around business. No, he was going to stand his ground.

Except that wisps of her hair brushed against the cream-colored curves of her jaw and neck and his throat suddenly got tight. He reached up, without even thinking, and pushed the hair aside, letting his knuckles graze her skin.

"It's not a request," she said, though she sounded a little less forceful. "It's my terms. If you wanna be here, you gotta help out."

"I'm here, Zoey, and I'm not going anywhere. I'm happy to help out. But you have to say please."

Her eyes locked on his, and he nearly buckled. But he knew she wouldn't respect the weakness. So he held on until, at last, her lips began to turn up in a smile. "Salt the damn driveway."

He arched a brow and folded his arms over his chest.

Something changed in her eyes. She sat the salt on the floor and then got in his space. Completely in his space. Her breasts brushed against his crossed arms. She grabbed him by the crotch and then licked his neck. She nipped at his earlobe and whispered, "Salt the driveway, Kellen. Now."

With a squeeze of his balls, she backed away, flashed him a grin, and disappeared inside. Time paused while Kellen stood there, brain-dead, his arms fallen at his sides, gaping at the space in front of him.

After he salted the driveway, Kellen went out for donuts and coffee.

When he got back, Sophie and Matthew were happy to see him only for as long as it took them to see the chocolate and sprinkle covered pastries. He set the donuts on the kitchen table and then leaned against the counter and watched them. Their faces were chocolate-smeared in an instant.

"Thanks. You can go now."

He turned to see Zoey coming past him from the hallway. She was freshly showered and wearing jeans and a grey Henley. She sat at the table with the kids and dug out a bear claw.

Kellen had never in his life seen a woman eat a donut so unapologetically and with such gusto. To top it off, she went and ate another. "Hey, before you go, pour us some milk, will ya?" she asked, her mouth full of the cinnamon roll she was halfway through.

This time he didn't do what she asked. Instead, he took the seat to her left and pulled a plain glazed from the box. "Where's Maya?"

"Asleep. She had a rough night."

"I'm sorry to hear that. What's her next course of action?"

She rolled her eyes at him. He wasn't sure if he was annoying her or if he'd just asked a really stupid question. "She's going to stay here until she recovers. Addy's taking her to the courthouse to get a protection order, so Damon'll be served today." She narrowed her eyes at him all of a sudden. "You're not going to make trouble, are you? Maybe I should keep you here until we get that done. So you don't go blabbing to him."

"I wouldn't...." He stopped himself. He didn't need to defend himself. Something occurred to him that made him smile. "If you want me to stay, Zoey, all you have to do is ask."

This got her. She sat up straight and glared at him. "I do not want you to stay. That's the last thing in the world I could ever want."

He held her gaze this time. He'd meant it yesterday

when he'd said he wasn't afraid of her anymore. He always had been, to an extent, because he hadn't understood her. Now that he'd gotten a peek beneath her bristly, outer layer, he wasn't quite as nervous. "Tell me to go, then. Tell me one more time."

She leaned in, hit him with those eyes, and said, "Go."

His expression fell. "Damn," he muttered, "I overestimated my play."

She grinned and slapped him on the arm. "You're growing on me, jerk face." She stood and went to the kitchen. He watched her wash the sticky frosting off her fingers and then pour herself another coffee.

Maya came in. Her kids stared at her, no doubt just as fearful and shocked as Kellen was. She looked about a hundred times worse than yesterday. Kellen jumped to his feet and hurried to her side. She was moving so stiffly. She was in a long-sleeved night shirt that hung down to her thighs. When he took her arm, his hand sank farther into the fabric of her shirt than he'd expected. How much weight had she lost? And when had she lost it?

She noticed him looking her up and down. "Damon didn't like me to gain any weight. I was afraid."

He gingerly brought her into his arms and stroked her hair. And then there was another pair of arms around them, or rather one around him and one around Maya. Zoey kissed Maya on the head. "We're gonna fatten you right up," she said. "You'll be up to a C cup before you know it."

Maya laughed and then winced, her hand going to her broken rib.

"Let's get her in the recliner," Zoey said. "She's gonna

camp out there for the day, aren't ya?"

Maya nodded, and Kellen helped her into the living room. Zoey brought her a plate of donuts and a big glass of milk. "Look what Kellen brought us."

"You're a generous god, Kellen," Maya said.

Zoey's phone buzzed in the pocket of her jeans. She looked at the screen for a long moment. As she was answering it, she walked out the front door. Kellen watched her go. He stepped back away from Maya and leaned against the wall so he could watch out the window. She was in her front yard, just at the base of the porch. Her head was down, her phone in a death grip. She was pacing back and forth, back and forth. Her hair was covering her face, so he couldn't tell what she was feeling.

"Oh, God," Maya groaned. "Kellen, she'll eat you alive."

He frowned, still watching Zoey. "What are you talking about?"

"You. Gazing with curiosity and interest. Run. Run the other way."

He let out a laugh and shoved his hands in his pockets. "I'm not crushing on Zoey."

She snorted and then winced. "Your face is an open book. I love her, but she'll demolish your soul. Don't let yourself even entertain the idea."

Zoey was holding the phone out in front of her, doing something with her thumb. And then all of a sudden she hurled it to the ground and started stomping on it. Startled, Kellen ran around Maya and out the front door.

Zoey's mouth was a volcano of profanities. Only this time, there was real anger behind the words. She stopped and turned her face up to him. There was more naked vulnerability there than he thought she was capable of. She covered it quickly, though. "Fuck off, Kellen!"

"What happened?"

"Did I invite you into my front yard to eavesdrop on me?"

"Honey, what happened?" he asked, approaching her.

She backed up a step. "Why don't you wipe that ridiculous expression of concern of your big, stupid face and leave me the fuck alone? No one wants you here, Kellen, just leave!"

He snapped. "God dammit, Zoey, what is your problem? I'm trying to be nice to you."

"Go to hell!"

"You really are demon-spawn, aren't you? Know what? You go to hell because that's sure as fuck where you came from. I'm glad they throw darts at your face."

She stopped shrieking at him. "What? Who throws darts at my face?"

He swallowed and shrugged. "Just some guys at some bar."

"Jayce's bar?"

He shrugged again.

"Jayce lets them throw darts at my face?"

He decided that the sky looked awfully interesting at that moment.

She huffed. "Anyway. That was my mom."

She had his attention again. He didn't know anything about her relationship with her mom.

"Apparently she's coming for Christmas."

"And…that's a bad thing?" he asked.

She glared at him, and he thought, for a moment, that she was going to shut him down again. But then she softened. "Yeah. It's a bad thing. I had these plans to give Sophie and Matthew this precious little Christmas. We were going to get a tree today while Addy took Maya to the courthouse, and I thought on Christmas morning maybe you could dress up as Santa."

Something tightened in his chest. "You were going to ask me to be part of your Christmas?"

"Yeah," she said. She leaned forward and patted his stomach. "You're halfway there. All you need's the suit."

He looked down at his perfectly flat belly. "What are you talking about? There's nothing but solid abs, there, see?" He lifted his sweater just enough to show her.

She bit her bottom lip and arched a brow at him. "So there is. My mistake. Yum, Kellen."

He felt his face go suddenly hot. Even in that moment he recognized the need for caution. This fire was extremely volatile and wildly unpredictable.

"Anyway," she went on, as though she hadn't just rocked his moment, "if my mom comes, I don't know how I'll be able to give them that Christmas."

"Why not?"

She leaned down and picked up her decimated phone. Then she sat on her porch step. Her breath formed little clouds in front of her. "I know in my head that my mom isn't a good person. I know she's selfish and that she'll hurt me, but for some reason, whenever I see her, I just want to throw my arms around her and beg her to love me. It's just the most pathetic thing. Basically, I hate myself when she's around."

Kellen sat next to her but not too close. The thread of trust being offered him was extremely fragile. "I didn't know you and she weren't close."

"As soon as I was old enough to start staying by myself, she started taking off. She'd have these phases of just acting like this really good mom. She'd bake cookies and get us matching Easter dresses. Other times, she'd find a boyfriend and disappear for days at a time."

Kellen watched her hands fidgeting with her broken phone. He desperately wanted to hold them. "That why you think nice people are fake?"

"Oh, God, don't psychoanalyze me, Kellen. Nice people *are* fake. I'd rather you just tell me to my face that you think I'm a bitch than to tip-toe around me out of fear."

"It's not always fear. Sometimes, I just don't want to upset you."

"Worse, then, because you think I'm too crazy to be trusted with the truth."

He smiled down at his hands. "Well, if it's honesty you want…."

She sat up straight and shoved him. "I'm not crazy. I just have a short fuse."

He laughed. "Playing fast and loose with semantics, aren't we?"

"You're an ass."

He glanced at her face and was relieved to see humor there. "Let me ask you this; do you think I'm an ass all the time, or is that just for this moment?"

"Just for this moment."

"Then why tell me? If you know that in the next

moment you might think I'm a pretty cool guy, why not wait for the bad moment to pass and avoid hurting my feelings?"

"Because it's too much work."

He laughed again. "All right. Well, I don't mind doing the work. That's what being nice is. It's about empathy."

She snapped her phone in half and then stopped fidgeting with it. Broken shards of glass and plastic were on the verge of falling in her lap.

"So…you want your mom to love you? Nothing wrong with that."

"You don't think it's pathetic? I do. I'm twenty-four years old. I've been on my own completely since I was sixteen. I think I'm fairly well adjusted."

He barked a laugh and immediately regretted it. He stared wide-eyed at her, not sure what she would do. She studied him for a moment before smiling and lifting her middle finger to him.

"I've got a job, and a home, and no debt outside a mortgage. That's more than a lot of people my age can say."

"You're right," he replied. "You're doing fine, Zoey."

She nodded, satisfied. "So, with all of that, why do I still crave her love? I'm secure. I don't need her. I don't need anyone." She blew out a wistful breath. "Anyway, I told her she had to stay in a hotel. So, maybe that will help."

She dug the toe of her shoe into the winter-dead grass at the base of the steps. After a few seconds, he realized she wasn't talking. Or yelling. Or pushing him away. He moved a little closer—a very little. He put his hand on the step behind her. Still she didn't push him away. He tried to think of something nice to say to her, when it suddenly sank in that she didn't like his nice talk. She'd only ever responded positively when he yelled at her. What the hell was he supposed to do with that information?

"She can't be half the crazy bitch that you are," he said. "Maybe Christmas won't be so bad."

She laughed and shoved him with her shoulder. "You sure know how to make a girl blush." At that, she stood up, smacked him upside the head, and went inside. He decided to take it as a compliment.

CHAPTER SEVEN

Later that morning, Zoey found herself alone with two traumatized children in a Christmas tree lot. "Um. That one's cool," she said, pointing to a six foot tall pine.

Matthew shrugged noncommittally. Sophie clung to his side.

"You know, you guys get to pick. Whichever one you want. Did you see that monster over there?" The Douglas fir she pointed out was well over six feet tall. She wondered if it would even fit in her house once she got it on the stand.

The kids didn't answer. Matthew took Sophie's hand and meandered around the lot. He stopped in front of a scrawny, little Spruce. "It's a Charlie Brown tree," Sophie whispered to her brother. Then she looked at Zoey. "Nobody will buy it because it's so skinny. Can we get it?"

"You want a skinny tree? No problem. Do you like it, Matthew?"

"Sophie picks the tree," he said decisively.

"All righty, then."

Zoey had told Kellen she was taking his truck and he could use her car for the day. He hadn't argued.

She found a guy to load the tree in the back of Kellen's truck.

She paid the tree guy and then helped the kids in. She liked driving the truck. It seemed out of character for Kellen, whom she'd never considered as outdoorsy or particularly macho.

There was a bag of trail mix in the cup holder and a pair of sunglasses on the visor. She put her hands on the wheel where his hands had been and wore his sunglasses.

"Hey, do I look like Uncle Kellen?" she asked the kids.

They laughed at her, which felt good. She had a hard time getting a smile out of them, normally.

"I'm Uncle Kellen, and I smile all the time," she said, in her best Kellen voice. "And I only say nice things and everybody loves me."

The kids laughed even more.

"Now you kids behave, or I might have to give you a stern talking to."

They were in gales and she found herself laughing, too. Kellen really was too precious. She wasn't sure what had changed. Maybe it was the way he'd taken care of Maya yesterday. Or the way he stood for himself when Zoey tried to push him away. Whatever it was, she decided she didn't mind having him around so much.

They went home. Maya and Addy were still at the courthouse. Kellen had gone to meet with his parents and explain the situation. So, she was on her own to wrestle the tree out of the truck. She laid it across her porch and found her stand in the garage. She screwed the stand onto the trunk of the tree and then stood it up. It was barely as tall as her and had lost about half its needles in the process of getting it home. The kids were grinning when she brought it inside, so she guessed it had done its job.

She sat it in the corner of her living room, at the end of the sofa. "You guys wanna decorate it?"

"Mom usually makes cookies and plays Christmas music."

She sighed. "Cookies. Hmm. I've never made cookies. Is it hard?"

They shrugged, looking wide-eyed and adorable.

"Maybe we'll go to the store and get the ingredients, and then your mom can help us when we get back."

"She should probably rest," Matthew said.

Zoey got a little twinge in the vicinity of her heart. "She should. But maybe she can tell us how to do it and we can make them while she rests on the sofa. Would that work?"

They both nodded. So they piled back into the truck and headed to the grocery store. Zoey didn't know what they needed or how much, so she just bought whatever the kids said. She was pretty sure they ended up with way more candy than was strictly necessary when making cookies.

They went home, again, and this time, Maya and Addy were there. Addy was settling Maya into her recliner. She was still so stiff and sore. Damon deserved to die.

The kids followed Zoey in, carrying bags of groceries. She couldn't believe how helpful they were.

"Hey, babies," Maya said.

The kids put the groceries in the kitchen and went to her, but stood back.

"Come here, Sophie," she said. "If you sit on my left leg like this, I'll be just fine."

Sophie carefully climbed onto her mother's lap and leaned against her.

"Matthew, I've got a spot right here." She patted the chair. There was a thin strip of space between her and the arm.

"I don't want to hurt you."

"You can't hurt me. I'm tough as nails. Besides, I need to snuggle with my babies."

He put his knee on the chair and wedged in next to her, keeping the jostling to a minimum. She didn't even wince as she put her arm around him and brought him to her side.

Zoey bit her lip. Maya's fingers gently stroked the cheeks of her two, little cherubs. Zoey blinked, trying to trace in her mind the journey that this woman had taken from the girl she used to hang out with in the gym after school. She'd gone from playing truth-or-dare at their slumber parties to breastfeeding a baby in her prom dress.

Zoey remembered that prom night.

Maya had dropped out of school to live with Damon and raise her baby, and Zoey had graduated early, but Addy was kind enough to ask them to be her dates to senior prom. Zoey and Addy drove in Addy's Camaro to Damon and Maya's apartment. Only a week before they'd taken Maya shopping for a dress. Now they would get to see her wearing it.

Maya opened the door to their knock. She smiled and hugged them. "I can't believe you're taking me to prom! This is so amazing."

She was in a shimmery, blue halter dress. Zoey whistled at her. "You look so hot. Your breasts are amazing."

"God, Zoey, boundaries," Addy grumbled.

"I know," Maya answered. "I love breastfeeding. I'll be sad when they go back to their normal size. Damon's even mentioned I should get a boob job. Come on in."

Zoey's mood faltered as she followed her friend inside. It didn't seem a very kind thing for a husband to suggest to his wife.

"Wow," came a male voice off to the right. "You girls look fantastic." Kellen was in the kitchen holding his nephew in one arm and wiping down the counter with his free hand. Maya went to him and took the baby. She sat in her rocking chair in the living room and unclasped her halter top, baring her breasts. Zoey glanced at Kellen. He was smiling adoringly at Maya, not at all ogling her breasts. Zoey wondered if maybe he was gay.

She and Addy took seats on the sofa. Zoey's tension rose when Kellen sat in a chair next to her. He smiled at her. "How's school?" he asked.

She glared at him and then rolled her eyes.

"School's going well," Addy said. "How's college?"

"It's cool. I wish I'd done what Zoey did and gotten dual credits and taken CLEP tests. She's eighteen and already a junior in college. I think that's just amazing, Zoey. A real accomplishment."

"Whatever," Zoey muttered.

"No, really. I truly admire you. I've never seen anyone work so hard."

"Jesus, what do you want?"

He blinked and sat back, his smile fading to a frown. "I don't want anything. I just thought—"

"I don't really care what you think." Zoey turned to Maya. The baby was sucking away, making little grunts and snorts. "He's really

hungry, isn't he?"

Maya smiled. "Always."

"She tried to nurse him in church," Kellen said with laughter in his voice. "She thought she could do it with a blanket there in service and no one would know. But he smacked and snorted like a pig routing around for food. Everyone was turning around looking for the source of the noise."

Maya giggled.

Zoey wished Kellen would just vanish. She kept her shoulder turned to him and pretended he wasn't there. "How long will you breastfeed?"

"Not much longer, I think. He's already doing bottles half the time. Which is why I can go to prom tonight. Mattie loves being fed by his uncle Kellen."

"Stay out as long as you like," Kellen said. "You've earned it."

Zoey wanted to break his nose again.

At last, Mattie finished nursing. Maya set him on a rug in the corner of the living room. He reached into a bucket for his toys and immediately began pulling them out.

Maya, having fixed her dress, strapped into her shoes and grabbed her purse. "Ready?"

Zoey and Addy rose and followed her out the door. Zoey was last out when a hand wrapped around her arm. She turned to face Kellen as she jerked her arm out of his grasp. "What?" she snapped.

His eyes widened. "Uh, nothing. I was just going to wish you a good night. I'm glad you get to go to your prom. You and Maya shouldn't miss out on something like that."

She gaped at him. "Yeah. Okay." She turned and followed her friends down to Addy's car.

Zoey had always remembered that moment for Maya's beauty; the incongruence of her child-like enthusiasm for a long-standing high school ritual, and her very adult responsibility in caring for her son. Now, looking at her holding her two children, the reality of Maya's womanhood washed over her. Maya had left an abusive husband for the sake of her children. There she sat, broken in body, but still nurturing her children.

"You have to tell me how to make cookies," Zoey said. If Maya could birth and raise these two, sweet children, Zoey could at least help them bake their Christmas cookies.

"You don't have to do that for us."

"I want to. We want cookies and music while we decorate our tree, isn't that right?"

Matthew and Sophie nodded emphatically.

"Okay," Maya said. "Well, first thing is, you have to get the butter soft."

"Love it when you talk dirty." She winked at Maya and headed to the kitchen.

Maya talked her through the process. Matthew and Sophie sat at the bar and helped, which meant they scooped globs of cookie dough out of the bowl and ate them. They apparently had to chill the dough before rolling it out to make sugar cookies, so they decided to make some chocolate chip cookies while they were waiting.

Since Zoey didn't know what she was doing, the whole ordeal was a major mess. But the kids had fun, which was all that mattered.

Addy, who had been crashing on the couch the past couple of nights, came and leaned on the bar next to them. "Mommy's taking a nap, guys," she said softly.

They automatically lowered their voices. Zoey leaned over the counter and peeked into the living room. Maya was reclined back with her mouth slightly open, looking like a beat-up angel.

"Hey, now that Aunt Zoey's got the cookies in the oven," Addy said, "why don't you guys get cleaned up and go watch TV in her room for a while."

Zoey had a ton more ingredients. She'd gone completely overboard due to her lack of knowledge on the subject of cookie baking, so she got started making some more dough. She was going to chop up a bunch of the candy the kids had talked her into buying and mix it all in.

"They couldn't find Damon," Addy said.

Zoey glanced up at her. "He'll crawl up out of whatever hole he's hiding in."

"They can't serve him until he does. They warned her that leaving an abuser often causes him to escalate. It could get dangerous here."

"Well, maybe she'll let me carry my gun, then. She made me lock it up yesterday and I don't know how I'm supposed to protect them if I'm unarmed."

"You and that gun. It's ridiculous, Zoey."

"I'm a single woman. You should have a weapon, too. You spend your time in that apartment in the city all alone, walking all over the place by yourself…you need protection. At least, carry some mace."

Addy shrugged. "Professor McDaniel either drives me or walks me when it's late."

"Oh, yes, Professor McSexyPants. Are you finally screwing him?"

"God, why do you have to be so crude?"

She shrugged and measured flour into her bowl of butter, sugar, and eggs. "I just want to see you get that guy out of your system so you can get back to the happy, friendly Addy we all know and love."

"This isn't high school. You've got to accept that we're all growing and changing. You're changing, too, Zoey. You just don't want to admit it. And, no, I'm not sleeping with the professor. I'm his TA and that would be completely inappropriate. It could also get him fired, so I'd appreciate if you could stop talking so flippantly about it."

"Fine, but if you're not going to do him, can I?"

"He would not be interested in you, I promise."

"You don't know. I have ways, Addy. Secret, sexy ways." She gave her a wink and finally got a smile out of her. "Okay, so how is Maya doing?"

"The pain killers have really got her mellow, but she's worried about the kids. She was a wreck the whole time we were out. I don't think she separates from them very often. The sheriff said he'd have your neighborhood patrolled regularly but they can't afford to post an officer outside your house or anything."

"Is custody going to be a problem?"

"Not yet. The order requires him to stay completely away from her and the kids until the court date, which will be January third."

"Great. So, if he shows up, we just call the cops."

"Yeah, here." Addy slid a business card across the counter. "Put Charlie's number on speed dial, and show the kids how to use it. That way you won't have to go through nine-one-one, and he's already apprised of the danger."

Zoey took the card by the corner and then grabbed her phone off the wall. As she put in the number, she heard a car pull into her driveway. Her car, driven by Kellen. Just like that, she thought back to prom night. Had he liked her, then, or had he just been trying to be nice?

For some reason, her body warmed. Her head lightened. Something like joy began to pulse through her.

Something was seriously messed up.

CHAPTER EIGHT

While Zoey was buying Christmas trees and attempting to bake cookies, Kellen was with his parents. They sat in the breakfast nook of their large, colonial home. Judging by the serene smiles on their faces, they had no idea what was going on.

Kellen grabbed a cup of coffee and sat down at the table with them.

"What brings you by, dear?" his mother, Lois, asked.

"Have you heard from Damon?"

"Not lately."

Kellen took a breath. "Maya's leaving him."

Their faces gradually fell around their in-tact smiles, morphing their expressions into something weird and grotesque. "Why?" Lois finally asked.

Kellen dreaded telling them what their son had done. He could barely wrap his own mind around it. He took a deep breath and lowered his head. "Damon's been...he's been hurting her. Last night he beat her severely and, apparently, it's not the first time. I don't know about the kids. Maya seems to think he's never hurt them. But with Matthew getting older, I'm afraid it's just a matter of time."

He lifted his eyes, daring to take in their undoubtedly hurt expressions. Bryan's mouth was hanging open. Lois looked almost amused. "Dear," Lois said, "I don't know what Maya told you, but Damon would never do that to her. Is it possible she was stepping out on him? Maybe her boyfriend did that."

Kellen gave himself a shake, trying to come to terms with this ridiculous thought. How could anyone think so little of Maya? "Mom, no. Look." He held up his phone with a picture of Maya as she'd looked yesterday. "He did that to her, and he's done it before.

Their smiles finished falling. Bryan, his dad, said, "That's not possible." At least he sounded like he had some doubt about his assertion.

Lois had absolute confidence when she said, again, "Damon would never do something like that."

Kellen understood the desire to believe the best in their son. But still. "Let's be realistic," he said. "We all know he's capable. Hell, he beat up on me all the time."

"You were children," Lois said. "Older brothers pick on their younger brothers. That's just how it works."

"Do they put them in the hospital? Knock out their teeth? Face it, Damon's always had a violent streak."

"No," Lois said, shaking her head. "I don't know what happened to Maya, but Damon didn't do that to her. He wouldn't. He loves her."

Kellen had expected shock, sadness, maybe even anger. Denial? No, he hadn't expected denial. "Mom, she wouldn't lie. I took her to the hospital. They apparently know her by name. They've questioned her about abuse in the past, and she's always lied to protect him. That's changed. Now she's worried for the kids' safety and we need to help her. She's staying with her friend, but I thought you might open up your home to her, since—"

"Let her hide here while she smears our son's name through the mud? How dare you even suggest such a thing!"

"Mom, come on. Dad," he said, turning to his dad, "tell her. We've gotta support Maya through this."

Bryan frowned, glancing between them.

Which was when Kellen realized he didn't know his parents nearly as well as he'd thought. "These are your grandchildren we're talking about."

"And they should be with their father," Lois said. "If she sues for custody, you tell her we're going to get him the best damn lawyer money can buy. She's not taking those kids from him."

The world came a little unhinged just then. His home suddenly felt like a place he wasn't welcome. He swallowed and tried to find something to cling to, something normal and sane. "My brother beat up his wife. I'm not supporting him." He lifted his gaze to each of theirs.

All he saw was disappointment and disgust in his mother's expression; confusion in his father's. He got up and left before the situation could get worse.

He drove Zoey's car back to her house. He went to the front door and was about to knock. But then he remembered that his family was in there and he didn't have to knock. Plus maybe Zoey would yell at him. For some reason, the prospect of getting yelled at by Zoey had become an exciting thing.

Their conversation yesterday had left a mark on him. In fact, it was like she'd taken residence in his thoughts and he couldn't evict her. He'd tried to forget the erotic dream he'd had last night. But the images were there to stay.

He walked in to find Maya snoozing in her recliner, Addy lounging at the bar, and Zoey with flour in her hair and clothes and cookie dough up to her elbows. Her wide, blue eyes met his. She lifted her fingers to her mouth, and then sucked the cookie dough off her middle finger, slowly and with a soft, "Mmm."

Kellen's brain immediately ceased functioning. He licked his lips and stared as she sucked yet another finger. Maybe she would offer him some. Maybe she would let him lick cookie dough off her and then, later, just lick her.

"Your parents take the news okay?" she asked.

"I'd love some," he answered, still hypnotized. His feet, completely on board with the goal of licking Zoey, walked him a few steps closer.

"Huh?"

"Cookie dough."

"Oh. Well, here." She grabbed a spoon and scooped some dough into it. "But no more. I'm making these for the kids."

"You're baking cookies for the kids?" He wasn't sure what to make of the fact that this brief, maternal moment only made her more attractive to him. He took the spoon and put it back in the bowl. He gently took her wrist and held up her hand. "How did you get this much of it on your hands?"

She shrugged. "It was really stiff, so I had to work it with my hands."

Kellen stifled a groan.

"Don't worry, I washed them first. Why are you scowling at me?"

He'd never noticed the beautiful shape of her full mouth…probably because she was usually using that mouth to shout obscenities at him. Not now, though.

Her lips turned up. Her voice changed, lowered and softened. "You want a taste?" she asked.

He caged her against the counter with every intention of taking a taste. He'd forgotten about Addy.

"Oh, my God, what is going on? Stop. Stop it! Do you hear me?" Addy shouted frantically.

She ran to Kellen, grabbed him by the shirt, and tried to pull him away. He let her, but only a few steps.

Addy stepped in front of him and put her arms out, as though guarding him. "Release him from the tractor beam, Zoey. I'm not even kidding."

"I'm not doing anything," Zoey said, making a mockery of the sweetness in her own voice. Her eyes never left Kellen's.

"He's a nice guy," Addy said. "Please, don't destroy him."

Zoey snapped out of it, then. She pressed her lips together and started gathering up dirty dishes. She turned her back to them a little too quickly. "I don't destroy men," she said. "They destroy themselves."

Well, Kellen had no intention of destroying or being destroyed. He moved to help her clean up. He regretfully watched her washing her hands. He helped her gather dirty dishes into the sink, and then he grabbed a towel and started wiping down the counter.

Zoey scrubbed dishes without looking at him. "So? Your parents?"

He leaned his hip against the counter, only inches from her. "They're struggling."

"What's that mean?"

"Means they're processing."

She dropped her hands and looked up at him. "Struggling? Processing? What's it mean?"

He sighed. "They didn't believe me. My dad…he'll come to terms with it, but I think my mom's in pretty heavy denial."

Zoey turned off the sink, flung the dish rag into it, and dried her hands. "I'll go talk to her."

He laughed. "Whoa, there, tiger. No way. I think you talking to my mother in even the best of circumstances would be a disastrous event."

"I'm going to bitch slap her with reality, Kellen. Her daughter-in-law and grandchildren need her support right now."

"You're not going to talk to her."

She just laughed and shook her head. She started to head to the door, but Kellen got in front of her. "You're not hearing me, Zoey. You're not going. I'm putting my foot down."

Shock first, then that wicked smile. "Putting your foot down. Mmm, I'm not sure you have the authority to do that. But I'm intrigued to see you try."

He was on the verge of grabbing her again, but Addy,

who was back at the bar, cleared her throat loudly. "Zoey, shouldn't you get the Christmas decorations out for the kids?"

"I've got cookies in the oven," Zoey replied, her eyes still on Kellen's.

"Kellen can keep an eye on them."

Zoey hesitated, keeping her eyes on him. "I won't go talk to your mom," she said.

"Damn," he said. "I was looking forward to showing you who's boss."

Her face turned red and her eyes lit up. But Addy cleared her throat. Zoey huffed and stomped past him toward the garage. Addy sent him a long look before following her friend.

CHAPTER NINE

Zoey loved Addy like a sister, but for the first time ever, Zoey wished she would just go away. Kellen Bradley had been flirting with her. More than that, Kellen Bradley had been sizing her up like a lion about to eat its prey. It had been a long, long time since anyone had stirred her up like he just had.

She sat on the edge of a box in the garage and buried her face in her hands.

The door clicked open and shut and Addy was there. "Kellen's our friend. You can't—"

"He's your friend. Not mine."

"Whatever. You can't do this to him."

"I can't flirt with him?"

"You remember what happened with Andy Crowley?"

Andy Crowley. Now that was a good memory. One of Zoey's hotter affairs. Funny, but the hottest sex with Andy hadn't been nearly as hot as that moment she'd just had with Kellen.

"Or Jess Landers?"

Jess had also been hot.

"You broke them. Both of them. And Terry Hale worst of all."

Zoey had been accused of this before, enough that she was beginning to believe it was true. Andy had fled, crying, and become an alcoholic. Jess hadn't dated since her, and that was four years ago. Terry, her most recent, was still dealing with heartache. The thing was, she didn't know what she'd done to break them. When the relationship ended, it was usually them dumping her, or it had been for Jess and Andy.

"What's wrong with me?" she asked. Such a pathetic question. One she'd never been brave enough to ask before. She began to wonder if there mightn't be something she could change, because she truly didn't want to hurt Kellen.

"You're too hard on them."

"How?"

"You don't bend, Zoey. You're a—a fucking Redwood. You just stand there, tall and solid and you refuse to give anything. These guys try, with you. You just don't let them in."

"I don't know what I'm supposed to do. Change who I am? What?"

Addy knelt in front of her and took her face in her hands. "You know how to do this, Zoey. You have two very strong relationships. With me and Maya. You know how to compromise in a relationship and how to let another person's needs dictate your behavior. You're doing it for Maya right now. You just seem to refuse to do that for the men in your life."

Her frown was impeded by Addy's hands squishing her cheeks together. Addy smiled and dropped her hands.

"I know what you're saying," Zoey said quietly. "But I just…don't want to lose myself in a man. None of them worked hard enough, you have to give me that, Addy. I'd give myself to a man who could prove he's got what it takes to stand by me. Why should I waste my time on men who can't take the heat?"

"There's a balance."

"I don't want to be consumed by a relationship."

Addy lowered her beautiful, dark lashes and nodded. "Maya."

"And my mom."

"Yes. I see." Addy sat and hugged her knees. "I think I'm afraid of that, too."

"Professor McSexyPants?"

Addy laughed and blushed. "He's so intense. If I ever gave in to my attraction, and if it turned out he returned my feelings, I'm not sure how I'd ever come out of it. I look at him and almost want to lose myself. It's sick."

Zoey propped her chin on her palm. "Men. Why must they make it so difficult to love them?"

Addy tucked a strand of hair behind her ear. "I don't know, but tell me this; does Kellen make you wanna lose yourself? Or do you just want to mate with him and then bite his head off?"

"Ha. Funny, Addy."

She arched a brow at her.

Zoey sighed. "I don't know. Something…clicked, yesterday. He's been on my mind ever since."

"He's a serial monogamist. He's long-term boyfriend material. You can't do this to him, Zoey. Not unless you're willing to take things to the next level. You'll hurt him."

All she knew was she definitely didn't want to hurt him. Not deeply, anyway. Maybe a little light bondage in the bedroom, but definitely nothing that would leave emotional scars.

They stood and each grabbed a box of decorations. They walked back into the house toward the kitchen. Kellen was there, facing them, placing a tray of freshly baked cookies on the counter, oven-mitts on his hands and a smile on his face. "Think I got the hang of this," he said.

"Damn," Zoey uttered softly. She shot Addy a pleading look, silently begging her to let her have a go at the pretty man.

Addy shook her head and moved into the living room. Zoey followed, feeling like a kid who'd been told no to a piece of candy.

Kellen joined them a few minutes later. They were untangling lights for the tree. The kids came in to help. Zoey put on some Christmas music, old stuff from Dean Martin and Frank Sinatra. It was about all she had, but the kids seemed happy with it.

"I would've been happy to pitch in for a tree, Zoey," Kellen said, as he and Addy handed the lights around, tucking them into the branches.

"What are you saying? You don't like our tree?"

"No, I didn't say that. I mean, it's a little skimpy, but—"

"It's a Charlie Brown tree," Sophie said. "We rescued it."

"You know what?" he said. "That's just what I would expect of you, sweetheart. You're a very compassionate little girl." He plugged in the lights and then lifted Sophie onto his hip.

"Thanks," she said. "It's a pretty tree, though."

"It is. Very pretty. It has an austere sort of elegance going on."

She giggled, and he tousled her hair.

Zoey's mouth was watering. She didn't know why she cared if he was good with kids. She certainly didn't want kids anytime soon, if ever. But something about his sensitive interaction with his niece was just— mouthwatering.

He caught her eye and grinned a little bigger. She looked away to keep from jumping him. A buzzer rang in the kitchen. "Oh, cookies are done," he said, and dashed off to get more cookies out of the oven.

"God," Zoey groaned, "I might have to excuse myself for a little private time."

Addy hit her with a couch pillow.

Maya woke up and inhaled deeply through her nose. "Cookies? You did it?"

Zoey grinned and shouted back to the kitchen, "Your sister-in-law wants cookies, Kellen."

"I'm on it."

He came back from the kitchen with a plate of cookies and a glass of milk for Maya. "These are chocolate chip," he said. "And this one is Zoey's concoction, so eat at your own risk."

"What the he—ck," Zoey caught herself before saying hell. These kids were killing her. "Those are candy cookies.

They have peanut butter cups, M&Ms, chopped up toffee bars, and bits of caramel. They're the best kind of cookie ever."

"Wow," Maya said. "Sounds good." She bit into one, smiled, and gave her a thumbs-up.

Zoey stuck her tongue out at Kellen, who grinned good-naturedly.

"You saved the sprinkles and stuff, didn't you Aunt Zoey?" Matthew asked. He was picking through the box of ornaments, handing them to Sophie to hang on the tree. "We need those for decorating the sugar cookies."

"I saved them." Being called 'Aunt Zoey' made her feel all warm and gooey inside. Which, in turn, made her long for Kellen all the more. Damn evolutionary instincts.

Kellen settled in on the floor next to Zoey. They sat there watching Matthew and Sophie decorate the tree. He gave her hair a tug. "You're a mess," he said. "Flour all over."

She turned and grinned back at him, feeling like a fool for blushing over the attentions of Kellen Bradley. Where was her irrational hatred when she needed it?

Their gazes remained locked until Addy cleared her throat and they both looked away.

A few minutes later, he stood and stretched. "I'm headed home. You need anything, Maya?"

Maya shook her head, a blissed-out smile on her face, likely a combination of good pain meds and cookies.

Kellen headed for the door. "Zoey, can you step outside for a sec?" He didn't wait for an answer.

Zoey pointedly ignored Addy as she shoved her feet in her boots and wrapped a shawl around her shoulders.

Outside, Kellen was leaning on his truck frowning down at his feet. He smiled when he saw her. "Hey."

"Hey."

"Would you maybe wanna have dinner with me tomorrow?"

Zoey's chest squeezed. She'd dated guys. Slept with guys. But she could never remember a time when a guy had formally asked her on a date. For a moment, one joyous moment, she had 'yes' on the tip of her tongue, but it vanished when she realized that Addy was right.

Kellen saw it, too. He brightened for a moment and then dimmed when he realized she wasn't going to accept.

"It's just not a good time," she said lamely.

He nodded, his brow furrowing for a moment. "Sure, I understand. Maybe once Maya's all better and doesn't need you?" There were those eyes, again. Wide and full of vulnerability.

She swallowed down a pain that was surprisingly strong. This was more than just mild regret. She'd expected to be sad in the way that she was sad when she couldn't buy a dress that was too expensive. This sad ran far deeper. "I don't think so, Kellen."

His frown held confusion this time. He nodded and reached behind him for the handle of his truck. Then he let go. "May I ask why?"

She hugged her shawl tighter to her body. "I just don't think it would work. I mean, I've been flirting with you, and it's been fun, but Addy's right. I shouldn't do that. It just wouldn't work between us. You understand?"

"Yeah," he said. His breath expelled a cloud in front of him. "Yeah, I understand."

He turned and opened his truck door, but then he froze. He looked back, just enough that she could see his perfect profile. "No, Zoey, I don't understand. I actually think it could work really well. I'm not afraid of you if that's what you're worried about. And I think you wanna be with me. So…I'm willing to try it out. Just give it some thought, okay?"

He climbed in his truck, slamming the door. She watched him drive away.

CHAPTER TEN

The next morning was Monday and, while the children had already gotten out for Christmas break, Zoey still had to go to work. Addy, who was getting her Master's degree and worked as a teaching assistant, was also on break, so she would stay with Maya while Zoey was gone during the day.

The accounting firm where she worked was small, but growing. She'd interned there while in college and now had her own client list. A list which was about to grow, by one.

There was cake on Albert's desk that morning. It was already half-eaten and everyone was milling around the office with their little paper plates and plastic forks. Zoey meandered past the fake Christmas tree and perched her hip on the edge of his desk. She cut herself a piece of cake.

Albert leaned back, a pleased expression on his face.

"So what did you decide on?" Zoey asked. "Alaskan or Caribbean?"

"Caribbean this month. Alaskan in the summer."

"Early retirement. How'd you pull that off?" He was only fifty-eight.

"Well, I got my military pension and twenty years here, so the two retirements together made it possible. Pretty sweet."

Zoey smiled, nodded, and bit into the cake. She was happy for Albert. She actually like him. One of the few people she had fond feelings toward. He was unemotional, and he minded his own business. His conversations were short and to the point.

"Had a request from one of my clients," he said. "He wants you to take over."

"He? Who?"

"Jayce Gilmore."

Zoey almost choked. "Jayce hates me."

"Really? He said you were friends."

She shrugged and bobbed her head side-to-side in thought. "Maybe friends who don't like each other very much. He requested me?"

"Yeah. Says he trusts you. You want him?"

"Yeah, I'll take him. He's got the bar and the gym and some rental property, right?"

Albert nodded and stuffed some more cake in his mouth. "I'll email you his files today."

Zoey went back to her desk mildly disgusted with herself for how pleased she was that Jayce wanted her for his accountant. After work, she drove to his bar to talk to him. She didn't admit to herself that the little niggling in the corner of her mind was actually hope. Hope that Kellen would be there as he so often was.

Jayce glanced at her when she walked into the bar but otherwise made no reaction. She stopped halfway to the counter, her eyes drawn to the dartboard where Rick, a regular there, was throwing darts at her face. "Son-of-a-bitch! Rick, I thought you were better than that." She stomped over, ripped the picture down, and then turned on him. "There's a special place in hell for you," she snarled. She crammed the photo into her purse and then made her way to the bar, which was mostly empty, being a Monday evening. "So are you a glutton for punishment, or what?" she asked Jayce.

He only glanced at her before going to work concocting some kind of drink that involved Vodka, Hot Damn, and Grenadine. He shook the mixture and served it to her in a martini glass. "What do you call this one?" she asked, taking a sip.

"The She-devil."

"Aww. After little ole me?"

Jayce didn't comment.

She liked the drink and took another sip. "Seem to recall last time I was in here you made me one called Hellfire and Brimstone. But that one sucked."

His lips quirked up just slightly.

"Why do you want me to be your accountant?"

Jayce shrugged and tossed a rag over his shoulder. "Talked to Albert and he said the firm would assign me to a new accountant. I didn't like the idea of someone new, so I asked for you."

"Just because I'm familiar?"

"Sure—and I trust you."

She nodded. "Okay. Well as long as you don't mind

seeing me around tax time."

"You got that backwards. You're the one who ain't gonna wanna see me around tax time. I got wads of receipts and ledger books kept in pencil that's smudged so much you can barely read them."

"I see. This was your way of punishing me, huh? Wasn't enough that I'm bound to hell for being such a bitch, you gotta make life on earth a misery, too."

"I do what I can."

Zoey sipped and glanced toward the door. She'd been stealing glances, not aware of how many.

"You waiting for someone?" Jayce asked.

"Oh, no. I just stopped in for a drink. And to make sure you hadn't temporarily lost your mind."

"Nope."

"Good."

She stared into her almost empty glass and swirled the drink around. Her coat was still on, her purse slung over her shoulder, poised to exit. Yet she didn't leave. "Has Kellen been by?"

When there was no answer, she forced herself to look up. Jayce was scowling at her. "Comes by all the time."

She swallowed. *Don't ask. Don't do it. This isn't high school. Stop, Zoey, stop!* "Has he said anything about me?" *Damn. It just slipped out.*

"Why would he mention you?"

Zoey hitched a shoulder. She should have known she wouldn't get anything out of Jayce. Her pride couldn't bear to ask any more questions, so she drained her drink and slid the glass to Jayce. "That was good. You should put it on the sign."

She stood.

"Hey."

She stopped and turned to face him. He was still scowling. "How's…." He paused and then lowered his voice. "How's Maya? And her kids?"

"As good as can be expected. Why?"

This time it was his turn to look away and act uncomfortable. Zoey saw what she'd never noticed before, but should have. Now that she was looking, she could tell it had always been there.

He shrugged. "No reason. But…if she needs anything…." He trailed off and frowned down at his hands gripping the counter.

"I'll keep that in mind," Zoey said. She wasn't one for physical displays of emotion but she suddenly felt she should reach out to him, or something. She knew how to help people and give to them, but she'd never really known how to be of comfort. Deciding to give it a try, Zoey reached across the bar and put her hand over his and gave it a squeeze.

He stared down at her hand and then up at her. "The fuck are you doing, Zoey?"

She quickly withdrew her hand. "Commiserating. Jeez, if you're gonna be an ass about it."

"Let's just stick to the arm's length rule of personal space, okay?"

"Fine, asshole. It's the last time I try to be nice to you." She hitched her purse up onto her shoulder and headed toward the door.

"Hey," he said again.

She huffed and glared at him over her shoulder.

"You want me to tell him you came by?"

Biting her bottom lip and thinking for a moment, she said at last, "No, better not."

He nodded and then moved down the counter to another customer. She went home to her little family and tried not to think about Kellen.

CHAPTER ELEVEN

Kellen's phone buzzed. He was watching a Discovery Channel show about Alaska, trying to take his mind off Zoey. It was Friday night and nearly a week since she'd rejected him. He muted the television, tapped his phone, and held it to his ear.

"Hey, it's Jayce."

"What's up?"

"Your brother's here."

"And he's alive?"

Jayce laughed darkly. "Yeah, I'm back in my office. I thought you could come get him, save us all some bloodshed."

"Sure. I'm on my way. But do me a favor and call the Sheriff. He's got a protection order for Maya that he needs to serve."

"My pleasure."

Kellen pocketed his phone and left his cozy recliner. The sky was pitch black, and the air sank its sharp teeth into his skin.

The highway dipped and turned with the roll of the hills. He tried not to think of Zoey and how much he wished she was by his side right now. His life had been rich and fulfilling. He'd never felt there was anything missing. Why there should suddenly be a Zoey-shaped hole in his heart was a complete mystery.

It might help if he didn't have to go to her house every day. He didn't see her, since he only went while she was at work, but there was evidence of her everywhere and of the surprising depth to her kindness. She'd stocked her DVD shelf with Disney movies for the kids. There was always a tidy tray next to Maya, with her medication, a bottle of water, and an assortment of snacks lined up or stacked neatly. Best of all, when she'd learned he was visiting in the mornings, she'd begun leaving him a plate of breakfast wrapped in foil and a thermos of coffee.

Through her house, Kellen learned that Zoey was a neat and organized person; that she loved playing hostess and that she cared about details. He learned that she liked reading thrillers, she watched a lot of romantic comedies, and she owned a pretty sick collection of PlayStation games downstairs. He didn't go into her room, but he did, one day, stand in the doorway and peek in. There was a huge quilt over her bed, cream colored with light blue flowers. Her pillowcases were yellow like the centers of the flowers. The only things on her nightstand were a lamp, iPhone dock, and a book.

All-in-all she seemed like a truly sane and stable individual. Kellen couldn't help wondering where all the fire came from, and if the passion she showed in her anger transferred to other areas of her life. These were the things he tried not to dwell on as he drove to Jayce's bar.

He arrived right behind the sheriff. Inside the warm, beer-scented tavern, the Sheriff went to stand over Damon and hand him a paper. Damon sat quietly, taking it and nodding along. At least he wasn't screaming and throwing things.

Jayce stood behind the bar, leaning forward and skewering Damon with his eyes. He turned and barely softened when he saw Kellen.

"Beer?" he asked.

Kellen shook his head. "Seems like he's not causing trouble."

"He's not. Got a lot of nerve, though, coming in here."

Kellen studied his friend for a moment. "Do you still have feelings for Maya?"

Jayce shot him a look but otherwise didn't answer.

"I'll take that as a yes."

Jayce's eyes narrowed.

The sheriff left, and Damon bellied up to the bar, sliding his beer glass across to Jayce. "Fill that back up, will ya?"

Kellen thought it best not to let Jayce speak. "All right, Damon, let's get out of here."

Damon snorted. "Where the fuck should I go? Home? It's not home without her there. And now I find out I can't even go talk to her. Why would she do that?"

Kellen felt the ripple of tension that pulsed from Jayce. "Let's go sit over there and talk about it." He led Damon to a corner table and lowered his voice. "You can't come in here anymore." He jerked his head toward Jayce.

Damon glanced back. His eyes widened. Then they narrowed. "What the fuck is his problem?"

"He wants you dead, so you can't come back in here again."

"Free country," he muttered.

"Not in here. Jayce is one of those guys for whom going to prison is not much of a deterrent when it comes to things he cares about. And he cares about Maya."

This time, Damon's expression mirrored Jayce's. "Boy better keep his goddamn hands off my wife."

"Damon, what are you doing here? Where have you been?"

He slumped in his chair. "Just been driving around. Slept in my car a couple of nights, 'bout froze my ass off. Then went to that shitty hotel down by the river. I gotta get her back."

"You're not getting her back. You broke her rib and beat the shit out of her face." His stomach clenched at the taste of the vile words. "You need to stay away from her. You can move back into your house, because she's not going back there ever again."

Damon's eyes narrowed again. "Whose side are you on, asshole?"

"Hers. I thought that was clear. I'm here right now to deliver you out of this place alive and make sure you know you can't come around Maya and the kids."

"What kind of a brother are you?"

"Right now, I'm her brother."

"She staying out with you? Are you fucking my wife?"

"Jesus, Damon! Listen to yourself. Just stay away,

okay?"

Damon leaned back in his seat. Then he leaned forward. His hands fisted and unfisted. His jaw muscles twitched. "She's not staying with you," he muttered to himself. "She's staying with that bitch, Zoey Odell."

Kellen tensed, recognizing the protective reaction for what it was. He had to deliberately remind himself that Zoey didn't need him to defend her. "All that matters is you gotta stay away."

"That redheaded whore always was trying to get Maya to leave me. She's poisoned her mind against me."

"Damon!" Kellen shouted, finally losing his cool. "Listen to me; stand up, walk out of here, and stay away from Maya. It's that fucking simple."

Damon stood, grabbed the edge of the table, flipped it aside, and grabbed Kellen by the front of his shirt. "You don't talk to me about my wife. She's mine, and I'll see her whenever I damn well please."

Spit and rank breath hit him in the face. Kellen's ears rang with rage. "Get your goddamn hands off me!"

Damon shoved him, reared his fist back, and swung. The punch connected with Kellen's jaw. His head snapped to the side and his vision went momentarily black.

The last time Damon had punched him, Kellen had been sixteen years old. Damon's punches had always knocked him either down or out. This time he stayed on his feet. He recovered and swung his own fist into Damon's face, slamming him in the eye. Damon stumbled back and then charged.

Kellen landed on the edge of a chair and thanked God Jayce was such a cheap-ass business owner, because the chair splintered and broke beneath him. Damon landed another punch to his face and one to his gut. Enraged, Kellen grabbed him by the hair and jerked his head back. He managed to roll Damon to his back and then land his own pair of punches.

On his third and fourth swing, he hit air before he realized Jayce was dragging him off his brother. No one was holding Damon, though, so when he charged, Jayce shoved Kellen to the side and swung his fist.

If Damon ran head-first into a brick wall, it would have done less damaged. He bounced backwards from the impact of Jayce's fist and fell to his back. Blood gushed down his nose and into his mouth. He choked and rolled to his side.

Kellen breathed hard through his teeth as the world came spinning back to a stop. The red in his vision cleared. Jayce stood over Damon, his eyes cold and his expression calm. Damon finally looked up at him and had the sense to stay on his back.

Someone had called the sheriff, who hadn't been too far down the road. He stepped into the bar and helped Damon off the floor. "They attacked me," Damon said, pointing at Jayce and Kellen.

Kellen started to defend himself, but Jayce rolled his eyes. "Come on, let's get this over with."

"What?"

"Down to the station for questioning."

"Why?" Kellen asked. "We didn't do anything."

"It's all right, Jayce," the sheriff said. "Y'all just have a seat and I'll get your stories here."

"Really?"

"Yeah, I figure with a nice guy like Kellen involved, this was probably a one-sided fight."

Jayce slapped Kellen on the back. "Awesome. I'll have to keep you around more often."

Kellen winced at the friendly slap. His entire back felt bruised.

The sheriff took Damon out to his car. He came back a few minutes later for Kellen's and Jayce's statements. After he left, Kellen dropped his head to the bar. The adrenaline abandoned him. He felt more hung-over than the morning after a drinking binge. "Pain," he groaned. "So much pain."

"You want whiskey or aspirin?"

"Aspirin."

A moment later, a bottle hit the counter. Kellen lifted his head and took the aspirin bottle. He popped four of the pills and downed them with the water Jayce handed him. Just then his phone rang and he found himself even more grateful for the aspirin.

"How dare you!"

Kellen closed his eyes. "Mom, he attacked me."

"Now your father has to go down and bail him out. After all he's been through, you have to go and have him put in jail?"

"He attacked me in a public place."

"Kellen, he's family. You need to think about that and get your act together." She hung up.

"I'm rethinking the whiskey," Kellen groaned. "Mom and Dad are backing Damon."

"What?" Jayce asked.

Kellen shook his head. "I showed them pictures of

Maya. They don't believe Damon did it. They're in some major denial."

"Shit." Jayce began wiping down the bar. His jaw muscles were tight, and Kellen could tell he was loaded with anger he didn't know what to do with.

"She's gonna be okay, man," Kellen said. "I'll take care of her. She'll be safe."

Jayce met his eyes. "If she needs anything…if there's anything I can do…."

"I'll let you know."

Jayce held his gaze for a long moment before nodding. He finished wiping down the bar, this time with less aggression.

Kellen went home, but found he couldn't sleep. He was too disturbed by his parents' behavior. Too worried about Maya. Too fascinated with Zoey. He wound up sleeping fitfully sometime around four in the morning.

CHAPTER TWELVE

The sobbing coming from the living room woke her up. Zoey hurried out in her nightshirt to find Maya clutching a phone to her ear and crying. Whoever was on the other end of the line was yelling.

Zoey marched to her, snatched the phone, and said, "Who the fuck is this?"

"How dare you!" shouted the female voice, and then the line disconnected.

Zoey slammed the phone onto the table. "Who was that?"

"My mother-in-law," Maya sobbed.

"She called to yell at you at seven in the morning?"

Maya's sobs were uncontrollable. Zoey couldn't take it. She'd had absolutely enough of this behavior from Lois Bradley. The woman was being deliberately obtuse, and she simply needed someone to hold a mirror to her face.

Zoey stormed back to her bedroom and dressed in jeans and a sweater. Once dressed, she grabbed her car keys, climbed in her car, and drove to the Bradley house.

Snow had been falling steadily for a while. The roads were dusted over. The Bradley's lived just a couple miles down a dirt, country road. Her tires slipped once or twice, but she was a woman on a mission. Nobody victimized her best friend like that.

The tires slipped and slid into the gravel before making it to the concrete carport. She got out, slammed the door shut, and stomped to the front of the house. She hammered her fist on the door, hoping the loud knock scared the shit out of them.

The door opened on the seemingly sweet Mrs. Bradley. She had the same demeanor as Kellen. Placid and nice.

Zoey shoved past her into the warm house, turned, and said, "What the fuck is your problem?"

Mrs. Bradley's smile faded, and she drew herself up. "Young lady, I suggest you watch your language in my home."

"Fuck you! That woman over there has been beaten and broken, and you have the nerve to yell at her? What kind of a sick, hateful person does that?"

Mr. Bradley entered from the kitchen to Zoey's left. He had a cup of coffee and a deer-in-headlights look. "I'm sorry, may I ask what's going—"

"Your bitch of a wife called Maya to kick her while she was down!" Zoey turned back to Mrs. Bradley. "Is that what you do? Steal candy from children? Knock crutches out from under injured people? Blame an innocent woman for what her drunken brute of a husband does to her?"

Mrs. Bradley's bottom lip quivered. Tears filled her

angry eyes. "You should leave."

"So it's okay for you to scream at a woman who's just lost everything, but it's not okay for me to call you out? Thanks, Mrs. Bradley, for setting me straight on the rules. Y'all have a great day." She flipped off Mrs. Bradley. Before leaving, she flipped off Mr. Bradley for good measure.

She muttered curses all the way to her car. She managed to turn it around and head back up the driveway. She got all the way to the turnoff for the road when her tires stuck.

"Oh, no," she muttered. She gunned the gas and her tires spun. She tried reverse. She tried rocking back and forth. "Oh, no, no, no, no…," she murmured as she climbed out of the car.

Mud. Her back tires were mired in mud. The snow was wet, the ground was too warm for everything to have frozen yet.

"Shit!" she shrieked. She pushed on the front, and then she pushed on the back. The damn car was going nowhere. She thunked her head on the roof of the car and took a moment to curse her incredibly bad luck.

Then she got back in and reached for her phone in her cup holder. Only her phone wasn't in her cup holder. It wasn't in her pockets. It wasn't in the passenger seat.

"Son of a bitch!" she screamed. "I hate my life. I fucking hate my life," she muttered as she trudged all the way back to the Bradley house.

She got to the front door, gave herself another mental kick in the ass, and knocked.

Mr. Bradley opened the door, this time, still looking

somewhat shocked. Zoey tiptoed up and saw Mrs. Bradley on the sofa sobbing violently.

"Hi," Zoey said, smiling as big as she could. "I'm so sorry, but I seem to have gotten my car stuck. Do you have a truck or anything?"

Mr. Bradley shook his head, nonplused.

"Shit. Okay, well, could I use your phone?"

She didn't wait for an answer because she was afraid of the door getting slammed in her face. She just nudged past him and scanned the room for the phone.

"Uh, in the kitchen," Mr. Bradley said, before returning to his wife's side.

"Yeah. Thanks." She headed to her right and found the phone. She couldn't help admiring the large kitchen. You could bake a lot of cookies in that thing. She looked at the phone and realized she didn't know who to call. Maya was out of commission. Addy's Mercedes wasn't going to help her get her car unstuck.

There was a phone book on the counter. She found a couple of towing companies and called them. Being a bad weather day, they were all two hours from being able to get to her.

With a sinking in her gut, she realized she only had one option. She dropped her head back. "God dammit!" she cried to the heavens.

The Bradley's turned to gape at her. She held up her hand. "Sorry!" she yelled to them. "No problems. Would one of you be able to give me Kellen's number?"

Mrs. Bradley glared at her, but Mr. Bradley said, "It's three on the speed dial."

"Thanks." She turned her back to them and hit the

number.

It rang four times, and she was beginning to fear he wouldn't pick up. But then he answered. "Yeah?" His voice was sexy raspy.

"I need you to come get me," she said, glancing nervously over her shoulder at the Bradley's who were now arguing and gesturing to her.

"Who is this?" he asked.

"It's Zoey, ass-face, I need you to come get me."

"What? Come get you where?"

"At your parent's house."

"What? Why—"

"Your mom called Maya and made her cry, so I came over here to yell at her, and as I was making my not-so-graceful exit, my car got stuck in the mud, so I need you to bring your truck and get me unstuck. Now."

Crickets.

"Kellen?"

Which was when she realized he was laughing. He must have dropped the phone.

"Listen, you son-of-a-bitch! Get your lazy ass out of bed and come pick me up."

"Oh, God," he laughed. "Yeah. Sure, Zoey, I'll come get you. Listen, I need you to ask me nicely."

"I beg your fucking pardon?"

"Say please, that's all. 'Please come get me, Kellen.' And then I'll be right over."

She just stood there with her mouth hanging open. "I'm sorry, at what point was it you thought you had the upper hand, here? Your poor mother is in severe distress. Come and get me so I can get out of her life!"

Zoey hung up and leaned back on the counter. She folded her arms over her chest and kept her head down. He would come. He cared too much not to come. In the meantime, maybe if she was real quiet, Mr. and Mrs. Bradley would forget she was there.

After three agonizing minutes, Mr. Bradley came in to refill his coffee cup. "Um," he said, "help yourself to coffee, if you want. There's plenty."

She winced. "Thank you," she said. He left, and she helped herself. She kept her back mostly turned to the room as she sipped her coffee.

This must be what time feels like in hell, she thought. Her cup was nearly empty when she heard the sound of tires on gravel.

A moment later, Kellen stumbled into the house, still laughing. "Oh, God. Zoey...where's Zoey?" He was looking at his red-faced mother.

She pointed balefully toward the kitchen. He turned and saw her.

The last thing she expected was to react to the brightness in his eyes. God, he looked absolutely beautiful as he made his way over to her, his hands in the pockets of his leather coat, his jeans hanging low on his trim hips. On top of that, he had a black eye and his bottom lip was slightly swollen. The effect was a more rugged version of the nice-guy. "Got a little flare up of foot-in-mouth disease?" he asked.

She straightened. "No. I meant everything I said. I just wasn't planning on getting stranded here."

His grin widened as he looked down at her. "It's things like this that get your picture put on the dartboard."

She narrowed her eyes. "What happened to your face?"

"Got in a bar fight."

She snorted. "Yeah, right."

"You don't believe me?"

"You? In a bar fight? No. I don't believe that."

"Well, it's true. You can ask Jayce." He gently tugged at a strand of her hair.

"Um," Mr. Bradley said.

Kellen turned and Maya saw Mr. Bradley standing there.

"Um, if you two want breakfast or anything…."

"Jesus, he's even nicer than you are," Zoey said to Kellen.

Kellen placed his fingers over her lips. "That's enough talking for today, huh?" He turned back to his dad. "We appreciate that, but we've imposed enough. I'm gonna get this little firecracker out of here and on her way."

His dad nodded. "Got more havoc to wreak, does she?"

Zoey's jaw dropped.

"Yeah, I think she keeps a pretty full schedule. Come on, Zoey." Kellen took her by the arm and led her past Mr. Bradley. She turned and smiled at him, though, and he smiled back.

"Your dad's cool," she said as she climbed in Kellen's truck.

"Mm-hmm." He drove them to the end of the driveway just past her car. "You wanna go put it in neutral for me?"

They climbed out and she put her car in neutral while

he hooked a wench under her car. She stood back as the wench slowly pulled her car forward and out of the mud. He unhooked it and then came to stand in front of her. "You're all set. Come have breakfast with me."

"With your parents?"

"No. God, don't you think they've been through enough?"

"Your mom was a real bitch to Maya."

He shrugged, clearly not wanting to get into it. "Let's go to Belle's for pancakes or something."

She recognized it for what it was. A date. "I can't. I need to get bagels for everyone at the house."

He looked her up and down, no trace of the humor that had been there earlier. "You can do that after."

"No, Kellen. Thank you, though."

His jaw muscles flexed, making his smile look tight and forced. "All right. Another time, then."

"No."

The smile vanished and his eyes turned hot. "Tomorrow."

"What?"

"Tomorrow I'm coming into town and take you to breakfast."

"No, Kellen, I said I don't want to."

"Well, I want to, dammit! I'm sick of always doing whatever makes everyone else happy. I don't care most of the time. It's fine. But I want this, Zoey, and you're gonna give it to me. So I'll see you at nine tomorrow morning. Give you time to get your family fed before I take you out. Okay?"

She fought as hard as she could to keep from smiling.

She loved the way he was trying to be aggressive. She loved that he called Maya and the kids her 'family.' Her lips quirked up and so did his. And then she was laughing.

He watched her for a moment. "So, is that a yes?"

She bit her bottom lip and looked up at him through her eyelashes. "Tell me what happened to your face."

His expression sobered. He blew out a breath. "Damon was at Jayce's last night. I went to talk him into leaving and we got into it. Mom was pretty pissed that I got my brother thrown in jail."

Zoey felt the rage build again. "I don't know if I'm angrier at him or at her. How can she be so blind?"

He shrugged, again. "So tomorrow. Nine o'clock. 'Kay?"

She studied him for a long moment before giving him a nod.

His smile made all the stress of her day worth it.

"Great," he said, "I'll see you then."

She nodded again. He got in his truck and drove a few yards down the road, waiting to make sure she got going. She made it onto the road and then followed him into town until he turned off down the highway that would take him home.

CHAPTER THIRTEEN

Kellen didn't get nervous dating women. It just wasn't something he dealt with. He'd always found it easy to be with them.

Naturally, he was perplexed by the butterflies in his stomach. He hadn't slept at all last night in anticipation of his breakfast date. He kept having nightmares. The kind where you're at the mall and look down and realize you're in your underwear. He kept snapping awake, dozing off only to have another dream.

He didn't look his best, even after splashing water on his face and drinking a half a pot of coffee. But it would have to do. He drove into town and pulled into Zoey's driveway. She didn't make him wait. She didn't even make him go get her. As soon as he put the truck into park, she was jogging out of the house. She had on a long, wool coat over her jeans and a red scarf wrapped around her neck. Her hair hung loose and wild.

"Hey," she said breathlessly as she climbed in the

truck. "Addy's sitting with Maya and the kids, and she is not happy, so you'd better go before she comes out here and talks me out of this."

Kellen didn't bother asking what Addy's problem was. He knew her heart was in the best place. She was afraid he would get hurt. More evidence that women equated niceness with weakness. Everyone just assumed that because he was nice, he was also fragile.

He drove them downtown to a little diner called Belle's. It was deliberately vintage. All the waitresses wore blue and white, plaid dresses with white aprons and bouffant hairdos. Kellen parked in the lot behind the restaurant. He wanted to hold Zoey's hand walking into the restaurant, but he wasn't prepared for the rejection if she pulled away.

She made it easy for him and tucked her mitten-covered hand into his. He smiled down at her and led her inside. There was a counter up front and then seating beyond it. They went to a corner booth. Patsy Cline was playing on the jukebox. Zoey took off her coat and scarf and said, "I love this place."

"Oh, good," he said. "I wasn't sure."

She gave him a funny look.

A waitress came and delivered their menus as she took their drink orders. Zoey opened her menu and nibbled on her bottom lip as she browsed. Kellen was entranced, waiting in suspense to see what would happen next.

Her eyes darted up. "Uh, what?" she asked.

He shook himself and opened his menu. "Nothing. Do you like pancakes?"

"Yeah, who doesn't?"

"I just know I mentioned pancakes yesterday, but you can get whatever you want."

"I'm gonna, so don't you worry."

He glanced at her again, and she was still engrossed in the menu. Then she slammed it shut, leaned back, and smiled. "Got it. What are you getting?"

"Uh—"

"Y'all ready to order?" the perky waitress asked. She sat two mugs of coffee in front of them.

"Yes," Zoey said. "I'll have the tall stack of chocolate chip pancakes, a side of home fries, and a slice of bacon. Could you bring me a glass of milk with that?"

"Sure, darlin'. What about you?"

Kellen gaped at Zoey. "Steak and eggs with pancakes instead of biscuits." He handed his menu over without taking his eyes from Zoey.

After the waitress left, Zoey leaned forward. "You got a problem with what I eat?"

"No. Not at all. It's just been a while since I dated a woman who was willing to eat in front of me."

"Oh, well, I'm not worried about what you think of me, so that's why."

He laughed. "Okay. Well, that's awesome."

"Besides, this isn't a date. Breakfast? No. Not a date."

He frowned. "I'm paying. Doesn't that make it a date?"

"Nope. Dates are romantic. There's no way to make breakfast romantic."

"But if I did pull off a miracle and make breakfast romantic, would it then count as a date?"

"Sure. You can't do it, though. It's impossible."

He leaned back and got lost in wondering how he could make breakfast romantic.

"See, now you're ignoring me," she said. "That's just seriously unromantic."

"I think I'm just so in awe of being here with you, it's left me speechless."

She twisted her lips and narrowed her eyes. "Hmmm. Nope. Not enough. Keep trying, though."

He leaned forward and grabbed her hand. She'd taken the mittens off, and her hand was warm and soft. "How's the family doing?"

Her guard went down. "Good. All the swelling in Maya's face is gone. She's just black and blue, now. Sophie and Matthew are taking good care of her, bless their hearts. Those are seriously the best kids I've ever met. How's your face feeling?"

"Hurts. I'll survive. You yelled at any defenseless, middle-aged women today?"

"Not yet. You carried groceries for any little old ladies today?"

"Not yet."

"Maybe that's what we are. Maybe your powers of good counteract my destructive forces, creating balance in the universe."

He grinned and stroked the back of her knuckles with the pad of his thumb. "I don't think you're as evil as you think you are."

"That's your mistake." She pulled her hand out of his and laid it in her lap.

He leaned back and studied her. How to get inside that fiery wall of protection? "What's it you're guarding yourself from?"

"Huh?"

"All the prickly attitude—it's a shield, right? What are you afraid of?"

"Oh, I'm not afraid of anything, jackass. I just am who I am, and if you don't like it, then fuck you."

He mouthed the last two words along with her and then laughed. "You're getting predictable—or I'm just figuring you out."

"There's nothing to figure out, Kellen. I'm just a bitch."

He frowned and nodded. "Maybe, or maybe you just want a man who will fight for you."

Her cocky expression faltered.

The waitress showed up with their food. Zoey pulled her hair back in a band and pushed up her sleeves. "You should try these," she said, cramming her mouth full of chocolate chip pancake. She nudged her plate toward him in offering.

He laughed and speared a bite with his fork. "Good," he said. "Hey, sharing food…that's romantic, right?"

Her eyebrow went up in a skeptical scowl. "Not hardly."

And then something suddenly felt wrong. Kellen glanced over to see Damon walking in the door with his arm around a woman. She had on a tight skirt over wool leggings and a shirt that barely contained her cleavage. Her skin was nicotine yellowed and her blond hair was black at the roots.

Damon grinned when he saw Kellen. "Hey, little brother," he said.

"Jesus," Kellen muttered.

"Mind if we join you?"

Before he could answer, Damon wedged in next to Zoey, forcing her to scoot down on the bench. She grabbed her food and slid it down the table with her, even as she glared hatred at Damon.

The woman pulled up a chair and sat at the end. She ran her hand up and down Damon's thigh.

Kellen felt sick for so many reasons. Seeing Damon cheating on Maya, seeing him at all, was nauseating. There was a very sudden, very real fear, now, as he truly saw his brother, for the first time, as a dangerous man. A dangerous man who was crowding in next to Zoey.

Kellen said a silent prayer that Zoey would keep her mouth shut. "Damon, what are you doing here?"

"Having breakfast. Just like you. Hey, how's your face? Sorry about that, by the way."

It was only a little satisfying that Damon's face was in worse shape. Though Kellen couldn't take credit for the broken nose. "That's fine, but maybe you could get your own table."

"Why? You two on a date or something? Not very romantic, a breakfast date. Or is this a morning after breakfast?"

"Christ, Damon, don't do this."

"Do what? I just wanna know what's going on in my little brother's life." Then Damon turned to Zoey and brushed his knuckles along her jaw. "Get to know my future sister-in-law, here."

Kellen's fight-or-flight kicked in and it was all fight. He gripped the table edge, trembling with rage. "Keep your goddamn hands off her."

Damon laughed. "Jeez, Kellen. You never used to be this aggressive. You must really have it bad for this one." He slid his arm around her shoulders.

Before Kellen could do anything, Zoey reached up and grabbed Damon's nose, twisting it out of shape. Damon screamed and tried to back out of the booth, but Zoey held firm until he was on the floor, his hands on his face, screaming in agony. "You crazy bitch!"

"Never put your hands on me!" she shouted down at him.

"I'm gonna kill you, you stupid cunt!"

That was when Kellen hauled Zoey against him. She kicked and flailed, but he held her tight. A moment later, two of the sheriff's deputies came in. They grabbed Damon and dragged him outside. The blond woman followed after him, shuffling along in her ridiculously high heels.

Kellen turned Zoey to face him. Zoey, who wasn't afraid of anyone, was shaking. Her eyes were red-rimmed with tears. She looked up at him and when her bottom lip quivered, Kellen's heart broke in two. "Come here," he said, as he gathered her into his chest.

"How dare he!" she screamed into his chest, her voice muffled. "How dare he touch me!"

"I know. You took care of it, though, didn't you?"

"You should have done something! You should have stopped him."

Her words cut him, but he swallowed down the pain and held her tightly. "It's okay. Everything's fine, now."

She sobbed into his chest for a couple of minutes

before she finally calmed. He could feel the tension easing out of her. She stepped back and dragged her wrists over her eyes.

One of the deputies came back in and they all sat in the booth, Kellen with his arm around Zoey. "He wants to press charges."

Kellen stiffened, but Zoey spoke first. "Tell him I won't if he doesn't. He was sexually harassing me. Touching me after being told to stop."

The deputy made a note and then stepped outside. They watched through the diner windows as the deputy talked to Damon. When he came back in, he wore a hesitant smile. "He's not going to press charges after all."

"Good."

"Maybe you should anyway," Kellen said.

Zoey shook her head. "I'm not going to add to the drama."

"Ma'am, if you feel you're in danger…," the deputy said.

"No. No, I'm not afraid," she said. Which wasn't exactly an answer. The deputy left and they leaned against each other for a few minutes.

At last they stood and Zoey cast a longing look at her breakfast.

"We'll get it to go," he said. He signaled the waitress, who hurried to the back for boxes.

"I can't believe you're related to that asshole. I can't believe there's not a bad name equivalent to cunt for the male of the species. It's so fucking unfair!"

"I know. I know it is. I'm so sorry, Zoey."

The waitress brought them their boxes, and he handed her his credit card. He and Zoey packed up their food and then headed out to the truck, grabbing his card and signing the receipt on the way out.

He drove toward her home. "I just don't understand why you didn't do anything," she muttered.

"You're mad at me?"

"You just sat there!"

"I'm sorry. I've never had to defend a woman's honor before. It's virgin territory for me."

"I don't need you to defend my honor!"

He jerked the truck to the left and parked in the gravel off the side of a gas station parking lot. "You're making my head spin. You don't want me to defend you, but you're mad at me because I didn't?"

"No! I don't need you to defend me, but I'm mad you didn't at least try."

He shook his head and stared out the windshield. The silence dragged out. At last he laughed in frustration and massaged his temples. "Jesus, Zoey."

She didn't answer and he couldn't bring himself to look at her.

"Listen, I was about to jump all over him. Maybe you don't believe me, but I've never wanted to hit someone so badly in my life. When he touched you, it just made me sick and angry beyond comprehension."

He turned to her, then, and saw she was listening.

"But you beat me to it, Zoey. You had him down before I could move. I think we both just have to accept that you're more badass than me."

She stared at him and a slow smile crept up her lips. "I am, aren't I?"

"Yes," he said, laughing in relief. "You're amazing. I'm sorry you had to go through this today."

"It was the least romantic breakfast I've ever experienced."

He shook his head. "I was a fool. As though I didn't have enough odds against me, I had to go and attempt the impossible."

She laughed, and he drove her home. They took their breakfast inside and ate at her kitchen table. The kids were as excited as ever to see Uncle Kellen. He loved the way they wanted to tell him about every little thing going on in their lives.

He and Zoey had come to a silent agreement to keep Damon's recent activities from Maya. When Maya asked what happened to his face, he told her he got in a bar fight with a drunk guy who wouldn't stop flirting with Jayce. The story was believable because Jayce always had a disproportionately large number of men flirting with him.

After a couple of hours of playing with the kids, Kellen decided to head home. He wasn't going to get anywhere with Zoey that day, and he had some work he needed to finish up.

"What work?" Zoey asked as she walked him to his truck.

"Gotta edit some photos for a magazine."

"Oh, yeah. Freelance photography. How well does that pay?"

He gaped at her and playfully shoved her shoulder. "It

didn't pay too well at first, but I'm doing pretty damn good for myself now, thank you very much."

"If it made you a millionaire, I'd still say it wasn't a real job."

"Well, I'd be a millionaire, so fuck you."

She dropped her head back and laughed. "You so stole my line."

"I did," he said, stepping toward her. He couldn't resist putting his hand in that thick, red mane of hers. As fine as her body was, that hair had always kept his attention ensnared, even in high school.

She sat in front of him in his AP Biology class. He was so impressed with how she'd worked to get here. Sixteen and wrapping up her senior year. She was easily the most beautiful girl he'd ever seen. He wished it wasn't so, because she clearly didn't know he existed. He tried to get her attention whenever she was with Maya, who was usually with Damon. But Zoey either ignored him or glared at him. He wasn't sure which was worse.

It was lucky getting to be in a class with her. Maybe this would be his chance to ask her out. He could ask her to prom. Sophomores loved being asked to prom. Maybe if she went to prom, he could get his hands in her hair. He'd always figured he was an ass-man, and Zoey indeed had a fine ass…but that hair.

He spent entire classes trying to come up with an excuse to get her attention and this day was no different, except that he finally had an idea. Maya and Damon were going to see The Hills Have Eyes *that night at the theater. He would invite Zoey to come with them and then maybe she'd get scared and hang on to him.*

Class was almost over. Mr. Snider was droning on and on. Kellen had been getting increasingly nervous. It was now or never. He reached up and tugged gently on a lock of her perfect, perfect hair.

He'd expected her to turn and raise a brow in gentle, silent inquiry. Instead, her spine stiffened. She spun, her hair whipping to the side, and pierced him with rage-filled eyes. "Touch my hair again and die, asshole!" she snarled in a harsh whisper

She didn't wait for a response, but turned back to her desk and scooted further forward, out of his reach. Somehow, Mr. Snider didn't notice. Kellen sat there, his hand still outstretched, his mouth open, and stared at the back of her head.

That night, Kellen found out about Maya's pregnancy. He consoled her and promised to help her even as Damon held her and promised to care for her. As the evening wore on, the talk turned from practicalities to dreams. Damon was promising white picket fences and two-car garages. Kellen was just excited to be an uncle. He'd never held a baby before. On a more selfish note, he was glad Maya was permanently in Damon's life because that meant always having Zoey nearby.

The next day, thrilled about everything, Kellen approached Zoey. "How crazy is it?" he said. "I'm gonna be an uncle."

At which point she broke his nose with her fist. She got in school suspension, which she fully deserved, but Kellen looked for a moment to speak to her, to figure out what had gone wrong. He found the moment a week later. She was walking to her car at the end of the day. He caught up to her. "Hey," he said, almost reaching for her arm, but stopping when he remembered how she'd acted over his touching a small bit of her hair.

She spun to face him. "What?"

He waited a beat, thinking she would do the decent thing and apologize. She didn't. So he did. "I'm sorry for upsetting you the other day," he said.

She laughed. "Seriously?"

"Yeah. I like you, Zoey. I don't want to piss you off. Maybe we

could go out for coffee, or something, and—"

"You're making me late for work."

"Oh. I'm sorry, but if you could give me a time—"

"I'm not giving you anything. Fuck off, Kellen." She turned and left. Even then, he was distracted by the way her hair lifted in the breeze.

He pushed it back over her shoulder and let it play through his fingers. "I love this," he whispered. "This alone is worth it all."

Her breath hitched. She folded her arms over her chest and took a step backwards. "Thanks. See you around, Kellen."

She turned to leave. He grabbed her arm and turned her to face him. She wouldn't look at him. She just stared at his chest, her teeth clenched shut like a stubborn child. He held her by the shoulders and rested his forehead atop hers. "I'll take care of you—"

"Stop. Just don't."

"Zoey, I want you. It's fun and all, but I'm starting to feel like this might never happen. I don't know what I'll do if this never happens."

She looked up at him, her brows furrowed. "I guess we could just go back to your place this afternoon. Just burn off all this energy so we can go on with our lives."

He dropped his hands and stepped back. "That's not what I want. Is that what you want?"

She hitched a shoulder. "Sometimes it helps to just get it out of your system."

That must have been what she'd meant when she'd said she would hurt him. She couldn't be that cold. No one could be that cold. "That's all you feel for me?"

She threw up her hands. "What else is there?"

It was a punch to the chest. "How about history? How about years of me trying to get past your walls and you finally letting me in? Zoey, I got nothing against casual sex, but what I feel for you…it's deeper than just attraction."

She laughed, but the sound was hollow. "You think that, but you can't handle me. I'm not…." She stopped and looked away. "I'm not as together as you think. I mean, I was in a relationship a little over a year ago. Terry Hale. You know him?"

Kellen knew who he was, so he nodded.

"I really liked him. Kind of like how I like you. I wanted something…more…than what I'd had, and I thought maybe I was ready. It went bad. You should, maybe, talk to him."

Kellen shook his head. "I don't have to talk to him. I can handle you, Zoey. I want to see where this goes."

She studied him long and hard before she stepped back. "I'm sorry. If you want to go away for a weekend and just, you know, tear into each other, just get this out of our systems, then I'm up for that. But I don't want to start something with you that's going to get you hurt."

"Quit worrying about hurting me and admit that you don't wanna get hurt yourself."

"All right," she said without hesitation. "I don't wanna get hurt. A guy like you has the potential to break my heart. I'm not ready for that risk. I'm sorry, Kellen. Let me know if you wanna hook up."

With that, she turned and went inside. He stood there, for a moment, and let the emotions flow through him. He was vacillating between frustration and pain.

He got in his truck and drove home, wondering what had possessed him to think he had a chance with her. Wondering why he even wanted one.

CHAPTER FOURTEEN

Jayce's bar might not have been the most romantic place to take a date for drinks after dinner, but Kellen had learned from past mistakes and wasn't straying too far from home for this one. After spending an hour in the car with Celeste crying and telling him how much she missed her ex, he wasn't taking any chances.

It had been three days since Zoey had blown him off. He'd put her out of his mind. Hadn't even given her a second thought. They would just be friends. No big deal. Besides, she was right—she was far too high maintenance. He deserved someone nice, like Amy.

He'd met Amy at the grocery store the day before. Her bag had broken on her way out the door, and he'd helped her pick up her things. She'd thanked him with the sweetest smile he'd ever seen.

She further impressed him by showing up for their date on time, dressed in an attractive, but practical, skirt and cardigan set. She looked like she'd walked out of an episode of Leave It To Beaver. Which was just right for his needs.

They'd had a lovely dinner and now, since he wasn't ready for the night to be over, he was taking her to Jayce's. He led her in by the elbow and smiled when he saw her looking around at the place like it was her first time at Disneyland. She was definitely over twenty-one, which he was glad to know, since her innocence might have given him second thoughts. Maybe she'd just never been in this particular bar.

Her ponytail bobbed back and forth as she took in her surroundings. He led her to the bar, because he wanted Jayce to meet her.

Jayce looked unimpressed as he jerked his head up in greeting. He was chewing on a toothpick and had a rag slung over one shoulder. "What'll it be, kids?" he asked as they settled in at the counter.

"Beer," Kellen said. "What about you, Amy?"

She shrugged, her arms close to her body. "Um, I don't know. What kind of drinks can you make?" she asked Jayce.

Jayce shot Kellen a look, which Kellen ignored. "Anything you want, sweetheart."

Amy blushed and giggled. She didn't interpret Jayce's 'sweetheart' in the cavalier manner in which he'd said it. "Um…I've always wanted to try a screwdriver."

Jayce arched a brow at Kellen as he moved down the counter to fix their drinks. Amy leaned in to Kellen. "Are you friends with him?" she asked in a reverent whisper, as though Jayce were a celebrity or minor god.

"Yeah, since first grade."

"Oh, wow."

Jayce returned with their drinks, and Kellen introduced him to Amy. "I really like your tattoos," Amy said to Jayce. "Where did you get them?" She rested her chin on her palm and stirred her drink absently.

Jayce glanced at Kellen.

"I mean, I hope you don't mind my asking," she said. "Did you get them in the Army or in prison or something?"

Jayce took his toothpick out of his mouth and stared at her. "Got them at the mall. From a nineteen-year-old girl named Tiffany with pink hair."

Kellen tipped his beer to his lips to hide his grin.

Amy's expression fell, and Jayce walked away to take care of another customer. "He's—different," Amy said, her eyes never leaving Jayce.

This was not the first time this had happened to Kellen. Certain women were more attracted to Jayce's image than his own, which just seemed wrong. Kellen felt his image projected dependability and stability. Jayce's image, though it was only surface deep, was that of a hard-drinking, heavy-hitting thug…the kind of man who ended up beating his wife. Kellen wondered if Amy would be disappointed to find out that Jayce had a heart of gold.

She sipped her screwdriver and made a funny face.

"Don't like it?" Kellen asked.

"I'm not really a big fan of orange juice," she said.

Kellen pressed his lips together and stared at her for a moment, wondering why she'd pick an orange juice based drink if she didn't like orange juice. Then he jerked his head up at Jayce.

Jayce nodded and a few seconds later, moved back toward them. "Not a fan?" he asked Amy.

She hunched her shoulders and made an apologetic face. "I'm sorry."

"No problem. What else you wanna try?"

"Um, maybe you could make a suggestion? Aren't you bartenders supposed to be able to guess a person's drink?"

Jayce leaned back, his face still devoid of expression. He kept his eyes on Amy as he flipped up a shot glass, poured it full of whiskey, and slid it over to Kellen. "I make this candy Cosmo for Janice," he said, nodding toward the buxom, blond waitress over by the pool tables. He was already pulling liquor off the shelves. "Should suit you."

"Is Janice your girlfriend?"

Jayce didn't answer.

Kellen shot back the whiskey and then reached across the bar and refilled his own glass. He filled in for Jayce, tending bar sometimes, so Jayce didn't mind if he helped himself.

Amy took the drink Jayce handed her and sipped. Her face lit up. "It's so good. You're so good at this. So do you have a girlfriend?"

He folded his arms over his chest. He looked at Kellen and shook his head. Kellen just shrugged. What could he do? He knew it was over. "Amy, I think after this drink, I'll take you on home. It's getting late."

"Oh," she said, her brow creasing. "I guess so. Maybe we'll come back again tomorrow?"

She glanced hopefully at Jayce.

Kellen laughed bitterly. "Maybe." Hell no.

"You okay to drive?" Jayce asked.

Kellen wasn't really feeling the two shots and the beer, but that didn't mean he should be driving. He turned his eyes up to Jayce. Jayce smirked. "You man the bar. I'll take her home."

"Really?" Amy squealed, as though she had a shot in hell of Jayce hooking up with her.

Kellen moved behind the bar and handed Jayce the keys. He handled the few customers who were there on a Thursday night until Jayce returned less than fifteen minutes later.

"You sure can pick 'em, man," he said, after reclaiming his spot behind the bar.

Kellen sat back down on a stool and drank the whiskey handed to him. "I saw her," he said, working on shot number four, "and I thought, this seems like a nice girl. She's, like, the absolute opposite of Zoey. That's what I want, and I went for it. Unfortunately…," He threw back the shot. "I was wrong."

"Opposite of Zoey? The fuck is that s'posed to mean?" Jayce asked.

Kellen shook his head, starting to not care. "You ever have feelings for a woman that you think are serious, but then she acts like they're not serious?"

Jayce just leaned on the bar.

"I mean, I've been with girls where all it was was just sex, and then they went and got all clingy and started acting like I owed them some sort of relationship when I'd been very clear that I was just looking for fun. To hear it said back to you…I mean, can you believe she actually said we should just fuck and get it out of our systems? And beyond that, shouldn't I be jumping at the opportunity?"

Six shots in, he was feeling philosophical.

Jayce didn't pour him another one. "I'm confused," he said. "Who are we talking about?"

Kellen dropped his head back and groaned. "No one. Just…I don't know why I want her, and I don't know why what she's offering isn't enough."

"So sleep with her anyway. Maybe she'll change her mind. If not, at least you got laid." Jayce shrugged. It was just as simple as that, for him.

"I wish I lived in your world, Jayce. So uncomplicated."

"The fuck does that mean?"

"It means that you don't dwell on your feelings and make everything all confusing. I admire that."

Jayce frowned. "Kind of sounds like one of those insults disguised as a compliment. I'm sorry…who is this we're talking about? Because you mentioned Zoey and I just want to clarify—"

"Fuck Zoey! She's on her own. She had her chance and she fucking blew it." Kellen felt a profound sadness that clutched at his chest and throat and eyes.

"Oh, shit," Jayce said.

Kellen fought it back, though. No tears escaped; however, the pain was plain on his face.

"Listen," said Jayce. "You crash upstairs, okay? Don't give her another thought. She's not the girl for you, Kel."

Kellen nodded then shuffled down the hall to the back stairs that led up to Jayce's apartment. He fell onto the couch and flipped the television on. He fell asleep.

CHAPTER FIFTEEN

It took Zoey four days to admit she'd done it on purpose. She'd pushed him away because he was right. She was looking for a man who would fight for her. Now she'd gone and blown it for herself.

She sped up the highway toward St. Louis on Saturday morning. She was headed to the Chesterfield Mall to fulfill the wish lists of two, displaced little angels. Maya had made her a list based on the kids' letters to Santa. Christmas was less than a week away, and Maya wanted to get some presents under the tree.

Zoey was glad for the chance to escape. She'd been moping around, feeling sorry for herself for too long. Kellen hadn't called or come by, of course. Why would he? Besides, she'd done the right thing. She'd ended it before it had even begun. It would have been wrong of her to string him along. Once she'd realized their attraction, she'd backed off. All was well.

Addy had offered to come shopping with her, but Zoey thought it best that she stayed and babysat Maya and the kids. Besides, it was good to be alone for a while.

She found the mall and parked in a spot way in the back. The ground was covered in a couple of inches of snow, which had become muddy slush in the parking lot. She hiked through it to the mall entrance and was blasted with noise. Never having had a family to buy for, she hadn't understood the concept of last-minute shopping, but now she saw what the big deal was. The weekend before Christmas. It was sheer madness.

She took a breath, squared her shoulders, and marched through the crowds to the nearest children's clothing store. She shopped for a couple of cute outfits for each of them then moved on to the bookstore and loaded up on books for the kids and a few novels she thought Maya might like. After that, she made her way to the toy store. Her Everest.

People weren't flowing through the store so much as they were being squeezed in and out of the doorway as the room reached capacity. In this store, she had specific needs. Matthew wanted a junior chemistry set and there was a certain doll that Sophie wanted.

Zoey shifted her bags, slung her purse strap over her head, so it wouldn't get knocked off her shoulder, and braced herself. "I'm going in," she mumbled.

She'd never considered herself to be short, but there were a lot of people in the world taller than her. She saw a toy that was on the list and had to grab it before the crowd moved her forward. She tucked it under her arm and then saw the chemistry set. She tucked it with the other toy. And then….

There was the doll. And oh, shit, there was only one left. She shoved past a large woman with too much makeup on. A man in a flannel shirt and beanie had a head-on collision with her. She shoved him out of the way and jammed her elbows into anyone who got in her way. Five more steps. Four. Three. Two.

"Yes!" she shouted, as she put her hand on the box.

Then she looked up into the eyes of a balding, middle-aged man with crooked teeth. "I'm sorry, miss, I got to it first."

His hands were on the doll. She grinned. "No, sir, you didn't. This is for my niece, I'm sorry." She pulled, but he didn't let go.

"Everyone wants this doll," he observed, "but I got here first, and you need to back off."

"Sir, you do not know who you're fucking with. If you don't let go of this goddamn doll, you're in for a whole world of pain."

"Are you threatening me?"

"You're damn right. Give me the doll." She pulled. He pulled back. She pulled again.

"Listen, bitch, I'm not letting this go."

She was fed up with being called a bitch. "Let. Go. Asshole!"

The guy let go with one hand, but then he wound his hand in her hair and yanked. She screamed and instinctively jammed her knee into his crotch. Zoey taken self-defense classes and had no fear of fighting back. She swung her elbow into his face. Finally she was free of him. She stumbled back toward the checkout counter. By the time she arrived, she'd regained her composure, if not her breath. She glanced back, looking for the guy, but he was gone.

She'd intended to have the store clerk call the cops, but since the guy was gone, she decided it was pointless.

She bought the toys and then made the long, painful trek out of the store.

"That's her."

She instinctively knew this voice was talking about her. She turned to find the man she'd allegedly assaulted hunkered over his damaged balls and holding a tissue to his bleeding nose. Mall security was next to him.

Zoey rolled her eyes. "Come on, man, you started it."

"I want her arrested."

"What?"

"I'm going to have to go to the emergency room." And then the man fell to the floor in a faint. Zoey was pretty sure it was all a big act, but that thought didn't alter her present circumstances.

She found herself ushered to a bench where one of the mall security guys hovered near her, detaining her for the police

EMTs arrived ten minutes later, with the police shortly behind them. The guy was conscious, not that she'd been worried. He'd only passed out from the pain. A policeman came at her with handcuffs.

"Seriously?" she said. "I'll cooperate."

"Ma'am, you're under arrest. You have the right to remain silent…." He recited her rights.

She could only laugh at the absurdity of it. Then she looked around and saw other policemen taking interviews from witnesses.

By the time she was pushed into the squad car, she'd stopped laughing. "Are you fucking serious?" she asked.

The cop driving didn't say a word. She slammed back into the seat. "This is ridiculous. He had hold of my hair and was pulling hard."

"Ma'am, you'll be given a chance to make a statement at the station."

She huffed in silence. She was taken to the station, finger-printed, and photographed. Then she was shoved in a cell with eight other seedy looking women. Zoey wasn't particularly a glamour girl, but next to these women, she looked like royalty. She immediately turned, grabbed the bars, and shouted, "When do I get my phone call!"

It was an hour before someone came. They took her to get her statement. Then she was allowed to make her phone call. She called her house. Maya answered.

"Maya, I need to speak to Addy."

"Oh, Addy's having lunch with her mom."

"You're home alone?"

"No, Kellen's here."

"Shit. Shit, shit, shit."

"What's wrong?"

She took a calming breath. "I need to talk to Kellen."

There was a shuffling as the phone was handed over. "Hey, Zoey."

"Okay, don't judge me, but…." She paused, not sure her pride was going to back down long enough for her to finish the sentence.

"But what?" he asked.

"But I need you to come to St. Louis and bail me out of jail."

Silence.

"Kellen?"

He was laughing again. "I'm sorry," he said, still laughing. "Are you serious?"

"I kneed a guy in the balls in a toy store."

More laughter.

She sighed and waited. A police officer gave her a wrap-it-up signal. "Seriously, Kellen, I have to stay in a cell with some very hostile looking crack-whores, so will you just hurry up?" She mentally prayed he wouldn't ask her to say 'please' because, in this circumstance, she might just have no choice.

"Yeah. Yeah, I'll be there in an hour. Try to stay alive. And don't rack up anymore charges, okay?"

She hung up. A policeman escorted her back to the cell. She rested her forehead on the bars and counted the seconds.

CHAPTER SIXTEEN

Kellen laughed off and on all the way to St. Louis. He found Clark Street and parked in the Justice Center garage. The building was plain, eight levels, with windows on the front and sides. Kellen had never been before. He'd bailed Jayce out a time or two when they were younger, but that was a small town jail, where he knew the Sheriff by name.

He quickly located the bonding window and asked after Zoey. He paid her bond and was directed to a visitor's waiting area. The room was full of people. Some looked despondent and worn down by life. Others looked like him, upstanding citizens there to visit their black sheep acquaintances.

Over an hour later, they brought Zoey out. When he stood, she nearly knocked him down as she threw her arms around his neck. "Aw, it's okay," he said, still finding the whole situation funny. He stroked her back with one hand and then took the bags being handed to him by a police officer with the other. "Looks like you had a successful shopping trip."

She punched him on the shoulder, but there was no fire in it. He slid his arm around her waist and led her out to the garage. He put her bags behind the seat of his truck and turned to find her standing almost against him. Her face was pale, her hands clenched together in front of her, her whole body shaking.

"Oh, sweetheart, come here," he said and took her into his arms. If she cried, she did it quietly, although she was shaking and clinging to him. Not so brave and badass after all, his Zoey. In that moment she'd looked like a scared little girl.

"I'm such an idiot," she said.

Kellen didn't answer her; he wasn't going to offer her false encouragement. What she'd done had been stupid and dangerous.

"The consequences could have been so much worse, you know?" she murmured into his coat.

He knew. He didn't want to think about it, but they could have been miles worse.

"Nobody's ever fought back. Nobody's ever used physical force against me. I've never felt so…vulnerable. And getting arrested? That was fucking humiliating, Kellen."

"I know, Zoey. I know."

She stepped back and shook out her arms. Her cheeks were red and her eyes, bright. "I've been a child. Throwing tantrums everywhere, assuming I would always get my way. What if I'd seriously hurt that man? What if he'd hurt me? Jesus."

For a moment, he watched her wrestle with reality. He waited for her to look at him, and when she did, he smiled. She poked him in the chest. "You're coming Christmas shopping with me next year."

"I insist upon it."

She smiled and climbed in the truck. He closed the door and kept his hand against it for a moment. Next year. He wondered if she meant it.

He went round to his side.

Once they were on the road, Zoey finally seemed to relax.

"You know," he said, "just this morning, when Maya told me you were in St. Louis doing last-minute shopping, the first thing I said was, 'I hope she doesn't assault anyone.'"

"You're a funny guy. You need to start heading west. My car's in the lot at the Chesterfield Mall."

"I'm taking you to dinner."

He heard a huff of breath. "It's too early for dinner."

"Nah, we'll just beat the rush. I wouldn't want to expose you to another large crowd of people."

"Ha ha. I don't want to have dinner with you, Kellen. I just want to get my car and go home."

"I think you do wanna have dinner with me. And if your offer still stands, I think we should get a hotel room."

"What?" she shrieked.

"You know—get this out of our systems—like you said. I think you're right. I haven't been able to eat or sleep right, and it's probably just this chemical reaction between us. We should just fuck, so we can forget it and move on. Don't you think?"

He smirked, proud that he'd shut her up. It had taken his ego a while to settle down, but then he'd recognized her words for what they were: a bluff. Or so he hoped. This was the perfect chance to call her on it.

Kellen swung down toward the river to a burger restaurant he'd been to once before. Inside were two, long tables that spanned the room. There were old-fashioned milk cans painted in various colors hanging over the table. Being an off hour, it wasn't too crowded. Still, it was the Saturday before Christmas, so they definitely weren't alone.

Kellen and Zoey sat across from each other. He watched as she concentrated on taking off her mittens and scarf. They browsed their menus. Everything here was local, down to the sodas and beers. A waitress came and they each ordered a burger and a beer. And then Zoey sat back and finally met his eyes.

"It's fine," she said. "If you want to get a hotel, let's do it. Did you bring condoms?"

He forced himself to keep cool. She was just bluffing. He was sure of it. "Yeah, I always have condoms," he said with a wink.

She rolled her eyes.

At this point, he wasn't worried about her going through with it. He was worried that she was going to make him actually pay for a hotel room before she finally gave up. Not that he couldn't afford it. He just hated to waste money if he wasn't really going to get laid.

The waitress brought their food and drinks. Zoey dove in like usual. He supposed this time she was probably genuinely hungry, given that she'd been shopping or in jail most of the day.

"So, I have a criminal record now, right?" she asked around a mouthful of burger.

"That's right. Unless you're found innocent."

She let out a laugh and shook her head.

"When's your court date?"

"Two weeks. I'll pay you back for the bail money."

"Don't worry about it, just make your court date so I don't have to send bounty hunters after you."

She flipped him off. It didn't even sting anymore. She flipped people off so often the gesture had lost all of its sharpness.

"Have you ever considered anger management?"

"I'm Irish; I don't think anger management works for us."

"You could give it a try. I know where to find a contact for you, if you're interested."

She frowned in thought.

"Zoey, you know those news stories you hear every Christmas about some crazy person doing some crazy thing? You do understand, don't you, that today you were that crazy person?"

Irritation and then shame. She sighed. "I did a few months of therapy not long after I emancipated," she disclosed. "Maybe I'll go back. If nothing else, it's a safe outlet to express my anger."

He smiled as she chomped into her burger.

"Awesome burger, huh?" she mumbled over the food in her mouth.

He grinned and watched her, taking in her little movements: shoving her hair over her shoulder, licking her fingertips, dabbing at the corner of her mouth with her napkin. Her cheeks puffed out when she took too big of bites and she looked like a freckle-faced chipmunk. When her blue eyes met his, though, time stood still. "What?" she asked.

He shook his head. There were no words that he could think of. Maybe 'unrequited,' because he wasn't sure if he would ever be able to make his way into her heart. She'd put up roadblocks everywhere.

But then her eyes softened and she gulped down the bite of burger she'd been chewing. "Everyone says I'll hurt you," she said.

Thank God. A real conversation. He leaned forward, so he could talk more quietly. "I'm a big boy, Zoey. I see you. I understand what I'm in for. And you…you can try, can't you? Your life doesn't have to be controlled by your anger, does it? Tell whatever voice it is that's trying to talk you out of this to shut the fuck up."

She almost smiled. But then her eyes went sad. "I don't want to get hurt. I mean, that kind of hurt. I've never met a guy I thought had that power, but looking at you, Kellen…well, you could definitely hurt me."

He shook his head. "I can promise you it'll be worth it. Just think about it. How great is this?" He gestured back and forth between them.

She smiled down at the table. "Pretty great. I mean, I have friends, but with you it's—different."

"Yeah, so let's go with it."

"You're such a nice guy, Kellen—"

"Fuck that. I'm sick of hearing that. Yeah, I'm nice, but I'm not made of glass. I can handle you, Zoey. I want to handle you."

She grinned. "I want to be handled."

His heart quickened, and he was suddenly out of things to say. She reached across the table and took his hand.

"Let's not have sex today," she said.

He laughed. "Music to my ears." He took her hand and kissed the backs of her fingers. "I wanna see you, though. I wanna date."

"Okay. We'll give it a try."

They finished eating and he drove her to her car. The parking lot was still crowded towards the front, but the back had opened up. He was able to park next to her and help her with her shopping bags.

He opened her door for her and she turned and hugged his waist. "Thank you."

He threaded his hand into her hair. He'd never felt anything so soft and silky, and there was so much of it. He wondered what it would be like with her on top of him and all of that hair falling down around his face.

She tipped her head back and his attention was captured by her lips. Her full, smiling lips over white teeth. He leaned down. Her smile faded as she met him half way and their lips touched.

Her small hands fisted in his shirt. The action undid him. He wrapped his arms around her, spun, and pressed her against his truck. He let her pull away long enough to gulp in a breath, and then his lips were back on hers, taking and taking, only to find that it wasn't enough. It was never going to be enough.

He pressed his body hard against hers, hating the

clothes that separated them. His hands roamed and squeezed up and down her waist and thighs. She broke away, turning her head. He kissed her neck, running his tongue along her jaw.

"Kellen!" she squeaked.

He wanted more. Needed more. He grabbed her ass and squeezed her hard against him. Her gasps and kisses drove him crazy.

"Hey!"

They froze and turned their faces. A mall security car. "You kids need to go somewhere else for that."

They both nodded and then, when he drove away, laughed. He let her go and took a half step back just so she could breathe. She smiled up at him with her red, swollen lips. There wasn't an ounce of mocking or flirtation in the smile, just pure, sweet Zoey. "God, I love this," he said, tracing her bottom lip with his fingertip.

This added a blush to her cheeks. She reached up, smoothed his sweater, and straightened his jacket. "Kids are making gingerbread houses Monday. You wanna come over?"

He nodded. "Yeah. I do."

"Good." She tiptoed up and kissed his neck just beneath his jaw.

With one, last, heated look, she stepped past him and climbed into her car. He watched her back out and start around the parking lot before getting in his truck.

CHAPTER SEVENTEEN

Her bed was a more than welcome sight. She fell face down into her fluffy pillows and screamed into them, punching and kicking for a moment. So many emotions. She'd had simultaneously her best and worst day ever. Kellen's kiss had definitely soothed her broken ego and temporarily made her forget her terrifying and humiliating arrest. In fact, it had lifted her to an exhilarating sort of peace.

She rolled to her back and let her body go limp. Upon arriving home, there had been questions to answer and kids to keep entertained. She'd held back everything she was feeling because for the first time in her life, she didn't want Addy and Maya to know something about her. She didn't want them to know that she might be falling in love.

More than anything, she was sure they wouldn't believe her. She already knew they didn't want her hurting Kellen. It was best just to do what she wanted and let them figure it out on their own.

She got up and undressed, showered, and put on some flannel pajama bottoms and a t-shirt. It was after ten, but she was too wound up to sleep, so she opened up her book and settled against her pillows.

She jolted when she heard a pounding at the front door. She jumped out of bed and peeked out the window. Damon was slamming his fist on the door.

Zoey's gun was in a locked safe on the dresser next to her phone. She dialed the sheriff with one hand while she unlocked the box with the other.

"Sheriff's office," the receptionist said.

"This is Zoey Odell. I need you to send someone to my house immediately. Damon Bradley is here in violation of his wife's protection order."

"Someone will be out there soon."

Damon was still pounding on the door. Zoey stepped out of her room and tip-toed down the hall, the gun held in both hands in front of her, aimed at the floor. Maya was sitting on the edge of the sofa, trembling. Addy had gone home to her parents' house, where she was staying for winter break. Poor Maya's bottom lip was quivering. "I hope he doesn't wake up the babies," she whispered.

Zoey shook her head. "The police are on their way."

"Open up! I just wanna talk to my wife! I got a right to talk to my wife!"

Maya's eyes were wide and dark. She held onto her elbows and rocked back and forth.

"You let me in, you worthless whore!"

Then the pounding changed. Now it was one, big, rattling thud. And then another. Zoey heard the wood splinter. An instant later, the door flew open, smashing into the wall.

Zoey snapped the gun up and trained it on his face. "Freeze!" she said.

For a moment he did, his eyes flying open in surprise. It wasn't long before he grinned. "You don't even know how to shoot that."

"Damon, I'll shoot you if you don't back out of my house right now!"

"The more you talk, bitch, the more it's gonna hurt when I give you what you deserve."

"Get out!" she shouted, suddenly terrified that he wasn't going to leave. She'd always envisioned that threat of the gun would be enough.

It wasn't. He charged. In that split second of decision, she recognized that she couldn't shoot him. She also recognized that his fists were clenched and ropey with veins; his eyes held nothing of human sympathy, but instead were blue pools of rage. She knew she couldn't fire a warning shot over his head. She lived in town, and the bullet could go anywhere. Instead, she aimed between his feet at the floor and fired.

The pop of the gun caused a pop in her ears and then there was only ringing. And screaming. The bastard had put his foot right where she'd been aiming. Now he lay on the floor, holding his foot and screaming at the top of his lungs.

Maya was backed against a wall, gaping, with her hands over her ears.

"Go be with your kids," Zoey said, her voice way more sturdy than the rest of her.

Maya nodded and shuffled behind her.

A moment later, the Sheriff and a deputy arrived. She was still standing over Damon aiming her gun. The ringing had begun to subside.

As soon as the officers saw her, they whipped out their pistols, holding them down and angled away from her. Randy, the deputy she'd gone to school with, said, "Zoey, put the gun down."

She was breathing deep and hard, her senses on alert, adrenaline coursing through her. She nodded and crouched to the floor. Once the gun was on the floor, she stood and backed away.

"Why don't you go have a seat on the sofa," Randy said.

Sheriff Carlyle, the other officer, was on his radio calling in an ambulance.

Zoey stared down at her trembling hands in her lap. The ringing in her ears was fading. Her front door was open, and cold, winter air flowed in. She began to shake.

A warm blanket went around her shoulders. A warm arm. She turned to see Kullen frowning at her. At the eye contact, his expression softened and he smiled. "Tough day, huh?"

She laughed in relief and leaned into him. "How'd you get here?"

"Maya called."

Zoey sat up. "Would you check on her? I'm sure the kids are terrified."

"The sheriff's talking to her. I'm staying with you."

"I'm fine. Go check on her, please? I feel so awful for those poor kids."

141

"Zoey, you're shaking. I wanna take care of you—"

She got up to check on Maya herself. She clutched the ends of the blanket with both hands. Maya was in the kids' room with the sheriff, but her kids weren't there.

"Where are Mattie and Sophie?" Zoey asked.

"In your room," Maya said softly. "They're watching Christmas movies on your television."

Zoey tip-toed down the hall and peeked in on them. "You guys okay?" she asked.

Mattie had his arm around his little sister. "Was that our dad?" he asked.

"Your mom will be in to explain everything—"

"It was our dad," Mattie said, his voice and eyes cold. "He was drunk. Is he dead?"

Zoey's throat tightened. "No, honey, I—"

"You should have shot him dead."

She went to the edge of the bed and sat. "I understand, Mattie," she said quietly. "But let's not say things like that in front of Sophie, okay?"

Mattie glared. "Can't say them in front of my mom, either."

"You can tell your mom anything."

"No, I can't. She tells me lies like how he's my father and he loves me no matter what. You think she thinks he loves her, too?"

Zoey didn't know how to answer. She brought him into her arms and held him, kissed his forehead. Sophie leaned into them and she gently rocked them both.

A throat cleared. She turned her head. Kellen leaned in the door with a blank expression. "Sheriff's ready for you," he said.

She released the children and left them to finish watching *Elf*. In the hall, Kellen put his hand on her back. She stopped and faced him. "Could you stay with them?"

"I'd like to be by your side for this—"

"I don't need you. They—"

"They don't need me either. But if you don't want me there, then—"

"I don't. Just stay with them." She walked away, not looking back to see if he complied.

The ambulance had come and gone, carting off a screaming Damon. A blood stain and bullet hole now resided in the entryway of her house. *Perhaps a long rug* she thought distantly.

After answering the Sheriff's questions, Zoey found herself alone on the sofa with a blanket wrapped around her in a very quiet, very still house. She stood and went to the front door, pushing it closed. She wedged a shoe underneath of it to hold it. And then she laughed. *Like a shoe is going to do any good.* Of course her deadbolt hadn't done much good, either, so maybe safety was an illusion.

Zoey picked up her gun and took it back to her room. The kids and Kellen were asleep. She returned the gun to the safe and then pulled a blanket over Kellen. One of his arms was draped over Sophie.

Across the hall, Maya was in her room perched on the edge of her bed, holding her arms around herself. She looked up when Zoey leaned in the doorway. "I'm so sorry," Maya whispered.

"I'm sorry. I keep trying to think of some way I could have handled that better. Lately, it feels like my life is a series of wrong decisions."

"Not tonight," Maya said. "Tonight you protected us all. Believe me, I know first hand what he would have done to you. And then to me. You did the only thing you could. Thank you, Zoey."

Zoey crawled into bed with her. They fell asleep holding hands.

CHAPTER EIGHTEEN

Once again, Zoey was startled awake by the sound of banging. Her heart rate shot up and she swung her legs out of bed. The sun was up, her house bright with it. She hesitated in the hallway trying to decide whether to get her gun first or check on the noise.

At last she recognized the sound. Hammering. She peeked in at the kids. They were still sleeping. No Uncle Kellen with them. She exhaled and turned left toward the living room. Immediately she was hit with cold air. Her door was off its hinges and resting against her front porch rail while Kellen and Jayce installed a new doorframe.

She stood in her pajama bottoms and tank top staring at them. At last, Kellen glanced her direction. His eyes dropped to her chest for a quick moment before he returned to his hammering. "Cold morning, huh?" he asked.

Jayce chuckled.

Zoey looked down and covered her chest with her arms. She didn't have a snide or witty remark available to her. They were fixing her door. She could only watch. "I'll make coffee," she said.

In her kitchen, she set the coffee pot brewing and then mixed up a pot of hot chocolate for the kids. Then she went to her room to put on a bra and a sweatshirt. There were a couple of space heaters in her hall closet, so she set one up in her room to keep the kids warm. It was only seven in the morning. Hopefully they would sleep for another hour or more.

"Where'd you find a hardware store open on a Sunday?" she asked, once she'd returned to the living room.

"Jayce's cousin owns the one over by Belle's," Kellen said.

Jayce was on his knees applying caulk to the floor where the subsill would be.

"If you'd awakened me, I'd have helped," Zoey said. "How much do I owe you."

"It's a Christmas present, Zoey," Kellen said.

She watched them work, not sure what to think of the whole situation. Jayce had just checked the level on the subsill when, for some reason, he glanced up. His eyes stayed on whatever was behind Zoey.

"What are you guys doing?" Maya asked.

Jayce stood to his full height and stared. Kellen answered, "Fixing your door, Sis."

"God, Kellen, you're just the best ever," Maya said.

Kellen grinned while Jayce just gaped at her. Zoey

turned and saw she was standing there in only her nightshirt that came halfway down her thighs. Even with the bruises on her face, she looked willowy and beautiful. "Aren't you cold?" Zoey asked.

Maya shivered. "Yeah. I'm gonna go change. Thanks again, Kellen."

Once she was gone, Jayce held out his hands. "It's like I'm invisible."

He and Kellen lifted the door into place. They were on the outside and now closed off from her view. She went back to the kitchen and poured some coffee.

A few minutes later, the door came back out and they began installing the hinges. Maya came in and wrapped her arms around Zoey's waist. Zoey hugged her gently, mindful of her broken rib.

"Kellen always takes such good care of me," Maya said.

Zoey forgave her because she was on pain meds. But it was hard not to get a little jealous. "He might be taking care of me, too, you know?"

Maya laughed. "Sure, Zoey. More like he's trying to keep you happy so you don't put a hex on him."

Zoey stiffened and turned away. She took her coffee to the table and sat. Maya joined her. Clearly she hadn't noticed Zoey's reaction since she was still smiling. When the kids woke up, they strolled into the kitchen in their pajamas, rubbing their sleepy eyes. Zoey stood and poured them some cereal. By the time they finished, Jayce and Kellen were swinging the door open and shut to make sure it was installed well. Then Jayce went to work putting in the deadbolt while Kellen stood back with his hands on his hips and watched.

When, at last, they finished and were cleaning up the mess, Zoey rose from the table, "You boys want coffee, or hot chocolate?" she asked.

"Coffee," Kellen said, at the same time as Jayce said, "Do you have marshmallows?"

Jayce then cleared his throat and lowered his voice. "I mean coffee. Black. Extra strong."

Maya giggled and Zoey didn't think she was mistaken when she saw his cheeks flush.

Zoey took a tray with four mugs on it into the living room. Hot chocolate and marshmallows for Jayce and Maya. Coffee for herself and Kellen.

They sat around her living room simultaneously exhausted and wound-up. Jayce and Maya sat on the sofa and Kellen sat next to Zoey on the love seat. Zoey had put all the kids' toys down in her basement so they could play as loud as they wanted and not worry about the clutter. After finishing their cereal, they ran down the stairs, talking about a superhero game they wanted to play.

As they disappeared down the stairs, the last thing Zoey heard was Sophie saying, "I don't wanna be Black Widow. I wanna be Spider Man."

Mattie replied, "You can't be Spider Man. You're not a man."

Sophie said, "I'm not a spider, either, so what?"

Zoey caught Jayce's expression. He was nodding. "Kid's smart," he said.

The little voices gone, Zoey said, "Thank you guys. Both of you."

Jayce cleared his throat, making Maya flinch. She was

hugging the end of the sofa like she was trying to keep as much distance as possible between her and the big, scary man. "Damon," Jayce said, "He had a protection order against him, right? This'll put him in jail?"

"For up to a year," Kellen answered. "I talked to the sheriff. Damon's under arrest for criminal contempt, so they'll hold him until his trial for violating the protection order."

Jayce blew out a breath and turned his head to look at Maya. "Is there anything I can do, Maya?" he asked.

She shrugged and glanced nervously at him, not holding eye contact. "I'll be looking for work soon. I don't suppose you're hiring?"

Jayce shook his head. "I wouldn't hire you."

Maya didn't have time to react because Zoey was on it. "What kind of an asshole thing is that to say? She asks you for a job and this is how you respond? Like she's not good enough to wait tables in your shitty bar?"

He pointed his finger at her. "I've about had it with your attitude. You jump to conclusions and start shrieking at people. Fuck you, Zoey!"

"Fuck you, Jayce!"

"Whoa, whoa, whoa," Kellen said. "Children are playing downstairs. Let's settle down."

Jayce glared at Zoey for a moment before turning to Maya. "I didn't mean that how it sounded. I just think with all of us looking, we can find you a better job than serving drinks in my shitty bar."

Maya smiled and lowered her head. She nodded. "Okay. Thanks."

Jayce and Zoey flipped each other off. But then he

sipped his cocoa, got marshmallow foam on his upper lip, and drained Zoey of her ire. She laughed.

"What?" Jayce asked, feigning innocence. He sipped again.

Maya even grinned.

Kellen leaned back and slipped his arm over Zoey's shoulders. Which was when Jayce and Maya froze, both of them with marshmallow cream on their lips in a comic tableau of shock.

Jayce didn't say anything, though his countenance darkened.

"Zoey?" Maya asked, dragging the name out slowly. "What's going on?"

Zoey felt suddenly exhausted. She sat her coffee mug on the end table and then leaned into Kellen, who took the hint and did the talking. "We've decided to start dating," he said.

Dating. It sounded so long term. Zoey smiled and nuzzled into his chest.

Jayce licked the marshmallow off his lip and leaned back, his expression going blank while his eyes observed all.

Maya shook her head. "I don't understand. Zoey, you don't even like Kellen."

"I do now."

"This is a bad idea. Such a bad idea. Kellen, you're smarter than this."

"Fuck you, Maya," Zoey said, responding to the hurt that Maya's doubt was causing.

Maya gasped.

"Easy," Jayce said.

"No, you take it easy!" Zoey was sitting up now, her face heating with rage. "God, some friend you are Maya. Thanks for being so damned supportive."

"I can't believe you expect me to support you while you hurt the most important man in my life! Kellen is my brother, Zoey. You don't get to treat him like he's just some guy you picked up."

"Nice! Thanks for just assuming that's what I'm gonna do."

"Oh, please. You use men, Zoey. You don't even think of them as humans…they're just sex objects to you, so don't act all offended—"

"Oh, my God, really?" They were both on their feet, now. "I made an effort with Terry—"

"Bullshit!"

"Whoa." Jayce stood and put his hand on Maya's shoulder. She flinched and he quickly withdrew his hand. "Let's just calm down."

"Fuck you, Jayce!" And since this came from Maya, everyone was stunned into silence. The generally stoic Jayce stood there with his mouth open in shock. Maya pressed her hands to her mouth. "Oh my God, I'm so sorry."

Jayce laughed. And then Kellen laughed. Zoey smiled down at her feet.

"Jayce, I didn't mean it."

"Maya, you can curse at me anytime you want," he said.

"I won't. I'm so sorry. Zoey, God, this is getting out of hand."

"Then apologize to me," Zoey said. "You apologize to

Jayce, but you just said way worse things to me."

"Was any of it untrue?"

"Yes!" she shrieked. Kellen's hands rested on her shoulders. "I do not treat men like that, Maya! I'm just really honest and if they can't take it then how is that my fault?"

"That is not what I'm talking about and you know it."

"Alright, that's enough," Kellen said. "Maya, I love you, sweetheart. Thank you for caring about me, but this is what I want. Okay?"

Maya huffed and folded her arms around her middle. "I just need you right now," she said, softly.

This made more sense to Zoey. She didn't understand her best friend attacking her. But she did understand Maya not wanting to lose Kellen to another woman. And now she could step back and perch on the edge of the loveseat, because this was about Kellen and Maya, and had little to do with Zoey.

Kellen took Maya into his arms and sat on the sofa next to her, holding her to him while she cried softly. Zoey felt a hint of jealousy. She caught Jayce's expression as he sat on the far end of the sofa and leaned his elbows on his knees. He was feeling a little jealous, too.

"I don't want you to think this is a romantic thing," Maya said to Kellen through her tears. "I don't have those kinds of feelings for you. But you've been my brother all this time and she's gonna mess you up and you won't come here and I need you. You're so strong and I can't do this on my own."

Jayce got up and went into the kitchen. Kellen gently rocked Maya and murmured to her. "I'm never going to stop being there for you. You know that, Maya. You're tired. You're healing. You're on medication. I've got you, okay? And so does Zoey."

Maya was nodding along and crying.

Zoey got up and joined Jayce in the kitchen. He'd found her liquor cabinet. "What say we booze up this hot chocolate?" he said with his back to her.

"A little early in the morning, don't you think?"

He arched a brow at her. "No such thing."

She sighed and poured herself a mug of hot chocolate, handing it to him. "Do your worst."

He pulled out vanilla vodka and Bailey's and poured generous amounts of liquor into each mug. They stirred, clinked their mugs together, and sipped. "Good luck with Kellen," Jayce said.

Zoey paused, her drink midair. "Thank you," she said softly.

He nodded.

"Good luck with—"

"Don't say it," he said.

Zoey smiled.

He shook his head. "Don't even say it."

"Well good luck anyway."

He nodded and drank. A few minutes later, Maya stumbled in and threw her arms around Zoey's neck. She sobbed her apologies while Jayce and Kellen stood uncomfortably by.

At last Maya stepped back and dashed her hands across her eyes. "I can't wait until I'm not crying so much. Seems like all I do is cry."

"Don't think of it," Zoey said. "Just heal, okay?" She

stroked her friend's hair and then nudged her back into the living room.

Jayce said, "Well, I'm going home."

Kellen cleared his throat. "Actually, could you hang out?"

Zoey turned in time to see Jayce's eyes go wide.

Kellen continued, "I thought maybe you could keep an eye on Maya and the kids while I spend some time with Zoey."

Jayce went pale. "Kids?"

Zoey stood. "I'm not comfortable leaving them. We can hang out here."

"No," Kellen said. "I'm taking you out. Jayce, you good?"

"Uh—" Jayce stammered.

"I'm not good," Maya said. "I don't need a babysitter, Kellen. I'm fine for a few hours."

"You can't lift anything," Zoey said. "What if one of the kids gets hurt? You can't get up and down those stairs or carry them."

"I can stay," Jayce said, hesitantly.

"Great," Kellen said.

"It's not necessary," Zoey said. "Because I'm not leaving—"

"We're going on a date. Right now, Zoey. So get dressed, grab your purse, and let's go."

She gaped at him, once again turned on by his attempt to boss her around. In that moment, she wasn't sure whether to put him in his place or obey. Her past boyfriends had all shattered when she'd pushed them and, until this moment, she'd always assumed that was their fault for not being tough enough. But maybe she'd never given them enough credit. Maybe this was her chance to try meeting a guy halfway.

She grinned. "Okay." She walked past him, trailing her fingertips across his abs, and went to her room to change.

Kellen turned to Jayce. "You're good, right?"

Jayce just looked at him.

"Kellen, I'm not comfortable with this," Maya said.

"With what, honey?" Kellen asked.

"With being alone with…." She stopped and cast a quick glance at Jayce.

Jayce laughed without mirth. "Great," he muttered. He turned to Kellen. "I could sit outside the front door so she doesn't feel threatened by my presence."

Kellen moved to the sofa and sat next to Maya. He knew the meds were messing with her emotions, but this was ridiculous. "You've known him as long as you've known me. He's my best friend. I feel safe knowing he's here with you and the kids. Is that good enough?"

She chewed her bottom lip. "I guess."

Jayce laughed again and shoved his hand through his hair, squeezing his hand into a fist. "You know, we went on a date once, Maya. You weren't afraid of me, then. Do you remember that at all?"

Her face turned pink. She shook her head. "I don't remember."

Jayce's arms dropped to his sides and his shoulders fell. "You…you're serious?"

Kellen couldn't watch this. He stood and went to his

friend whose heart was taking yet another kick-in-the-ass by a woman who barely knew he existed. "Maybe you can hang out in Zoey's room," he said. "She's got a television. Just listen for if Maya needs you and around lunch time, if we're not back, help her make something for the kids."

Jayce was still staring in horror at Maya who had moved on and was now channel surfing. He swung his gaze to Kellen.

"I know," Kellen said, giving Jayce's shoulder a squeeze.

Jayce's jaw muscles twitched.

"I'm sorry, man. I know it hurts," Kellen said quietly.

Jayce slumped back on the counter and shook his head.

"You just gotta give her some time."

Jayce stared ahead and nodded, but Kellen could tell his words had meant nothing.

Zoey came out in jeans and a pretty, green sweater. "Ready?" she asked.

Kellen placed his hand on the small of her back and led her out the front door, smiling with pride as the door swung open and clicked shut flawlessly.

He helped her into his truck and started driving.

"Now, it's almost lunchtime," she said. "I feel the need to tell you that lunch dates are no more romantic than breakfast dates."

He smiled, keeping his eyes on the road as they left town and headed down a curvy, back highway.

"Kellen, where are we going?"

"Home."

She laughed. "This is a booty call?"

"Don't cheapen it, Zoey. You want this just as bad as I do." He reached over and rested his hand on her thigh. She made no effort to reject him.

"I thought we were going to date?"

"We are. But tomorrow is gingerbread decorating day. Tuesday is Christmas Eve. Wednesday is Christmas. I need some alone time with you."

"You mean sex."

"Doesn't have to be sex. Probably will be…but doesn't have to be."

She chuckled and put her hand over his on her leg.

He pulled down the dirt driveway to his cabin and listened to her gasp. "What?" he asked.

"I thought you lived in some one-room, log cabin or something. This is really nice."

He climbed out of the truck and went to open the door for her. He held her hand and led her inside. The cabin was two stories with a loft, so the entryway ceiling was high and full of light and air. She seemed to want time to look around, but he dragged her straight up the stairs to his loft bedroom.

She laughed when she saw where they were going. "Kind of feels like you brought me here to, I don't know, establish dominance or something," she said.

"I did." He turned and pulled her hard against him, taking her mouth with his. "I feel like you don't fully grasp how much my girl you are."

She chuckled against his mouth, her hands pawing at his chest and shoulders.

He covered her with kisses and slid his hands beneath her sweater to her back. "Last night you kept pushing me

157

away," he said.

"Mmm."

"No more, Zoey. I want you. I wanna take care of you."

She let out a breath when his hand moved to cup her breast. Her own hand had wandered down to the front of his pants. He'd never been with a woman this aggressive. He'd never been this aggressive with a woman.

"So what are you gonna do next time I try to stand by you?" He shoved her sweater up and over her head. She jerked at his t-shirt, and he helped her peel it off.

She pressed her lips to his chest and his blood sang in his ears.

"Answer me."

She slid her hand down his jeans, taking his length before he had a chance to react. He forced through the blinding urge to fuck her and grabbed her by the wrist. He spun her to face the bed and pressed against her back, bending her over the bed. God, he'd never done this. It felt freaking great. He unclasped her bra and shoved it off her shoulders, tossing it aside. He grabbed her hips and ground his erection against her ass. "Fuck," he murmured. "Next time I offer to help you or hold you, Zoey, what are you going to do?"

"Let you," she answered.

He was pleased with the answer. He pulled her upright with her back against him, and took her breasts into his hands. Blood surged from his brain and he groaned.

She pushed back, turned, fell to her knees, and ran her teeth over his dick through his jeans. "Holy fuck," he gasped.

The triumphant grin she gave him was a challenge. He grabbed her by the hair and pulled her to her feet. She cried out and then moaned when his bare chest pressed against her bare breasts. He massaged his fingers into her scalp. With his free hand, he dipped into her pants and massaged her clit. She cried out.

"I need one more thing, Zoey," he said.

"Don't push your luck." She grabbed him by the balls. "We both know I'm the one in control."

"Wrong answer." He spun her again, this time capturing her wrists behind her back. He held them in one hand and then pinched her nipple with his free hand. "I want you to ask me nicely to fuck you."

She threw her head back and laughed.

"And say please," he added.

She fought to free her arms, but he held her tightly. He reached down and unfastened her jeans. He shoved them down with her panties and she kicked them off. "Like you're not going to fuck me anyway?"

He didn't argue with her. He bent her back over the bed, her arms still pinned to her back. Ah, the sweet view he had. He cupped and caressed her ass.

She laughed and then, when he slid his hand up her slit from behind, she moaned. He drew his wet fingers away and fumbled with his jeans, getting them pushed down just enough to free himself. He took himself in hand and pressed his tip against her opening. Then he leaned over and nibbled at her ear. "Zoey, you're so beautiful."

"Fuck me!" she cried through gritted teeth.

"I love the way you make me feel, Zoey. Not when you're yelling at me or pushing me away or making unreasonable demands. But when we're talking, laughing, kissing. Like now. I love the way I feel with you now."

A frustrated sob escaped her lips.

"Just say please, Zoey. I want you so bad. I hate waiting like this. Your ass pressed against my dick like this is driving me crazy." He moved a hand beneath her and cupped one of her breasts. "God, you're fucking perfect."

"Kellen, just do it!" She fought, trying to free her hands. Her hips arched up and back, inviting him, begging him.

He broke into a sweat. He rested his forehead against her spine and groaned. "I won't give in to you," he said. "This is where you have to meet me."

"Fuck!" she cried. "Please! Please, God, Kellen, fuck me already!"

He stood up, released her hands, and reached in his nightstand for a condom. She arched her back and rocked her hips toward him. He grabbed her hips and slammed into her. They both cried out.

The way she rocked against him, meeting him move for move, he knew he wasn't going to last long. He hooked an arm around her waist and lifted her so that her back was against him, her head dropped back on his chest. He sat her on her knees on the edge of the bed, thrusting into her hard and fast. One hand stayed on her left breast, the other snaked its way between her legs.

"Oh, God!" she sobbed.

A second later, he felt her muscles contract as she cried out and writhed in his arms. He let her pleasure carry him over the edge. He sucked in a breath, gritted his teeth, and held on through the waves of orgasm.

He dropped her onto the bed and took a step back, breathing heavily. Her back was to him. He disposed of the condom and waited. She rolled toward him. The smile on her face was the sweetest thing he'd ever seen. Until she reached for him, which was even sweeter.

CHAPTER NINETEEN

Zoey chugged a glass of water and then dragged her arm across her sweaty brow. She'd stripped down to a tank top and was considering trading her jeans for shorts.

"I know it's hard work," Maya said. "You don't have to do it."

"I'm halfway there. Just gotta get over this hump." She had the pieces baked to one of the gingerbread houses. It took three batches to finish them. The dough was stiff, the oven was hot, but she was not giving up.

Besides, it was good distraction. Kellen had brought her back home yesterday and then left. She'd hinted that he should spend the night, but he hadn't taken the bait. No, he'd dragged her to his cave, broken her in like a wild stallion, and then left her here wanting more. The more she thought about it, the more she realized that was exactly what he'd done. He'd planted his flag. Staked his claim. He'd wanted her to know that she was his girl.

She picked up the rolling pin and started rolling another batch of dough. It helped that out of the corner of her eye she could see the most gorgeous man on the planet sitting on her sofa, concentrating hard on whatever was on his computer screen. He'd come over, as promised, bringing his camera and laptop with him so that he could get pictures of the kids—his Christmas present to Maya. But aside from a quick peck on the cheek, he hadn't shown any indication of being nearly as smitten as she was.

Maya snapped her fingers. Zoey realized she'd stopped rolling and started gazing. "Sorry," she said and focused with renewed determination.

"No, I think it's cute," Maya said. "I've never seen you like this."

She lowered her voice. "He's so intense over there."

"He gets that way."

Zoey sighed, but it was masked under her heavy breathing from rolling out the impossibly stiff dough. At last she got it where she wanted it and started cutting out the pieces using cardboard templates she and the kids had drawn.

Addy came by. Though she was staying with her parents over the break, she much preferred to be here with her friends. She came in the door without knocking and headed straight for the kitchen. "Kids look like they're having fun in the snow," she said. When she approached the counter, she lowered her voice.

Zoey tip-toed up so she could see out the front window. The morning had yielded about four inches of snow, so far. The kids were running around bundled in their coats, hats, and scarves, trying to catch snowflakes on their tongues.

Zoey smiled and then filled a deep bowl with powdered sugar, egg whites, and lemon juice to make the icing. She put the beaters of the hand mixer she'd just bought in the bowl and switched them on.

Powdered sugar poofed in a cloud all over the kitchen. She immediately switched the mixer off and stood there while the sugar settled. Maya and Addy sat there gaping at her. Kellen had fallen to his side on the sofa laughing.

"You can laugh while you're cleaning up this mess, funny guy!"

He pulled himself together and came into the kitchen. He held up that damn camera and shot a picture of her. "Oh, that's a good one," he said. "Captures the full potential of your rage."

"I'm gonna shove that thing up your ass, Kellen."

He set the camera down and picked up the mixer, turning it on to it's lowest speed until the mixture was wet. Then, he kicked the mixer up higher and gestured for her to take over. She did, casting him a skeptical glance along the way.

He went to the sink, wrung out a cloth, and started cleaning the sugar off the cabinets and countertops.

By the time she finished the icing and took out the last of the cookies, he was pulling a mop and bucket out of her utility room. Zoey worked on cleaning up the clutter on her counters and then helped Addy and Maya assemble the first house. Kellen mopped around her feet until she hopped up on the counter. When he finished, he put the mop and bucket away, and then came back in.

He gave her hair a tug. "Your turn," he said.

"My turn for what?"

"I've cleaned your kitchen and your floors. Now, it's your turn."

Without warning, he picked her up, tossing her over his shoulder, and carried her back to her bedroom and into the bathroom. He sat her on her feet, turned on the shower, and then started stripping.

"Just what the hell do you think you're doing?" she asked, even as she peeled off her tank top and started on her jeans.

"Taking a shower. What are you doing?"

"Taking a shower. Do you think you're going to get lucky in there?"

He crossed his fingers before shoving his jeans off. His boxers went next and that left him totally, gloriously naked. Zoey froze, her jeans halfway down her thighs, and stared. He dug a condom out of the pocket of his jeans. She had no will to fight or tease as he came toward her and finished yanking her jeans down. And then her panties. And lastly her bra, which he unclasped and slipped off of her almost reverently.

Their eyes met for a moment. They both smiled. Their smiles slipped away as they held hands, and climbed in the shower. He turned her, putting her back to the water. Gently cupping the back of her head, Kellen tilted it away from him, into the water. She closed her eyes. His fingers massaged as they threaded their way through her water soaked hair.

When he tilted her head forward, she couldn't help but marvel at him. His blue eyes, hot and potent, focused on hers. His jaw, strong and tense. His massive erection pressed into her belly.

Touching him was an evolutionary imperative. Without thought of any kind, she reached for him, wrapped her hand around his length, because that was what she was meant to do. It was what he was meant for. He hissed in a breath and the tendons in his neck popped out. He dropped his forehead to hers, his eyes squeezed shut.

He reached behind her for something. The shampoo. He lathered some into his hands and then began working it through her hair. She was lost again. Hypnotized by his power. Lulled by his strong, knowing hands, caring for her. Pleasing her.

He tilted her head back again and rinsed her hair. She closed her eyes as the water sluiced down her scalp and hair and back. His tongue on her neck had her gasping and opening her eyes. He held her against him while he kissed and licked her neck, nipping at her jaw and ears. He grabbed her knee and brought her leg up over his hip.

She panted frantically, already on the edge of orgasm and he wasn't even touching her there. She arched her hips, seeking more of him.

Kellen lifted her up, turned, and pressed her back against the wall. She wrapped her legs around his waist, struggling to keep from sliding off of him. He had her, though. One arm braced beneath her ass, the other wrapped around the small of her back. He wasn't going to drop her.

He dipped his head down and sucked her nipple between his teeth.

"God!" she sobbed. She thrust against him, struggling

to quell that insane need.

He took her other breast and she dropped her head back in frustration. Detaching his lips from her nipple and raising his head until his mouth hovered just in front of hers, he whispered, "Say please, Zoey." His voice was harsh and hungry.

"Please!" she gasped. The game was over. He could have anything he wanted from her.

He chuckled against her mouth. "That's getting easier. What is it you want?"

"You know," she groaned. She lunged at his mouth, wanting to kiss him, but he pulled back.

"I wanna hear you say it."

"I want you inside of me. God, Kellen, please!"

And then she felt him, the tip of him at her entrance. She thrust her hips, bringing him into her an inch.

"Slow down," he said.

She shook her head. "I can't. I want you."

"Open your eyes."

She hadn't realized they were closed. She opened them and looked at him. Into him.

"Say it again," he said.

Her breath was ragged and shaking. She was shaking. "I want you."

"Tell me I'm different, Zoey. Tell me I'm not like other men."

"You know you're different. You know what you're doing to me. I'm sorry I never saw you before, Kellen. Come inside of me, please."

His expression turned determined as he pushed all the way inside of her. They cried out together and then held each other, still and trembling for a long moment. "I can't get you out of my head. I've never wanted anyone like this, Zoey."

She dug her nails into his shoulder blades, and he began moving into her. Pounding into her. She gave herself up to his control in a way she'd never experienced before. There was nothing for her to do, no need for her to think as he brought both of their bodies to the height of pleasure and then sent them scrambling and gasping over the edge.

The shower spray hissed. Their panting breaths gradually slowed. They were collapsed on the floor of the shower, him on his knees between her legs, her splayed out in front of him with her back against the wall.

He leaned forward and kissed her. Their lips were familiar together now. There was no more tentative tasting. No more discovery. Only blissful ownership.

He leaned in and kissed her again. Then he turned off the shower and helped her to her feet. They dried off and dressed, casting bashful smiles at each other. He tackled her onto the bed, his weight a warm comfort, and made out with her for a few minutes.

When he at last rolled off, Zoey sat up and checked the clock. It was only noon. She stared at the time. "I feel like my whole life just changed. But we're still in the same day as we were before."

He stood and pulled her to her feet. "See, that's about the nicest thing I've ever heard."

"It's weird. I'm actually feeling nice."

He kissed her on the forehead. "Don't worry. I'm sure it'll pass."

She laughed and took his hand as he led her back into the kitchen.

CHAPTER TWENTY

Kellen propped his chin on his palm at the kitchen table. The kids were decorating their houses with candy, but he couldn't take his eyes off Zoey. She, Addy, and Maya were all helping with the decorating. Zoey wasn't even paying attention to him, but he couldn't stop being aware of her. He'd feel her from now on. Everywhere he went, he'd feel her in his skin, in his bones.

What was this? Not love. Surely not love. Though, he didn't know what else it could be. She'd completely knocked him out. It was like she'd said, his whole life had changed.

"So what's changed?" Addy asked. She was lining the top of Sophie's roof with cinnamon candies, so Kellen wasn't sure who she was talking to.

"Who are you talking to?" Zoey asked.

"You guys. Maya says you want to be together and that I should relax about it. So, I want to know what's changed. How do you go from hate and indifference to suddenly gazing at each other like puppies?"

Zoey sighed. "I think we just didn't know each other before."

"You had plenty of opportunity, but you were bound and determined to hate him and pretty much every man in existence. Now, all of a sudden he's made it into your inner circle. It just seems abrupt."

Zoey and Kellen both covered up laughs at the 'inner circle' remark.

"What?" Addy asked. Then she rolled her eyes. "God, you guys are sick. You know what I meant."

"Having only recently made it into her inner circle," Kellen said, with a wink at Zoey, "I'd kind of appreciate not talking this to death. It's still unreal to me and I just want to relax and enjoy it."

Zoey folded her hands over her heart. "Aww. You're so sweet. Isn't he sweet?"

"Alien abduction is the only scenario that makes any sense," Maya said. "Some sort of bodysnatchers situation. Or maybe she's turned into Stepford Zoey."

"The question is," Addy pondered, "Do we like Stepford Zoey?"

"She definitely doesn't shriek as much. And she's got a nice, pleasant aura about her."

Zoey flipped them both off, and they laughed.

"There she is," Addy said.

Zoey lowered her fingers before the kids looked up from their houses.

"So what are you doing here?" Kellen asked Addy. "Thought you were going to be with your parents through

Christmas."

"I just wanted a break."

"Your folks doing all right?"

"Oh, they're perfect. They're always perfect."

Kellen nodded. He knew Addy's tone. They'd grown up together, all of them, and Addy had been a better friend than most. Certainly better than Zoey up until recently. He knew the power her parents had over her, and the way she simultaneously despised their perfection and wanted to live up to it.

He also knew that when she stopped making eye contact, she was upset about something. Her voice tone didn't change. Just the fact that she suddenly became highly focused on whatever she was doing. Which, in this case, was piping swirly decorations on the side of Sophie's house. "Went to dinner in St. Louis last night," she said.

Kellen caught Zoey's eye and for the first time, experienced that silent communication that lovers enjoy. She winked at him. "Oh?" she said to Addy.

Addy nodded and kept piping. "Saw the professor, so that was cool."

"The professor? Really? Did he look hot?"

Addy huffed. "Would you stop? He's not that good looking."

But even as she spoke, her cheeks were reddening. Zoey shared another look with Kellen before returning her attention to Addy. "Did he join you?"

"No. He was on a date."

"What?" Maya and Zoey both shrieked.

This was where Kellen got lost. The facts, as he knew them were: Addy worked for the professor; Addy and the professor weren't dating; the professor was on a date last night. He couldn't fathom why the women were reacting so dramatically.

"That bastard!" Zoey said.

Addy shook her head. "He's not a bastard. He's a single man who can date whomever he wants."

"Who was she?" Maya asked.

"I didn't know her," Addy said. "She was beautiful."

"He has no business dating. And behind your back like that!" Zoey's face turned as red as her hair.

Addy didn't answer, so Kellen was lost in confusion. Curiosity warred with self-preservation. Curiosity won. "I don't understand. Why shouldn't he date?"

Zoey and Maya honed in on him, their eyes round. He got the sudden sense that he'd asked the stupidest question on earth. "They have an understanding," Zoey snapped.

"Oh," he said. "I didn't know. Well, then, he was cheating?"

Addy sighed and shook her head. "There's no understanding. He's free to date whomever he chooses. It wasn't cheating. I don't even know why I mentioned it."

"There is, too, and understanding," Maya argued. "What about that time he acted all jealous when you were dating that soccer player? You broke up with that guy. You could have had a perfectly good relationship, but the professor didn't like it, so you gave that guy up for him."

"He never asked me to."

"But he didn't tell you not to. He's been stringing you along for way too long."

"No, no, that's not right," Addy said. "I mean, yeah, there's some attraction there, but we both care too much

173

for our careers to act on it. Besides, Joel wasn't right for me. I didn't break up with him just for the professor."

Maya and Zoey shared a look and rolled their eyes. "So what did he do when you saw him?" Zoey asked.

Addy shrugged. "He was his usual, charming self. I introduced him to my parents. He introduced us to his date. Then we went to our table."

Kellen watched the women exchange glances and grow silent. He didn't understand. But he felt he'd already treaded too deeply into those waters, so he bit his tongue.

Addy's phone beeped. She pulled it out, read her text, and turned red. Zoey and Maya were fixated on her.

"What did he say?" Maya asked softly.

Addy could only shake her head.

Zoey snatched her phone. "He says, 'She was a colleague. It was a work date.'" Zoey's grip on the phone tightened. "Well, that's bullsh—crap, and I'm gonna tell him so." She started thumb-typing until Addy took her phone back.

She typed out her own message, sent it, and pocketed her phone.

Kellen felt like he was watching a soap opera. He was on the edge of his seat, dying to know what Addy had replied. But no information seemed forthcoming and he was left with the somewhat less interesting gingerbread house show.

"When's your mom coming, Zoey?" Maya asked.

"Christmas day. She's supposed to stay in town for a couple of nights, but she said she'd get a hotel."

Kellen thought Maya's next breath sounded like a sigh of relief. "Do I get to meet her?" he asked.

"Well, big boy, by the looks of it, you're not gonna have much choice." Zoey jerked her head toward the window.

He stood and crossed into the living room. He pulled back the sheer curtain. Snow still fell steadily. It reached nearly the top of the tires on his truck. The drifts were much deeper.

Arms came around his waist and a warm cheek pressed to his back. "You're stuck with me," she said. "You're all mine."

He could totally drive home in that snow with his big truck. But if she needed an excuse to ask him to say, he'd let her have it. He said, "I can live with that. It just so happens I brought my overnight bag, just in case." He turned and took her and kissed her. Then he sank onto the couch and brought her onto his lap. She covered his face in kisses and pressed her lips to his. He rubbed her back and waist, keeping his hands in neutral territory, but on her—always on her.

Later, Kellen went outside with the kids.

He, bundled in his coat and boots, stepped out into the snow and paused in surprise when he saw it was already shin deep; and still coming down hard. The kids tumbled into the front yard, squealing with laughter. He moved to the middle of the yard and started piling up snow for the base of a snowman. The kids joined in and piled on snow while he shaped it. By the time the bottom was finished, Zoey had come out to join them.

They rolled a big ball of snow for the middle, and a smaller for the top.

"Hey, I got something," Zoey said, jumping up and running toward her garage. She came out with a small box and opened it up. Inside were a bunch of pieces: eyes, noses, mouths, eyebrows. They were like giant Mr. Potato Head pieces for a snowman. "It was gonna be a Christmas present, but you guys need it now, so—"

"Thanks, Aunt Zoey!" Matthew cried.

Kellen sat back and watched while they assembled a face for their snowman. Then he went inside to get his camera. He took pictures of the kids posing by Howard the snowman. After that, they agreed to have a boys versus girls snowball fight. So Kellen helped Matthew build a snow barrier to hide behind. Zoey and Sophie went straight to work making snowballs so that they wound up with more ammunition than the boys. But they had no defensive structure.

"You're gonna regret that!" Kellen called.

"The best defense is a good offense. Ready, Sophie? Attack!"

Sophie's snowballs flew in a gentle arc and landed in soft puffs. She missed them nine times out of ten. But damn if Zoey didn't know how to throw. Her snowballs came in straight lines with intense accuracy and made an impact even through their heavy coats. Every time Kellen or Matthew popped their head up, they got hit.

"You seem to have forgotten that I took our softball team to the state championship, Kellen, my man!" she shouted before beaming him in the face with a snowball.

At last, the boys ducked down, their backs to their

snow wall. "Okay," Kellen said. "Can you hit her if you've got time and a clear shot?"

"Yeah, but she's too fast."

"It's okay. I'll lay down cover fire and give you a chance to really nail her. In the face with the biggest snowball you can throw. Can you do it?"

Matthew nodded and started packing up a snowball. Kellen built himself a supply of a dozen. Then he counted, "One...two...three...Go!" He got to his knees and started chucking snowballs as fast as he could. Because Zoey hit him first, and kept throwing, he couldn't even get one across the yard. But then Matthew stood, took careful aim, and threw.

There was a satisfying smack as the snow splattered all over her face. She was stunned.

"Get her!" Kellen yelled. They abandoned their barrier and began throwing snowballs as hard as they could until Zoey was on her knees with her arms around her head yelling, "Stop! I give! I give!"

They stopped and laughed. Zoey fell to the ground and splayed on her back. "I'm sorry, Sophie, I let you down."

"It's okay. You did your best, Aunt Zoey."

Matthew crowed over Zoey. "In your face, Aunt Zoey. Girls stink! Boys rule!"

"Uh-huh. That's fabulous." She was smiling, but her voice was dry. She was clearly exhausted.

The snow was falling so hard that her coat was already dusted over. Kellen knelt next to her and grinned. She reached up, grabbed him by the front of his coat, and pulled him down for a kiss. Their frozen lips quickly warmed. Somewhere in the background Matthew and Sophie cried, "Eww!" But then they ran off to play.

Kellen pulled back. Her lips were bright red against the backdrop of the snow. Her hair fanned out around her. Her eyelashes had snowflakes in them. The back of her left hand rested on her brow. "My God. Don't move."

"What?" She started to move her hand and he reached out to still it.

"Do. Not. Move." He ran to the porch for his camera.

"Oh, Lord, Kellen, don't photograph me."

He held up his camera and waited for her to relax. "What are you worried about? You know you look hot."

"I do not," she said, but her smile and blush were perfect. He snapped three pictures.

"You are beautiful, but frankly, I think it was my kiss that made you so photo-worthy."

She arched a look and he snapped another photo.

"What's the snow look like, falling straight down on you like that?"

She blinked up at the snow and he snapped five more pictures.

Then he stood over her, his feet on either side of her waist, and aimed the camera straight down at her. "Look at me, Zoey," he said.

She did, but her lips were tight with amusement. He held her gaze for a long moment. That was all it took for her guard to go down and her lips to part, just slightly. He snapped the perfect photo and then stood back and admired it on the screen.

He forgot about everything else as he took his camera toward the house.

"Hey, are you gonna help me up or anything, asshole?" she shouted.

He barely heard her. He stomped the snow off his boots before going inside and settling onto the sofa to edit his photos.

CHAPTER TWENTY-ONE

Christmas Eve dawned all the brighter for the snow on the ground. The sun glared off of it, through the window, and straight into Zoey's eyes. She threw her arm over her eyes and blinked until she adjusted to the light. Something heavy was draped over her waist. She smiled.

Kellen was asleep face-down. He was facing her, but still completely zonked. She grinned. "It's Christmas Eve," she said.

When he didn't stir, she climbed on top of him and sat on his bare ass. They were both completely naked. She dug her palms into his back and shoulders and rubbed, waking up the blood flow and jostling him. "It's Christmas Eve," she said, louder than before.

"Mmmm," he groaned.

She leaned forward and pressed her breasts to his back. She caught a flash of dimple on his cheek. She reached beneath him, took him in her hand, and stroked until he was erect. His groan was different this time. He began to move. She lifted on hands and knees, so he could turn over underneath of her.

He grinned, though his eyes were barely slitted open.

She didn't wait. She slid down onto his hot, hard length, taking him to the hilt. His smile vanished. He threw back his head and groaned. "Fuuuuck." He reached above him and gripped the headboard. His biceps bunched, and the muscles in his abs and obliques lengthened. Zoey ran her hands over every muscle as she began moving on top of him.

She shoved her tangled hair out of her face and dropped her head back. She swiveled her hips, grinding against him, and taking control of her own pleasure. She covered her breasts with her hands and massaged.

"Look at you," he whispered.

She snapped her head up and opened her eyes. He was on his elbows watching her, his blue eyes nearly black. She slowed and lengthened her moves, her lips curling up in a wicked smile. She tweaked her nipples between her thumbs and fore fingers and let her lips part. She'd figured this out last night. This drove him crazy. In a moment, he would shed all pretense of civility and become a complete animal.

She slid one of her hands down her belly and to tease her clit, slipping her fingers between their bodies and massaging. His eyes followed the path of her hand and then went wide and fiery. His jaw muscles ticked, and the pulse in his neck quickened. Then he snapped.

The world spun as he flipped her to her back and pinned her wrists over her head with one of his hands. His mouth went straight to her breasts, sucking and teasing them each in turn. She thrust her hips, seeking pleasure. He slid back inside of her and then fucked her harder than she'd ever felt. So hard she couldn't stop the cries that escaped her throat. He grunted with the effort and ground his pelvis into her with each thrust.

As orgasm screamed through her, she felt his mouth on hers, swallowing her cries. He wasn't finished, though. "Christ, woman, there are children in the house," he snarled as he pulled out of her. He flipped her onto her stomach, knelt between her legs, and pulled her hips onto his lap. Then he slammed back into her.

"Oh my God," she moaned.

"You like this?"

"Ah! Yes!"

He fucked harder. It was almost painful, and she lost complete control of herself. She was crying actual tears and using a pillow to muffle the noise. She was on the verge of orgasm, but just couldn't get there. How was he lasting this long? "God, come already!" she sobbed.

His only response was a low, guttural sound, so utterly masculine and so utterly undone that her pleasure heightened another notch. She felt a sudden surge of power and energy. She got up on her hands and knees and pushed back against him. He grabbed her ass, his fingertips digging into her flesh. "Oh, yeah," he moaned. He moved harder and faster. When he snaked his hand beneath her and between her legs, she lost it. He came with her as wave after wave of pleasure hammered her senses.

At last he fell to the bed next to her, and she collapsed onto her belly. Sweat drenched her. His hair clung to his forehead. His eyes were once again barely open and his smile was ridiculous. So was hers. She couldn't stop smiling, in fact.

"You were crying," he said, his voice raspy and his breathing still heavy.

"Why didn't you stop?"

"You'd have told me to stop if you wanted me to."

She dragged her hand up to pat his cheek but ended up just slapping him and letting her hand slide off his face. "I like that," she said. "I'm a big fan of your work, Kellen."

He let out a breathy laugh and covered her hand with his. "Merry Christmas Eve, Zoey." His eyes drifted shut.

"You too, Kellen." She watched him for a few minutes. Then she kissed him on the cheek, covered him up, and went to the shower.

She knew within seconds of standing, that she was going to be sore for a while. She used the shower massager to ease away some of the soreness in her muscles, and by the time she got out, she felt like putty. They were snowed in, anyway, so she put her pajamas on and went out for coffee.

The kids sat in front of the television that was turned up way too loud. Maya and Addy sat at the kitchen table and looked up at her. Addy probably could have gotten home, given that her parents only lived a few blocks away. She'd used the snow as an excuse to stay.

"Mind if I turn this down?" Zoey asked. She stepped into the living room and grabbed the remote without waiting for an answer. Once the television was no longer ear piercing, she got herself a cup of coffee and then sat across from her best friends. "What's up."

"We had to turn the television up," Maya said.

Zoey frowned. "Why?"

"Because of the two jungle beasts in the back bedroom. Jeez, Zoey."

She winced. "I'm sorry," she said. "We'll be more careful. I didn't know you could hear."

Maya blushed and sipped her coffee. Addy rested her cheek on her fist. "So glad you're having a good time." Her tone was flat.

"You jealous?"

"Of course not. Why would I want a man who makes me scream and gives me multiple orgasms for Christmas?"

"Okay, but just to be clear, you're not jealous that I have Kellen, right? You're just jealous that I'm having sex?"

Addy sank lower. "Yep."

"Get a man, Addison," Zoey said.

Addy stirred her coffee with a spoon.

"Seriously," Maya said. "I know you're waiting on Dr. McHotAndBothered, but you can find someone to be casual with, can't you?"

"I don't know," Addy said. "I don't even know what I'm waiting for. Just that I couldn't bear it if I did something to ruin whatever possibility there is."

"He's an adult," Zoey said. "A worldly one at that. He's not expecting you to remain celibate based on a crush you have on him. Besides, if you do find someone, maybe it will spur him to either make a move or back completely off."

Addy shrugged and didn't appear to have more to say

on the subject. "So what's Kellen like?" she asked.

Zoey felt silly having this conversation, but she was in such a good mood. "He takes some coaxing, but then he's an animal."

"Really?" Maya asked, scrunching up her nose.

"Yeah, he's just like you would think. Very polite and kind, just wanting to make you feel good and do something nice for you, but push the right buttons and he goes all savage."

Maya's smile faded some. "Savage in a good way."

"Oh, definitely. Such a good way."

She nodded and went back to staring down at her hands. "You're not the kind of woman who would let a man hit you, anyway. If he did, you'd kick his ass and walk out, right?"

"I would. But I can't say how I would react if I had children." Actually, she was quite certain that children would only heighten her will to defend herself. But Maya was a different person and Zoey didn't want her feeling any more judged than she already did.

Maya chewed her bottom lip, "I didn't have children the first time Damon hit me. What was my excuse, then?"

"You were a frightened teenage girl caught between an abusive father and an abusive boyfriend. Don't go down this road, Maya."

"It would have been easier to leave, then."

"There are two very positive results of your staying. It is what it is, Maya. You're doing the right thing now, and that's all that matters."

Her eyes welled as she looked away. "If only I'd left even a couple years ago. I'm afraid for Mattie. He's going to remember all of this. How's he not going to be messed up?"

Addy reached over and took her hand. "We all have shit to deal with. He'll deal with it because he has a strong, loving mother he can depend on. You take care of right now, and the future will work itself out."

Maya nodded, clearly wanting to believe. "There's just so many what-ifs. What if I can't provide for them? What if I never find them a father? What if they wind up hating me? What if I'm one of those women who repeatedly gets in abusive relationships? What if…?" She choked up. Then she buried her face in her hands. "I'm so selfish," she murmured.

Zoey and Addy rubbed her back and quietly assured her that she wasn't selfish.

Maya gulped in a breath. "It's just that I'm already so lonely. I mean, I love you guys, I really do, and I couldn't do this without you, but Damon, as much as he hurt me, loved me."

"That's not real love," Zoey said.

"It is! You don't know, Zoey, because you weren't there. He stood up for me. Nobody hurt me with Damon around. He took care of me, provided for our family. He loved me at night and in his arms, I felt safe. It was just outside of his arms that I got scared again. As long as he was holding me, I knew it was okay."

Zoey just sat there, staring into the middle distance, worried for her friend.

Maya's breath, this time, was calmer. "I'm not idealizing it. I know you're worried about that, but there were good times. And the love is real. Maybe it's unhealthy, but it's real. Whenever he...raped me...it was always from behind. Whenever he wanted to love me, he took me in his arms and took comfort from my body, and gave me comfort with his. That was real. Okay?"

Zoey didn't like it. Didn't want to acknowledge it, but she nodded.

"I just want you guys to know I'm giving up something. You think I've left a bad guy and I'm finally free...but I'm giving up something that I may never have again. So...I just want you guys to know that."

Addy and Zoey took turns hugging her. "I can't pretend to understand," Zoey said. "But I'm here for you if you need to cry about it or anything. I hate that your heart is breaking."

Maya nodded against her shoulder. Addy gave Zoey a proud nod.

Later in the morning, Zoey's cell phone rang. Since everyone she loved and cared about was in her house, she got a little chill at the sound. She stared down at the name on the screen for a moment before lifting it to her ear. "Hey, Mom," she said.

"Hey, baby doll! Would you be up for us dropping by a day early?"

"Us? Early?"

"Yeah, me and my boyfriend, Mark. We just got into town."

"You just got into town? Mom, it's a freaking blizzard

out there."

"Well, that's part of the problem. We're kind of stranded at this gas station, just on the north edge of town. Know where I'm talking about?"

"Yeah. Mom, we've got a foot of snow. This is Missouri. We don't know how to drive in that kind of weather."

"Well, the highways have been plowed, honey."

"Great. Then can you drive as far as the intersection at the end of my street? Because then you could probably hike it."

"See, we're kind of out of gas and the station is closed."

"Don't they have pay-at-the-pump?"

"We only have cash."

Zoey slumped. Her eyes wandered to the window where Kellen's big, black pickup truck sat buried halfway up the tires in snow. "Hold tight," she said. "Let me see what I can do."

"Oh, thanks, babe. You're the best."

She hung up and went back to the bedroom. Poor Kellen was still out cold. She shook him. "Hey," she said, "wake up."

"Mmm?"

"Wake up, I need a favor."

He grinned.

"Not that kind of favor."

He frowned.

"Open your eyes, Kellen, jeez!"

He did and his brow furrowed as he sat up. "What's going on?"

"My mom and her boyfriend are stranded at a gas station. You've got that big truck, could you go pick them up?"

His eyebrows went up, and he glanced out the window.

"Your truck can handle it, can't it?" she asked.

"I guess. I mean, I don't know, I've never driven in snow this deep."

"If you get stuck you can just hike back. It's not a big deal."

He let out a laugh that didn't seem rooted in amusement. "Uh, okay. I guess that's true. Can I get a shower first?"

"No! She's stuck at a gas station in the freezing cold." Zoey gathered his jeans, t-shirt, and sweater and hurled them at him.

He hurled them back at her and then climbed out of bed. Zoey bit her lip and tried not to get distracted by how good he looked naked. He grabbed his duffel bag off the floor and began digging through it for fresh clothes. He was moving so slowly.

Zoey bounced on the balls of her feet. "Could you speed it up? Jesus."

This time his laugh was fully frustrated. "You need to tone it down a notch, Zoey. I just woke up. Let's talk politely to each other, okay?"

"I need my mom picked up. Can you do it or not?"

He shot her a look as he pulled up his jeans. She closed her eyes and let out a breath. She couldn't bear to keep her mom waiting. "Can you please hurry?"

She still had her eyes closed when he came to her and

189

pressed his lips to her forehead. Before she knew it, he was gone.

CHAPTER TWENTY-TWO

Kellen figured he'd make it a few yards down the road and then get stuck, but his tires handled the job, and once he made it to the highway, it was smooth driving. A little slick, but there were no other cars on the road, and he knew how to drive on ice.

He regretted arguing with Zoey. Every little tiff they had made him uncomfortable. They'd just started doing whatever it was they were doin, and, in his mind, he figured they should have a honeymoon period longer than five minutes.

He supposed he'd been unreasonable. Her mother was stranded in the middle of winter, so of course he didn't have time to take a shower. There had just been something about the way she'd pushed him into this that bothered him. She'd been frantic. There'd been a crazy little glint in her eye that he didn't recognize.

The gas station was indeed deserted. A small, red

Toyota was parked to the side. He turned into the drive and felt his back tires fish-tail just a bit. He pulled up behind the car and hopped out, leaving his truck running.

A man and woman got out. The man wasn't much older than him with dark hair and a strong jaw. The woman looked like a caricature of Zoey, as though all her features had been aged and exaggerated.

"Kellen?" she asked.

"Yes, ma'am." He frowned when he saw her unloading two rather large suitcases and one smaller one.

"Oh, God, please call me Tracy. I am way too young to be a ma'am. This is my boyfriend Mark."

Kellen shook hands with the guy and helped him load the suitcases in the back of his truck. Once they'd all piled in, Tracy in the middle, Kellen asked, "Do you want me to drop you by your hotel first, so you can drop off your luggage?"

"Oh, we're just going to stay with Zoey," Tracy said. "No sense spending all that money on a hotel when our daughter's got a nice, roomy house in town."

"Yeah, I get that," he said, not wanting to offend her. "The only thing, is, she's kind of got a houseful already. Addy and me. Maya and her two kids."

"Oh, I'm sure there's plenty of room. It'll give me a chance to get to know you. I must say, Zoey's got exceptional taste." She ran her hand up and down his arm.

Kellen smiled tightly and kept focused on the road.

Tracy suddenly squealed. "Look at me!" she said, "sandwiched between two, hunky young men."

Her hand slid across his shoulders. It was little comfort that she was doing the same thing to Mark. With

Mark, it was consensual.

He wanted to ask if Zoey was aware that she was getting more houseguests, but again, he didn't want to hurt Tracy's feelings. Instead, he focused on the road, only talking to answer Tracy's questions.

At last he pulled into Zoey's driveway. Mark and Tracy exited the truck. Zoey stepped out, looking adorable in an oversized sweatshirt. Tracy ran into her arms. "Baby doll!" she squealed.

Zoey hugged her, and Kellen, who had just stepped out of his truck, froze at the sight of her expression. Her chin rested on her mom's shoulder, her eyes were squeezed shut, and her smile was sheer, girlish bliss. "I've missed you, momma," she said.

He wanted to be happy about it, but there was something off. Some underlying pain, just under the surface of her smile. Tracy stepped back. "Look," she said, turning her head side-to-side. "I went red. You've inspired me."

"It looks incredible. Better on you than on me."

"Oh, stop," Tracy said.

Kellen slammed the door shut and hovered by his truck. Now that he knew his tires could handle the snow, he was seriously considering going home. Even long-standing marriages built on a bedrock of love and commitment still rattled in the presence of in-laws. He wasn't sure his fledgling romance with Zoey could withstand the pressure. He desperately didn't want that heartbreak.

While he was standing there deciding, Tracy, Mark, and Zoey all disappeared inside. The door slammed shut, almost in answer to his thoughts. He cocked his head and frowned. A moment later, it opened again. He blew out a breath and smiled when Zoey popped her head out. "Grab their luggage, Kellen. Don't be rude."

She vanished back inside.

"You've gotta be fucking kidding me," he muttered. He turned and hauled out the two suitcases.

Inside, their pieced-together little family that had been so cozy over the past week took on a more chaotic air. It was louder, primarily due to Tracy, whose voice was sharp and demanding of attention. Maya was cowering at the end of the sofa closest to the corner in the living room. Addy smiled politely and chatted with Mark even as she stood between Maya's family and the newcomers, subtly shielding them.

Zoey was nowhere to be seen. And then she was there, hurrying out of the hallway with her mom in tow. "God, Kellen, you're so slow. Mom's exhausted, bring the suitcases back here so she can shower and get some rest."

He dropped one of the suitcases, took her chin in hand, and forced her to meet his eye. He didn't say anything, only arching a brow. This time she didn't think his assertiveness was cute or attractive. She glared at him, pure vitriolic hate. "Please," she snarled.

He dropped his hand, gritted his teeth, and took the luggage back. He stopped in the hallway when he realized he didn't know where he was going. The kids were in one of the spare rooms. Maya and Addy in the other.

"Back in the master bedroom," Zoey said. "You and I can sleep on the hide-a-bed downstairs."

He glanced back over his shoulder, but did as she

asked. He dropped off the suitcases and then left Zoey and her mom in the room. He waited in the hall, listening to Zoey in the background. "I'll get the sheets changed while you're showering."

"Thanks, sweetie," Tracy said.

"If there's anything you need, just let me know."

As soon as Zoey rounded the doorway into the hall, he grabbed her arm. She didn't even look at him. She pulled her arm away, and when he caught her other one, she pulled away from him again. This time he held tight, and she started slapping at him. "Let go. I have to get sheets."

"Stop. Zoey, I need to talk to you."

She fought harder, shoving and slapping. At the same time, he knew if she really wanted him to let go, she'd kick him in the balls or something. She wasn't acting like herself right now, and he remembered what she'd said about how she hated who she became when her mom was around. "Let. Go," she said, her voice quiet and tight.

He grabbed her by the shoulders and pushed her against the wall. She hit harder than he intended and stared up at him, dazed. Her eyes were wild. Frightened? Panicked? He didn't know what it was he was seeing. Her bottom lip quivered.

"Oh, baby, calm down," he whispered. He cupped her cheek and stroked it with his thumb.

Her whole body buzzed and trembled. "I need to change the sheets."

"Hey," he said, "calm down. Go sit down and adjust, and I'll change the sheets. Where are they?"

Her eyes softened at last, and he felt her relax just a

shade. "They're in a cabinet in the utility room."

"Okay, I got it. Go sit down and get to know Mark. He's our age, so we should have a lot in common."

Her lips quirked up, and he gave her hair a little tug. At the last second, she threw her arms around his waist. "Thanks," she said.

"It's not free. We're gonna give that hide-a-bed a run for its money tonight, you hear?"

She laughed and shoved him away. "You're insatiable." She walked away, and he slapped her on the ass as she went. Then he found his way to the utility room between the house and garage and gathered some sheets. The bathroom door in the bedroom was closed, so he went ahead and switched the sheets.

He was about to gather the pile of used sheets in his arms when the bathroom door opened. Tracy, wrapped in a towel with another towel twisted around her hair, leaned against the doorframe. "Well, hello there," she said.

He gave her a quick nod before scooping up the sheets.

"I hope I'm not putting you out," she said.

He was only two steps from the door.

She strolled out of the bathroom and fell face down onto the bed. She folded her hands under her cheek and kicked her feet back and forth.

"Not at all," he said. "Anyway, it's Zoey's house. If she's happy, I'm happy."

"Mm, that's sweet." She rolled her eyes shut and moaned. "God, this bed is orgasmic."

Well that pretty much ruined any chance he ever had of getting off in that bed again. "Glad you like it," he said, and hurried out of the room. He threw the sheets in the wash along with a few towels.

When he finished there, he returned to the living room. Zoey was chatting it up with Mark, but then Mark stood and joined Tracy in the bedroom. The door clicked shut, and Kellen's stomach churned. At least he had a few, beautiful memories from that bed. He collapsed into a recliner.

"Send her to a hotel," Addy said.

Zoey glared at her. "If you don't like her, you can leave."

Kellen sat up. "How do you talk to your best friend like that?" He'd snapped before he had a chance to talk himself down. How dare she turn on Addy out of the blue?

Addy interrupted before Zoey could jump down his throat. "It's okay, Kellen. I understand what she's going through. And Zoey, I am going to leave, because I can't watch you do this to yourself. I've learned already there's nothing I can do to stop hurricane Tracy from fucking with your life. I just have to make one last-ditch effort to save you from yourself. That's why I'm begging you…send her to a hotel."

Zoey deflated. "I can't. I don't want to. She's my mom, okay? Sure she's a selfish hag, but she's my momma. She used to run her fingers through my hair to put me to sleep. And she'd take me shopping and we'd have the best time together. I love her, okay?"

Addison smiled gently and put her hand on top of Zoey's. "I understand."

"Do you need me and the kids to go?" Maya asked.

Suddenly, Zoey snapped out of it. "God, no. You're staying right here. This is your home, now, for as long as you need, okay?"

Maya smiled and nodded. Addy looked relieved. Kellen was definitely relieved, though he still didn't feel secure about his own position in her life.

"And Addy, don't go," Zoey said. "Christmas at your parents' is just freaking depressing. Stay here, and we'll make this fun no matter what."

Addy hugged her.

"What about me?" Kellen asked. "You want some space?"

She turned to face him, grabbed his hand, and said, "Please, don't leave me."

He grabbed her face and kissed her. "Never, unless you ask me to."

"Not even then."

He wanted to tell her that she had to take some responsibility. That he couldn't hold up against her if she pushed too hard. That what she said to him mattered, no matter how patient he was, no matter how he tried to listen to her heart rather than her words. But it didn't seem the time, so, instead, he just held her.

He turned to Maya. "Can I take the kids to Grandma and Grandpa's for a little while in the morning?"

She stared down at her hands. "You'll stay with them? You won't let your mom talk to them by herself?"

"Absolutely, I'll stay with them." He and Maya had already discussed this. He was only waiting on a definite decision.

She sighed. "Okay. They really wanna go and I can't

bear to tell them no. Just so long as you swear you'll stay close to them."

"I swear, Maya. I only want their Christmas to be as normal as possible. We won't stay long, either, just long enough and then we'll come right back here."

She gave him one of her soft, shy smiles. "You're the best brother-in-law ever."

He grinned proudly. Zoey squeezed him tighter, and he looked down to see that she was proud of him, too.

CHAPTER TWENTY-THREE

"Time for *A Christmas Story*!" Zoey shouted.

Matthew and Sophie cheered as they ran into the living room. It was seven o'clock. Dinner had been havoc, since Zoey had two extra people and she wasn't that great of a cook to begin with. Kellen had jumped in, faithfully helping her no matter how many times she snapped at him. She could see it was wearing thin, though. She wondered how long she could get by with being a bitch to him before he gave up.

She'd made a pot of hot chocolate for the kids and a pitcher of eggnog for the adults. She poured hot chocolate for the kids and topped it with marshmallows. They were bundled on the couch on either side of their mother. Maya had her feet up on the ottoman and a look of sheer peace on her face. Zoey went back to the kitchen and returned with a mug for Maya. "Here you go, beautiful momma," she said.

"Hey, what about me?" Tracy said, pretending to be offended.

That was Tracy's anthem. Her motto. *'What about me?'* Zoey despised it, but she so desperately wanted something from her mom. Some connection. Some validation. She couldn't figure it out, she just knew she had to keep trying. "Eggnog?" she offered. "I was generous with the rum."

"In that case, I'll take some," Tracy said. Mark and Addy also wanted some, so Zoey delivered it before popping in the DVD of *A Christmas Story.*

Once everyone was settled, she ran out to the garage where she'd sent Kellen to wrap presents. As in everything he put his hand to, he turned out to be quite competent. So she sat on the step and watched him. "Looks good," she said.

"Thanks." He taped up the end of the last package. "Looks like the kids are gonna make out pretty good."

"I hope so. Such a rough time to have their home broken up. What did you get them?"

"I made a photo collage for Maya. Got a skateboard for Matthew and roller skates for Sophie. I'm pretty sure Maya's gonna kill me, but they've been asking for ages."

Zoey smiled. "It's good they have you in their lives."

He gathered up the leftover rolls of paper, tape, and scissors and piled them in a corner. He reached down and pulled her to her feet. She sank into his chest and inhaled his scent. "It's getting crowded," he said.

"You can't go. The kids will be heartbroken."

"The kids see me all the time. I'll come back in the morning. They'll be fine."

She tip-toed up and caught his bottom lip between her

teeth.

He kissed her, taking her mouth with his. "God, you've been exhausting today," he whispered in between kisses.

"I'm sorry. I'm so stressed."

He kissed her jaw and neck. "I'll share it, Zoey, but I won't take it all. Work with me, okay? I want you so bad. I want you more than just for now. I want you for a really, really long time."

She shoved her hands up his shirt and dragged her nails down his chest. He hissed and sucked hard at a spot on her neck.

"Well, look at you two go at it."

Zoey jumped back. She hadn't even heard the door open. "Hey, Mom," she said, pulling her hands out of Kellen's shirt.

Tracy smiled, all acid sweetness. She nodded towards the gifts. "Anything I can help with?"

"No, thank you. Kellen got it all finished."

"Isn't Kellen just the most helpful thing?" Tracy leered at him.

Zoey felt her face go red. "Yeah, I guess." She turned to him. "You may as well go get the hide-a-bed set up, since you know where the sheets and blankets are."

He frowned at her, and she silently begged him just to go and do it. She didn't know why she was being so punitive toward him, but she did know she wanted him as far from Tracy as possible. His eyes held so much conflict, she just knew he was going to walk away any second.

He didn't. He leaned down and kissed her, softly at first, and then with a sweep of passion. He buried his fingers in her hair and drained her of all her stress. She stared up at him, at a loss for words. He stroked her cheek with the backs of his knuckles and then went into the house.

Zoey blew out a breath and pressed her hand to her chest.

"Wow, what was that?" Tracy asked.

For the first time in her life, she had to stop herself from saying something harsh to her mother. Never in her life had she so much as thought about pushing Tracy away. But just then, after Kellen had given her an invisible, undefinable gift in that kiss, she wanted nothing but to be away from her mom and in his arms.

Still, she stopped herself. "Just a kiss," she said.

"Mark kisses me like that. Drives me wild."

Zoey smiled and moved past her and into the house. She doubted Tracy had ever been kissed like that. She doubted many people had. She poured herself some eggnog and settled into the couch next to Sophie. Kellen joined her a few minutes later, and she snuggled against him. Strange that in the few minutes they'd been apart since that kiss, she'd felt somehow incomplete. Like her world was fractured. Now, with him against her, by her side, at her back, everything seemed…right.

"You look hot in that t-shirt, Kellen," Tracy said.

"Thanks," he said flatly.

Tracy had always flirted with Zoey boyfriends. Somehow, this was different. It felt like a personal attack and she found herself getting angrier by the moment.

"This has been going on, what, a week?" Tracy asked. "That's a record for you, isn't it baby doll?"

Zoey forced herself to smile.

"You know, Mark and I have been together three months, now. Tell them what you do for a living, baby."

"I'm a stripper," Mark said in his deep voice. But his eyes were glued to the television. "Ha," he laughed. "Here comes the flagpole."

"What's your man do?" Tracy asked.

"He's a freelance photographer."

"Freelance? As in code for unemployed?"

"No…I mean, he doesn't have an employer, but he earns a good living."

"Well, if he ever needs extra, he could definitely strip. Bodies like that are in high demand."

Kellen sat up. "You know what, Tracy, tonight is about Matthew and Sophie. We're just trying to give them a Christmas as close to what they're used to as we can, so if you don't mind letting them watch the movie, maybe you could move your conversation to the kitchen?"

Tracy gaped at him. She barked a laugh. "Are you serious?"

Zoey opened her mouth, but Kellen clamped his hand over it. "I'm not meaning to be rude. This is just their tradition. So, if you don't mind?"

Tracy rolled her eyes and slumped back in her seat. Zoey felt Kellen relax, and she was grateful not to have to intercede. She leaned against him, resting her head in the crook of his shoulder.

After the movie, they played a couple of board games and then it was bedtime. The kids sat cookies out for Santa along with a note. Zoey thought the whole scene was über precious. She clung to Kellen's side and for the first time in her life, felt a stirring of something she could only describe as maternal longing.

Maya tucked them in, then they all sat around chatting until they were sure the kids were asleep. Maya and Kellen brought the presents out and arranged them under the tree, so the kids would have something exciting to wake up to.

At last, Maya sat back on her heels and sighed, holding her injured rib in the process. "Guys, thank you so much for this. Zoey, Addy, Kellen…I wouldn't be here without you. You guys are truly my family."

Kellen knelt next to her, slipped his arm beneath her shoulders, and helped her back onto the sofa. Addy sat next to her and kissed her on the cheek. "I love you, Maya. No matter what, I'm here for you."

"Me, too," Kellen said.

Maya looked up, and Zoey nodded to her.

A few minutes later, Maya was ready for bed. Addy went with her to help her into the bed. That left Zoey uncomfortably alone with Kellen, Tracy, and Mark. The latter two were whispering and giggling to each other.

Kellen was perched on the edge of the sofa, his elbows leaning on his knees. "You ready for bed?" he asked.

"Yeah."

She offered her hand, and he took it. "Goodnight, Mom," she said. "Goodnight, Mark."

"'Night," they both muttered without looking up at her.

She led Kellen downstairs and did a little strip-tease for him before climbing under the sheets. There was a dip in the middle of the bed, so they couldn't help but roll into each other, which was fine while they were making love. Late in the night, she found she was either shoving him or he was shoving her. Sometime after midnight, they got up and dragged the mattress onto the floor. There was still a dip, but it wasn't quite as deep. But, since the floor was hard and unforgiving, they both woke up stiff and exhausted on Christmas morning.

CHAPTER TWENTY-FOUR

Kellen couldn't speak, he was so tired. He took Zoey's hand and led her to the downstairs shower. They held each other and stood under the hot spray until they finally became alert. They dried and dressed. Then they heard a child's squeal above them. They grinned at each other and raced upstairs to see Sophie.

She jumped up and down in the living room. "Santa came! Santa came!"

Matthew came out, bleary eyed, but grinning. "Hey, Uncle Kellen."

"Hey, bud."

Zoey leaned into Kellen. "Can they open their presents?" she asked.

"They usually wait for their mom."

Zoey nodded, then she asked, "Can I tell Sophie I got arrested getting her one of those presents?"

He whispered back, "You'd ruin the whole Santa

thing."

Zoey snapped her fingers. "Darn."

He kissed the top of her head. Maya and Addy filtered out, headed straight for the coffee pot, and then moved into the living room. After a few sips, everyone seemed awake and ready to go. Maya let the kids tear into their gifts.

They were the most grateful children Kellen had ever seen. They stopped after each gift to show their mom and gush over how excited they were.

It was over too fast. When the kids were done, they simply spread out on the floor and began playing with their toys.

Addy gave Maya and Zoey each a small, rectangular box. They ripped them open. "A Kindle!" Maya shrieked. "Oh, Addy, thank you!"

Zoey lunged at Addy, tackling her on the sofa and kissing her face. "You're the best!"

"Ick! Stop! Jeez."

"Okay, my turn," Zoey said. "Only, maybe you shouldn't open these in front of the kids." She handed Maya and Addy each a box.

"Mattie, honey," Maya said, "Would you and Sophie mind playing with your toys in your room? We'll have breakfast in just a few minutes."

"Sure, Mom," Mattie said cheerfully. Kellen stood and helped them. They sprawled out on their bedroom floor with their new things, and Kellen smiled, for a moment, as he watched them.

He returned to the living room where Maya and Addy were ripping open their presents. He lounged back on the sofa next to Zoey.

"Yes!" Maya shrieked, pumping her fist. "I've read great reviews on this."

Addy gaped at her. "Are you kidding me? You've researched…personal massagers?"

"It's really great, Addy, you'll love it," Zoey said.

Addy shook her head as though she couldn't believe Zoey had done this. "You're crazy, you know that? Who gives these things out on Christmas?"

"The best kind of friend. You'll be thanking me soon. You'll be all, 'Thank you, Zoey, oh, oh, ooooohhhhh!'"

Kellen had a hand over his mouth, his face turning bright red. There was a knock at the door and Zoey hopped up. "I invited Jayce," she said, as she made her way to the door.

"Really?" Kellen said. "That's so sweet."

"Yeah, well, I hated to think of him all alone and pathetic on Christmas." She had the door open for most of this sentence.

Jayce, with a case of some kind of liquor propped on his hip, pressed his lips together. "Thanks," he said flatly.

"You're welcome. Come on in." Zoey stepped aside.

He stepped inside and carried the clinking bottles to the kitchen.

"What did you bring?" Zoey asked.

"Your favorite wine. Kellen's favorite beer. And Addy's favorite scotch."

Addy laughed. "I don't drink scotch, Jayce."

"Yeah, well, you said the professor does. Keep it at your apartment just in case." He winked at her and she blushed to her ears, then he passed a bottle of RumChata to her and plopped down on the couch between her and Maya.

Addy hugged the bottle to her chest. "I love this stuff."

"I know." Jayce turned to Maya and handed her a card in an envelope. "Merry Christmas. Open that later, okay?"

Maya blushed and hesitantly took it. "Thank you."

"What do you like to drink, Maya?"

"Um. I don't really know. I like wine. I haven't tried much else." She glanced at Jayce but wouldn't hold eye contact. Kellen felt sorry for her, seeing how nervous she was with someone she'd known forever sitting next to her just because he was a guy. But, at least, she didn't move away.

"What about your kids?" Jayce asked. "Matthew seems like a Jack Daniels man to me."

Maya laughed. "My precious boy is definitely still in the chocolate milk phase of his life."

"You're right," Jayce said. "Sophie, though: closet drinker. She's shooting tequila every time you turn your back, admit it."

Maya laughed harder and then hissed as she pressed a hand to her injured rib. "You're funny, Jayce."

Jayce sat a little taller.

Zoey brought in a tray with mugs of coffee. She sat it on the coffee table and Addy immediately poured RumChata into hers. Jayce held his mug out to her and she boozed up his coffee for him. "My kind of woman," he said.

Addy clinked mugs with him.

"Between Zoey's present and Jayce's," Maya said,

"your Christmas is looking very promising, Addy."

Kellen grinned, because he knew it was the embarrass-Addy portion of the morning. She was already bright red.

"What did Zoey get you?" Jayce asked, reaching for the package tucked into the arm of the couch on the other side of Addy.

"Nothing," Addy said as she tried to grab the gift. "Jayce, come on."

But he was already peeking inside. He grinned and shot Kellen a look. "Ah, the Power Stud. Janice has one of these. Of course, she had to retire it after she started sleeping with me." He leaned back and splayed his legs out in front of him. "Ain't no substitute for Jayce."

Addy glared at him from behind her glasses. "You're a pig."

He just shrugged. "You know how to use that thing? You want me to give you a few pointers?"

Maya was giggling, and Jayce flashed her a smile, clearly pleased to be entertaining her.

"Have you all no decency?" Addy said, her face bright red. "What normal people talk about stuff like this?"

"It's nothing to be ashamed of, Addy," Kellen assured. And then he stopped talking because Zoey sat on his lap. He hugged her against him and felt suddenly overwhelmed with warmth. He nuzzled his cheek against her soft sweater.

All three adults on the couch sarcastically said, "Awww."

Zoey giggled, and Kellen buried his face in her neck, about as happy as he'd ever been, surrounded by his friends and family and holding a warm woman in his arms.

And then a sharp, smoke-scratched voice disrupted the tranquil mood. "Hey, y'all opened presents already?"

Everyone turned to see Tracy coming from the hallway in her robe. She poured herself a cup of coffee and sat in one of the recliners. "I'm so disappointed," she said. "I really wanted to see the kids open their gifts."

"I'm sorry, Mom," Zoey said. "I didn't know."

"Oh, well," Tracy sighed. "Jayce Gilmore, is that you?" She leaned forward, flashing a view of her cleavage.

Jayce was already sitting up, stiff as a board, his eyes wide and his face red. He cast a desperate glance at Kellen, who had no clue what was going on. "Uh, hey, Ms. Odell," he said.

"Oh, honey, please. After that night in your daddy's pickup truck, I think you can call me Tracy. Come here." She stood, and he met her halfway for a hug he obviously didn't want.

Kellen clamped his arms tight around Zoey who was already beginning to vibrate. As soon as Jayce sat back down, he turned to Zoey. "I did not have—I didn't—we didn't—I swear to God, Zoey—"

"Oh, relax," Tracy said. "We only made out a little."

Jayce nodded vigorously. "And I was seventeen, Zoey. Seventeen. And drunk."

"A very mature seventeen," Tracy added.

"Oh, God." Jayce fell back against the couch and closed his eyes.

"I'm sorry, Jayce," Zoey said in a tense and scarily quiet voice, "but you're going to have to die."

He sighed. "I understand."

Kellen couldn't stop gaping at his best friend. "Why

did you never tell me this, man?"

Jayce sat up. "I believe I did. I was practically living with you, back then. I'm sure I told you."

"No. No way. I would have remembered."

"Does it matter?" Zoey shrieked. And then for no reason at all, she punched Kellen in the shoulder.

Maya and Addy were both staring at Jayce. He glanced at each of them. "Well, I think I'll go," he said, leaning forward.

Addy grabbed him by the back of his shirt and pulled him back down. "I made out with you, too. Remember?"

"He made out with everyone," Zoey said.

"Only when he was drunk," Kellen said.

"He didn't make out with me," Maya said.

Jayce turned to her, his expression more hurt than Kellen had ever seen it. "Yes I did. You don't remember?"

Maya frowned in thought.

Jayce's jaw dropped.

Kellen felt for him. Probably the one make-out session that had meant anything to him and she didn't remember.

"Well I'm about to take the kids to Mom and Dad's," Kellen said. "You wanna come with us?"

Jayce tore his gaze from Maya, who was still trying to remember the most important moment in Jayce's life. "Uh, no. Thanks, man. Your mom hates me. Plus I gotta take the old man out to breakfast."

"You don't gotta."

Jayce shrugged. "He called yesterday. Said, 'Hey, shithead, we having Christmas breakfast?' And I said 'yeah.' How could I not? I mean, all the love…it just gets ya right here." He pounded his fist to his heart and grinned.

Kellen shook his head. He never could understand how Jayce could be so nonchalant about that relationship. "If you change your mind, come on by."

"Thanks." Jayce stood, casting one last, longing glance at Maya.

Kellen walked him out the front door and closed it behind him.

Jayce turned to face him.

Kellen laughed. "Don't you hate it when your youthful mistakes come back to humiliate your ass?"

Jayce's expression shuttered. "Yes. Yes I do."

"Was she any good?"

Jayce looked at him like he'd lost his mind. "I don't remember. But gross. What the hell was wrong with me?"

"You were horny and had abandonment issues. You had that phase there where you were chasing women in their forties. Remember that?"

Jayce nodded. "Yeah, I guess I do."

"Don't worry about it. I won't let Zoey murder you in your sleep."

He laughed bitterly. "May as well let her." He frowned down at his feet. Then he shook his head. "How's she doing?"

Kellen understood the subject change. "You saw her."

Jayce nodded; his hands clenching into fists. Kellen knew he'd be thinking about how beaten Maya looked and how much he wanted to punch Damon. "She seemed pretty relaxed."

"Good painkillers."

"Shit. I thought she just found me charming."

"I'm sure she did."

Jayce shook his head. "Doesn't matter. Look I'm going. You have a cozy Christmas with the new girlfriend, okay?"

Girlfriend? That stunned Kellen into silence. He watched Jayce's truck disappear down the road as he mulled it over.

Kellen went back inside to find Zoey handing her mom a small box.

"I got you a present," she said. "If you want it."

"I love presents!" Tracy said. "Of course I want it." Tracy opened it. "Oh, earrings," she said. "I love them. Did you see the earrings Mark got me?"

She sat Zoey's earrings on the table and then pushed her hair back to reveal the ones in her ears.

"They're lovely," Zoey said, disappointment tainting her voice.

Kellen went for more coffee. He wasn't sure how much longer he could sit here and watch this woman he cared so much about throw herself at someone who obviously didn't love her. He heard Tracy follow him. She held her coffee cup out, and he topped it off for her. Then as he was returning the carafe, she cupped his right ass-cheek and squeezed.

He turned and looked straight at Zoey, silently begging her for permission to tell this woman to keep her damn hands off of him. However, Zoey's wide, frightened eyes, and a shake of her head, told him she wanted him to be silent. He would do his best.

Tracy didn't notice the interchange as she moved back to her recliner. Kellen stayed in the kitchen with his arms folded over his chest.

"You know," Tracy said, "I dreamed last night that I was in a Kellen and Mark sandwich. It was so hot."

Zoey's face paled. The smile she wore was a sad mask.

"Isn't it great that we can date men of the same age?" Tracy asked. "It's like we're more like sisters than mother and daughter."

"Yeah," Zoey said. The earrings sat on the table, ignored.

"Maybe we can double date while we're here," Tracy said.

Kellen finally made his way back to Zoey's side. "Exactly how long are you here?" Kellen asked.

Zoey whipped her head around and said, "She's here as long as she wants. You got a problem with that?"

Kellen wondered how she could make mere words feel like a slap in the face. "Nope. No problem."

She held eye contact for a long moment before turning back to her mom. "A double date sounds fun," she said.

"Great! Maybe tomorrow night?" Tracy replied.

"Sure."

Kellen supposed it was time to have a conversation with Zoey about communication within a relationship. But this wasn't the place. He did want to get away, though.

"Hey, Matthew? Sophie?" he shouted. The kids came running out of their room. "If you guys get dressed, we'll go over to Grandma and Grandpa's for breakfast."

"Really?" they both asked.

He laughed. "Yeah, really."

"Is Mom coming?"

"No, she's gonna stay here and rest."

"Is Aunt Zoey coming?"

"Why would Aunt Zoey come?" he asked. It came out of his mouth without any thought, and then he sat there wondering why it had.

Zoey was also frowning, clearly confused and slightly discomfited. They looked at each other.

And then Matthew answered the question. "Because she's your girlfriend. Ain't she?"

This thing between them had happened so strangely. Fast and sneaky. They stared into each other's eyes, and he wondered if she was doing the same thing he was—calculating his obligations to her and where exactly she belonged in his life. This cocoon they'd been living in wouldn't hold them for long.

"No, Matthew," Zoey said. "I'm staying here, but I hope you kids have a great time."

Matthew and Sophie jumped up and ran to their room to get dressed.

Kellen did the only thing he could think to: he kissed her. There was something in the kiss that said what he couldn't find words to say. At least, he hoped it did. Her lips certainly responded. With words, she was prickly and often cruel, but when he kissed her, she submitted. She accepted him and gave of herself. She became soft and sweet.

He slipped his tongue between her lips and she joined him. Tracy made some off color remark and Addy responded to her, but Kellen didn't care. He needed this.

It was the only way to understand Zoey and to be understood by her. He wrapped his arms around her and held her tightly against him, plundering her mouth. Here was connection, even more than the sex they'd had. Even more than the conversation.

He kissed her until he sensed that she'd completely given herself to him, then he pulled away and cradled her against him, looking down into her blue eyes. She was his, right then. There was nothing but pure, anger-free Zoey in those eyes. Her lips were parted, red, and swollen. He kissed her forehead. "I'd invite you to my parents', I really would, but I couldn't guarantee you a good reception. My mom thinks you're the devil's bride."

She grinned up at him. "Talk me up. When you think she'll be receptive, I'll apologize."

"Really?"

"Sure. I should have just politely told her that she didn't need to do what she'd done, and then asked her not to call anymore without apologizing to Maya first. That would have been the sane way to behave, right?"

"Yes," he said, laughing, "it would have."

"I think you're rubbing off on me, Kellen."

He kissed her again and then untangled himself from her arms. She dropped her head back against the sofa. Her arms lay where they'd fallen when he stood. He grinned down at her. "You're beautiful, Zoey."

Her smile faded and her eyes widened. She didn't speak, so he moved on, checking on Matthew and Sophie. Once they were dressed, he helped them into their coats and snow boots and then led them out to his truck.

CHAPTER TWENTY-FIVE

Zoey sat there, paralyzed with contentment. She felt her eyes stinging and then two tears spilling over. At the sound of his truck leaving, something broke inside of her. Her chest swelled and she leaned forward, struggling to breathe. She could only stare in front of her, feeling like she was suddenly free-falling with no net to catch her.

Addy and Maya appeared at her sides, both touching her and stroking her hair.

"You never had a man tell you you're beautiful?" Addy asked.

Zoey shook her head. "Not like that. No. Not like that."

"You can trust him," Maya said. "Kellen is the best man I know."

Zoey suddenly gasped. "Oh, my God. Oh, God, I'm gonna fuck this up. I can't be with him. What was I thinking? He's too good for me!" She jumped up and paced, trying to keep up with her pounding heart.

"What are you talking about, baby doll?" Tracy said. "You're plenty hot enough for him."

"I'm certain that's not what she means," Addy snapped at Tracy before turning her attention back to Zoey. "Calm down."

Zoey paced and shoved a hand into her mass of hair. "I just figured we'd fool around. I mean, I figured it would fizzle. But, it isn't going to fizzle, is it? This isn't just a fling, is it?" She turned to her friends. "Is it?" she shrieked.

They both jumped back. Maya laughed. "Jeez, Zoey, everything is so intense with you. Of course it's not just a fling. He's clearly crazy about you, and you about him. So just relax into it. Everything's going to work out."

"No," Zoey said, shaking her head. "No way. No, I can't do that. I can't do this. He's too good, do you hear me? Too good." She leaned on the last word, trying to convey to them that it was his goodness, his virtue, his pure-heartedness that she couldn't handle. "I'll forever feel inadequate. He'll figure out he can do better and he'll leave. I couldn't possibly please him. I couldn't be good enough. Shit, what was I thinking?"

Addy stood, grabbed her by the shoulders, and shoved her onto the sofa. "You need a drink."

"I need medication."

Addy ignored her and went to the kitchen. She returned with wine, which Zoey gulped down in one breath. She held out the glass to Addy, who laughed and brought back a refill. She drank this one more slowly.

"I don't see what the big deal is," Tracy said. "You're the one who's too good for him. I mean, he's hot, but you can do better. Have fun with him while you can, and then ditch him before he ditches you. Simple."

Zoey ignored her, because she knew that Tracy had no idea what love was. Love. God, had the word really entered into the conversation? Yes, she was certain of it. Love was what he was saying with those kisses. What neither of them could say with words.

She shook her head. "I can't do this to him. You guys were right."

"No, we weren't," Maya said. "This is it, Zoey. He's it. He was there all the time, all you needed was to open your eyes and your heart. Now that you have, the hard part's over."

Zoey kept shaking her head. "He doesn't know what he's getting into. I'll hurt him." She was repeating the words she'd been told by others, only now she understood them. Now she had a proper fear of them.

"Stop it, woman, for the love of God!" Addy shouted. "He likes you. It's done. Enjoy it."

Zoey met Addy's eyes, wanting to believe her. She nodded. "You're right," she said, not believing a word of it. "I'm overcomplicating it. Whatever happens happens, right?"

"That's right," Addy said. "Be grateful for it. Enjoy it, okay? I mean, Kellen Bradley…you'd be a fool to throw that away."

Zoey nodded along. She would go with it. She would fail, but she would enjoy being with him for as long as he was willing to put up with her. It was too late to save her heart: Her heart was already lost.

Somehow the morning evolved into Zoey and Addy

trying to cook breakfast, while Maya sat at the bar and Mark and Tracy danced in the living room to some really loud, hip-hop music.

"This is a fucking travesty!" Addy shouted. "There should be children and Christmas music! Call Kellen and tell him to come back!"

Zoey agreed, but she was too busy trying not to burn the pancakes to call Kellen. Addy was frying bacon again after burning one batch. The second was on it's way to black. When it did, she took the pan and dumped it into the trash can. Then she stomped into the living room and ripped Tracy's iPod out of the stereo. "It's Christmas, goddammit!" she shrieked.

Everyone turned to her.

"We're going to listen to Elvis sing Christmas songs, and somebody is going out to buy us cinnamon rolls and other delightful pastries because the good Lord did not put me on this earth to cook and watch you two—" she flung her arm out, pointing at Tracy and Mark, "—fornicate via dance to music that's at least two generations younger than you! Fuck!" She shoved her hands in her hair, squeezed her eyes shut, and breathed.

"Jesus," Maya said. "This is a tirade of Zoey proportions."

"Hey," Zoey whined.

Meanwhile, Tracy was riled. "You'd better watch your language, young lady," she said to Addy. "As you so insensitively pointed out, I'm a lot older than you, and it would serve you right to treat me with respect."

"Respect?" Addy laughed. "Really? You deserve respect about as much as you deserve a Nobel Prize."

Tracy hauled back and slapped Addy across the face and then, of all things, Addy tackled her. Mark jumped out of the way as the two women hit the floor and rolled. Addy landed on top. Tracy flailed beneath her while Addy started ripping out her extensions.

Zoey, stunned silent for a moment, finally ran to pull Addy off, while Mark dragged Tracy away. "Get that little bitch away from me!" Tracy shouted.

Addy was just crying, crying like a little girl. Ugly sobs and tears streaking her face. "I'm just having a really hard time, and I fucking hate your mom," she sobbed.

Zoey, who had only seen Addy break down like this one other time, didn't know what to do. She shoved Addy toward the bedroom she'd been sharing with Maya. Addy fell face down on the bed. "Holy shit," Zoey said. "What the hell was that?"

"I don't know," Addy moaned into the pillow. The sobs were mostly over. "I'm sorry, Zoey."

"Are you okay?"

"Yes. I feel better now." A long, red extension hung on her class ring. She shook her hand hard, trying to fling it off; her face still buried in the pillow.

Zoey reached for her wrist and untangled the strands of hair. "What happened?"

Addy rolled to her side. "I wanted to kill Damon. I mean, you don't know…I really think I could have done it. I can imagine squeezing the life out of him for what he's been doing to Maya. We've always been so helpless watching it. I don't get upset about much, but people hurting my loved ones…that just drives me crazy."

"What's that got to do with Tracy?" Zoey asked.

"Everything, Zoey. She hurts you and you just take it. Then you hurt the people around you, like poor Kellen. I can't stand it. I can't." She reached to the nightstand for a tissue and dabbed at her eyes and nose.

Finally Addy sat up and said, "I'm really sorry. I can't believe that just happened. I'm just so tired and stressed over Maya and now you."

"It's fine," Zoey said. "She likes it when people apologize to her. So I'm sure when you do that, everything will be fine."

Addy barked a laugh. "You serious? I'm not apologizing to that bitch."

Zoey flinched. "You can't call my mom a bitch."

"I can call her anything I want. The only one I'm sorry to is you. Tracy can go to hell."

Zoey stiffened. "If you were really sorry, you'd make up with her. You know how much she means to me and how much I want us all to just get along."

Addy laughed again, but it lacked amusement. "Yeah, I know, but I'm not apologizing."

"Then leave." Zoey felt sick, saying it.

Addy looked sick, hearing it. She stood and poked Zoey in the chest. "You're being an idiot." Then she grabbed her overnight bag, threw her things in it, and walked out the door.

CHAPTER TWENTY-SIX

The kids didn't want to leave Grandma's house, but Grandma was pushing the limits with Kellen. She kept circling around the subject of Damon, clearly wanting to talk about him with the kids.

They ate their breakfast, a feast comprised of muffins, eggs, sausage, and bacon. There was a bowl of pomegranates in the middle of the table, too, which Matthew and Sophie had fun pulling apart and eating. Then they opened their presents while The Grinch played on television in the background.

When he'd first walked in, he'd been taken aback by a bruise across his mother's cheekbone. She'd refused to talk about it, but Kellen had pulled his dad aside and asked him. Apparently Damon had visited his parents before going to Zoey's and getting shot in the foot. Bryan had, at last, taken a stand in favor of Maya. He and Damon had had words and when Lois had stepped in to calm the dispute, a drunk Damon had hauled back and smacked her.

Now, here she was, hovering around the kids, hanging on to a delusion. At last, she couldn't take it anymore. She pulled Kellen aside. "Damon should get to see his kids on Christmas," she whispered.

Kellen sighed. "Damon's in prison where he belongs. Good Lord willing, he'll never see those kids again."

She frowned and her chin quivered slightly.

"If he wanted to see his kids, he wouldn't have hurt Maya," Kellen said.

"He didn't hurt Maya. He said she was fooling around with someone else and that's who hurt her."

Kellen actually laughed. "Maya? You believe that? Mom, I can't do this with you right now. If you don't want to see the truth, that's your business. Until you do, though, I just can't talk about this with you."

Her eyes filled with tears and she left the room. Sophie was playing with her miniature dolls, and Matthew was reading a comic book. Kellen leaned against the bar separating the kitchen from the living room. His dad got up from the floor where he'd been playing with Sophie.

"She'll come around," Bryan said. "I think she already doesn't believe her own words. She just doesn't know how to admit to herself that her son is capable of this."

Kellen felt his chest tighten. "I'm just thankful you've come around."

Bryan nodded. "It took me a while to come to terms with it. You don't ever want to believe your child turned out bad. There's a lot of self-blame. A lot of questioning everything you've ever believed in. But you talked about him hurting you when you were kids and…and you're right. I turned a blind eye to it, because I didn't want to make waves with your mom. We chalked it up to sibling rivalry, and then we just kept spoiling him."

Kellen blew out a breath. "Is there anything you can do to help Mom along? Maya needs all the support she can get."

Bryan shook his head. "I don't know. I'll try to sway her, but I've never been very good at that sort of thing."

Lois came out again, holding two, small picture frames. "Hey, kids," she said. "I thought since you don't get to see your daddy for a while, you might like to have a photo of him for your nightstands. You can wish him goodnight and give him a kiss, just like if he was there."

Kellen cursed quietly and moved toward them to intercede. Turned out he didn't have to. Sophie moved behind Matthew and neither child accepted the gifts. "He hurt Mommy," Matthew said.

Lois shook her head in sympathy. "I know that's what everyone has told you, but—"

"I was there!" Matthew jumped to his feet. "Me and Sophie both. He always hurts her. We've seen him. I tried to help, once, and he hit me, too. Sometimes he grabs handfuls of Sophie's hair and drags her to her room when he doesn't want to listen to her crying. We don't want to see pictures of him."

Matthew had tears streaming down his face and his bottom lip quivered, but he stood strong.

Kellen hadn't known about Damon hurting the kids. At the moment, he wished he still didn't know.

Lois broke down, falling to her knees and crying into

her hands. Matthew gaped at her and then turned to Kellen with confusion in his eyes.

Kellen smiled supportively. "Guys, tell Grandma and Grandpa thank you for the wonderful Christmas. Give hugs and kisses and then get your coats and boots on."

The kids obeyed while Kellen gathered up the toys and books they'd gotten. He packed the things behind the seat of his truck and then bundled the kids into the truck.

When he pulled into Zoey's driveway, he saw Addy sitting on the porch step next to her duffel bag. She had on a hat, coat, and gloves, but she was still shivering. Kellen helped the kids out of the truck and once they'd gone inside, he turned to Addy.

She smiled sadly up at him. "Don't suppose I could impose upon you for a ride?"

He picked up her duffel and helped her to her feet. Then he tossed her bag in the back and opened the door for her. Once he backed out of the driveway and made it onto the plowed road, he asked, "What happened?"

"Oh, I got in a fight with Tracy. It was my fault. I snapped."

"You? Snapped?"

She shrugged. "It happens."

He frowned, wanting more information, but also afraid to ask. Her parents' home wasn't far, though the snow slowed them down. They arrived in less than ten minutes. He pulled into the driveway of the two-story colonial.

Addy hesitated. "You mind if I offer some advice?"

"Sure," he said.

"Go home until Tracy leaves."

Kellen's hands slid off the steering wheel and he sank back into his seat. "Yeah, I've been thinking about that. But, she asked me to stay. She begged me to stay."

"Listen, you're not getting out of this without her getting pissed at you. The only thing you can control is how you piss her off. I'm speaking from experience when I say, piss her off by saying you're tired and need to sleep in your own bed, or something like that. Because if you stay, something's going to happen with Tracy, she *will* take Tracy's side, and then the repercussions for you could be a lot worse. A lot."

He frowned at her. "Is it really this dire? She kicked you out and you seem okay."

"I am okay. I've been through this before. Once Tracy leaves, she's going to show up on my doorstep and offer tearful apologies. Then we're going to go shopping, get mani-pedi's, and be best friends again. But, with you, I don't think it'll be that simple. It's a huge deal that she's opened up to you. If she perceives even the first hint of betrayal in you, that door will slam shut forever."

He shook his head. "She's more reasonable than that."

Addy burst into laughter. She laughed so hard she had to hold her stomach. She reached over and patted his shoulder. "Oh, Kellen. So precious. So innocent."

He started to bristle. He hated being treated like he was naive just because he preferred to see the best in people. Or rather, because he preferred to hope for the best.

"Listen," she said once she calmed. "If you want to hang on to her, you might have to move a little faster than you want. Beneath all of her bitchy veneer lies a pit of massive insecurity, so go ahead and let her know that you're here to stay. Tell her you love her. Whatever you need to do—"

"Whoa, what?"

She stopped and gaped at him, much as he was doing to her.

"Love?" he asked. "We just started this…whatever this is. I don't even have a word for it yet. I mean, I don't know if I'd even introduce her as my girlfriend at this point. We haven't talked about any of this."

Addy's expression was blank for a moment. Then she closed her mouth and put her hand on the handle. "God, never mind, then. I thought you were in love with her."

"I'm not *not* in love with her. I was just kind of going with it."

This time she glared at him, clearly disgusted. "She's my best friend. I thought you'd be good for her. I thought you were serious about her."

"I am!" he said, irritated to suddenly be on the defense. "I'm very serious about her. It's just, I can't go saying stuff like…like love stuff. We haven't had any kind of meaningful conversation on the subject. We've just been doing whatever feels right, and I figure it'll eventually work its way into a relationship."

"Kellen, you knew right from the beginning you were going after a high maintenance girl. You need to think a lot farther ahead than her, or she's gonna destroy you. And worse than that, she'll end up hurt and I'll have to hate you. Thanks for the ride." She hopped out and grabbed her duffel.

He sat there and watched until she got all the way in

the door. He drove back toward Zoey's house, feeling like he was about to walk into a trap. He seriously considered passing her street and going straight home. But he didn't.

He parked in her driveway and sat for a few minutes, trying to make sense of Addy's words. When he went inside, it was to find Zoey sitting next to a crying Tracy on the sofa, rubbing her back and attempting to soothe her.

Maya and the kids were nowhere to be seen. Mark was in a recliner reading an issue of Cosmo. Kellen hovered in the doorway a second too long. Zoey snapped her head up. "Close the door, dammit, you're letting the cold in."

He shut the door but kept his shoes on. He wanted to be able to bolt if things got bad. "Where are the kids?" he asked.

"Downstairs."

He headed to the basement rather than running for the hills. Maya was lounging in a chair with a book while the kids played with their toys. There was a television mounted to the wall playing *White Christmas*. Kellen sat on the floor next to Maya's feet. "Should I go home?" he asked.

"Probably."

"You wanna come with me?"

"Yes," she said. "I'm worried about the pain on the drive, though."

He nodded. "It'll be rough, but the cabin's quiet and comfortable."

"Zoey will hate us."

"The kids don't need to be around that crazy mother of hers. And if Tracy grabs my ass one more time, I'm gonna snap."

Maya laughed and tousled his hair. "Your fault for looking so good in those jeans."

He shook his head. "I feel so objectified."

Her fingers lingered in his hair and he rested his head on her knee. "Being friends with Zoey can be exhausting," she said.

He could only nod, his eyes on the kids.

"It's not wrong to take breaks from her. Me and Addy do it all the time."

"So I should take a break now?"

"Do you want to?"

"Yeah. I'm—confused."

"Then you need a break. You can figure everything out and then decide whether you want to do this with her."

He hated to even think about not doing this with her. His heart hurt just imagining breaking this off. But, Maya was right. He needed some space. "Can we get out of here without her hating us forever?" he asked.

"Probably not."

He sighed. This was not going to be pretty. He stood and took a fortifying breath. "All right," he said, "I'm gonna get you and the kids packed up. Then…prepare to run."

Maya laughed then she sighed.

CHAPTER TWENTY-SEVEN

When Kellen topped the stairs and rounded into the hall, he ran smack into Zoey. She shoved him. "Watch where you're going, asshole."

"Hey!" He grabbed her wrist and then squeezed his eyes shut. Now was not the time to lose it with her. He took a breath. "Zoey, it was an accident."

"Fine. Just move because Mom needs aspirin." She shoved past him and to her bedroom. Kellen shook his head and went to Maya's room to pack her stuff. His next stop was the kids' room, which was a mess. Packing them up took a little longer. He wasn't sure he could fit all their Christmas gifts in his truck. It was a struggle enough to fit the whole family.

He was zipping up their suitcase when Zoey walked in. "What the hell are you doing?" she asked. Well, more like shrieked.

He turned to face her. He reached out to touch her

cheek, but she pulled back. "I thought I'd take Maya and the kids and give you some time alone with your mom."

"You're ditching me?"

"No, Zoey, I'm giving you space."

"Did I ask for space? No, I didn't. I asked you to stay with me."

"Listen," he said, treading very carefully, "this isn't a big deal. I'll come back tomorrow and hang out a while. I just want to be able to sleep in a bed that isn't trying to eat me, okay?"

There was a flicker of amusement in her eyes, but it quickly got swallowed up by her anger. "Fine. Go."

He'd take it. He knew 'fine' didn't mean fine, but, at this point, he was just grateful she wasn't screaming and throwing things. "Thanks," he said. "Call me if you need anything."

She folded her arms over her chest and stepped out of his way. As he walked past her carrying the luggage, she said, "Seems like if you were concerned about my needing anything, you wouldn't be leaving me."

He didn't touch it. Right now, the game was keeping his head down and getting out. Except when he went back inside after loading the suitcases in the truck, she was sitting on the edge of the kids' bed crying. Nothing terribly dramatic, just a few tears and a red nose. He did not want to engage. He knew nothing good would come of it, but he couldn't bear to leave her there by herself.

He went and sat next to her. He slipped his arm around her waist and she leaned into him. "You're done with me," she said.

He wrapped his other arm around her. "God. No."

"Yes, you are. I can feel it."

"I'm not."

"I can hear the question in your voice. You're gonna leave and then realize you're happier without me, and then that'll be it."

"Zoey, how is it you manage to make me feel like you're pushing me away and clinging to me all at the same time?"

She pulled away and frowned up at him. She shook her head, either because she didn't know the answer or because she didn't understand the question. He said, "I'm gonna take a risk, here, and be brutally honest with you."

She paled but nodded him on.

This was sheer idiocy, but it was who he was. Honest and transparent. Reasonable. "The fact is, Zoey, it's a challenging enough struggle navigating your moods when you aren't under stress. With your mom here, I just don't—"

She jumped up and threw her hands in the air. "I might've known. This is because of Tracy. You can be nice to every other person in the world, but, for some reason, you've got it out for my mother."

"That's not what I was saying."

"You know, if you hate her so much, then there's no way you can like me. She and I are so much alike. You think she's this awful bitch, but she's just trying to find happiness in a world full of people who just want to stab her in the back."

He stood and approached her slowly. "You've got the ability to reason past this, Zoey. I've seen you do it. Set your anger and your fear aside, and think."

"You're saying I'm stupid? Irrational?"

He closed his eyes and blew out a breath. "I'm saying you're better than her and you know it. A few wrong moves and yeah, you'll turn into your mother. But, Zoey, you've got it in you to be better."

"Fuck you, Kellen. How dare you talk down to me like this? You think you're so perfect?"

"Not at all—"

"You're not. You're a coward and a people pleaser. I wouldn't be you for all the money in the world. I can't imagine going through life simpering and bowing to everyone else's wishes. You think I'm afraid? You're the one who's afraid."

Anger flared out of nowhere. "I'm afraid? Why the fuck wouldn't I be? I have to live among a bunch of people who could snap and fly off the handle at any moment and I'm just here, trying to live my life, minding my own business, hoping I don't piss someone off. I take a chance on you and you rip me to shreds, Zoey."

"So why are you still here?"

"There you go again, pushing me away. Which is it? Do you want me or don't you?"

"You said you could handle me!"

"You're not giving me anything back. I'm the only one putting out any effort."

"That's a lie. I'm giving everything I have."

"Then it's not enough." He regretted the words as soon as he said them. She stepped back and all the anger drained out of her, leaving her pale except for her red nose and eyes. He wanted to take it back, but as soon as he heard the words, he realized they were true. He didn't have what it took to hold up a relationship with her by himself.

She stepped further back. "All right," she said, defeat heavy in her voice. "Well, it was fun while it lasted. You're amazing in bed, Kellen."

He didn't know what to do. Didn't know what to say. So he just watched as she turned and left the room. She went to her room and stayed there. He loaded Maya and the kids into his truck and they set off on the snowy drive to his cabin. He was aware the whole trip that he was frowning. He just couldn't get her words out of his mind.

Maya was kind enough to wait until they'd settled into his cabin before interrogating him. The great thing about his house was that there was no setup. The kids had spent the night there, plenty of times in the past, and knew exactly where to put their things and where to find the controllers for the game console. With the kids settled in the den, he and Maya had coffee in the sitting room.

"So quiet here," she whispered.

Kellen could only nod. His head was throbbing.

"Is it over?" Maya asked.

He sighed. "I can't figure out how to be with her. I didn't want this to get too deep too fast. I wanted to just have fun with her for a while. But I'm pretty sure by the time I waded through the shit she throws at me, I'd be a hundred percent committed, whether I wanted to be or not. And even then, there'd be no telling how she would treat me. Shit, I should have listened to you and Addy and Jayce. I don't know what got into my ego to make me think I could handle her."

He closed his eyes and let the silence sink in. Maya was kind enough to allow it. She stood and kissed him on the forehead. "Merry Christmas, Kellen."

"You, too."

After she disappeared into the den, he realized how incredibly selfish he was being. Poor Maya, beaten and uprooted from her home, on Christmas no less, was offering him comfort. He resolved to have his act together by morning. He'd allow himself tonight only to wallow in self-pity.

CHAPTER TWENTY-EIGHT

Zoey was too numb to cry anymore. She came out of her room when they left and went into the kitchen to fix dinner for Tracy and Mark.

"I hope they didn't leave on account of us," Tracy said.

"They just wanted some family time to themselves."

"But Kellen's not really Maya's brother, is he?" Tracy made her way into the kitchen and hopped up on the counter. Zoey stood at the stove, waiting for a pot of water to boil so she could make spaghetti.

"He's her brother-in-law."

"Hmm," Tracy said. "You think they'll be sleeping in separate bedrooms tonight?"

"Don't do that, Mom."

"Do what?"

"Try to stir up unnecessary drama. I'm drama-ed out."

"I was only wondering, is all. Didn't mean to upset

you."

Zoey dumped a box of pasta into the water and then stuck a jar of store bought sauce in the microwave. She wasn't the least bit hungry, but Tracy and Mark were. She got a loaf of French bread out of the freezer, wrapped it in foil, and put it in the oven.

"You don't have to cook, baby doll," she said. "We could go out."

Zoey wondered how her mother intended to pay if they were to go out. She wondered if her mom realized how annoying an offer of going out was when she was already halfway done with dinner. She settled for, "Too much snow. Without Kellen's truck, we won't be going anywhere for a couple of days."

Zoey managed to get dinner on the table, choke down a few bites, and get the kitchen cleaned up before pleading a headache and going to the guest room. She showered and lay in bed, where she composed two dozen texts to Kellen and deleted each one. She had no business communicating with him. He'd gotten out, and rightly so.

Still, she couldn't help feeling disappointed in him. She wanted him to be Superman. She wanted him to stand up, strong and immovable even when she railed in anger against him. She wanted someone she could say and do whatever she wanted to without hurting him.

But, he was right; she hadn't given him enough. And she was right, too; she'd given him everything she had. It just so happened there wasn't much to give. Between trying to take care of Maya and the kids, being bombarded with her mother, and dealing with her own, massive insecurities, she just didn't have anything worthy to offer to Kellen.

She slept intermittently that night. When she woke up, she didn't feel like she'd slept at all.   She'd taken the kids' room and the pillows smelled like them. She got up and headed to the kitchen where Tracy and Mark were having a fight. She didn't pay attention. Just took her coffee and retired to the living room to read on her new Kindle.

Before too long, she was ten percent through a book and she had no idea what she was reading. She turned it off and looked out the window. She sat there for the next four mornings. Each morning, the snow had melted a little more. Each morning, Tracy and Mark were there, lounging in their underwear, eating all of her food.

If Kellen wasn't going to talk to her, she needed to at least go see Maya. She also needed to go to the grocery store. She made herself get dressed and cleaned up. She drove to Addy's, first, simply because she was closest.

Addy greeted her at the door with a smile and a hug.

"Can I come in?" Zoey asked. It was only ten o'clock, which, on a winter break, seemed early.

"Absolutely. I'm having coffee in the breakfast nook. Come on.

Zoey followed Addy through her parent's house. "I came to apologize—"

"Oh, stop. You know I forgave you the moment it happened. And I'm sorry for snapping when I did. I should have gone home before I lost it."

Zoey sat in a chair at a little, round table. Addy went to the kitchen and prepared her a cup of coffee. She joined her at the table. "So is Tracy gone?"

Zoey stared at her blankly. "No. She says she and

Mark are on vacation. They haven't even gone back to the station for their car."

"God, Zoey. I'm so sorry."

Zoey sank into her chair. "I love my mom, I really do, but I'm not sure what I'm going to do if she stays much longer. I mean, Maya's with Kellen, but when school starts back up next week, it just makes more sense that she stays with me. Plus, she's going to be looking for jobs. She should just be in town, but with Mom and Mark in the house, I just don't know how it's going to work."

Addy didn't say anything. She sipped her coffee and stared out the window. Little tufts of dead grass were showing and water dripped steadily from the trees and the eaves of the house.

"Say it," Zoey said.

Addy shook her head.

Zoey huffed.

"If you already know what I'm going to say," Addy said, "then you shouldn't need me to say it."

"That's never stopped you before."

"Yeah? Well I'm tired, now. I've been through this thing with your mom several times already and I'm just tired. There's nothing more to say."

"You think I should turn her away."

Addy pressed her lips together.

Zoey turned her gaze to some movement out the window. A cardinal perched on a pine bough, bobbing up and down from his landing. "You think I've sacrificed too much for a woman who will never love me." It hurt saying it. The pain was sharp but expected. She'd been preparing for it over the past few days. "I never had to lose you or

Maya. You'd never give up on me, but Kellen's gone. He's seen me at my worst, and he couldn't take it. Nor should he have to. If I'd given up on her, I'd still have him. That's what you wanna say."

Addy studied her through the lenses of her glasses.

Zoey was on a roll, though, and no longer needed her friend to point out her flaws. "You think I was afraid of how much I felt for Kellen. You think I pushed him away so I wouldn't have to experience the disappointment of his leaving. This is typical daddy-issue stuff I inherited from my mom, isn't it? This is textbook abandonment issues. And I cling to my mom because I want so badly to have that kind of relationship. A real mother-daughter relationship. But she doesn't want that at all; she's just using me."

Hot tears slithered down her cheeks. She took in a shuddering breath and sat her coffee cup on the table. She looked down at her lap and screwed up her face, fighting against the tears. They came anyway, silently purging her system. Addy mercifully sat by in silence.

When she was done, Zoey grabbed a napkin from the middle of the table and dried her eyes and nose. "Okay," she said. "Good talk."

Addy laughed. "You're strong on your own, Zoey."

Zoey shook her head. "I fake it, but I'm not. You know, I secretly long for a man just so I can hand off some of the responsibilities. Like—wouldn't it be nice to have someone mow the lawn and take out the trash? Or a pair of arms to hold you so you can just let go for a while? It's pathetic."

"That's not pathetic, Zoey. That's human. We all want

a partner. I think you, me, and Maya are so lucky to have each other—but as great as our relationship is, we each still want lovers. A committed lover to share our lives with full-time. It's not a weakness."

Zoey shrugged. "My mom has to have a man. She can't be happy without one. I don't want to be like that."

"Your mom is a lost woman. She lost herself a long time ago. You're not unhealthy like that. You like yourself. You're not afraid to be left alone with your own thoughts. You're stable, minus these insecurities that you've let rule so much of your behavior. And you know what? You're only twenty-four. It's okay that you haven't gotten it all figured out just yet."

Zoey leaned back. She smiled just a hint. "Yeah. There's still time to change."

Addy reached over and gave her hand a squeeze. The two women stood and hugged. And then Zoey drove down the highway toward Kellen's place.

CHAPTER TWENTY-NINE

Kellen thought it was coincidence that Terry Hale showed up at the gym, but, as it turned out, Jayce had invited him.

It had been four days since he'd walked away from Zoey. Starting two days ago, he'd been getting up in the mornings and going to Jayce's gym. Usually he just met Jayce there on Sundays to hold the punching bag for him. But today Jayce held the bag while Kellen punched. He took tips on his form from a guy named Ace, a professional boxer who'd been working out there for several years.

"That's good," Ace said, standing by. "Keep that wrist strong, let the power come from your body. Good."

Kellen felt sweat drip down his back. He'd never done much of this. Jayce loved boxing, but Kellen had generally stuck to weight lifting. Now he thought he might make this a regular part of his workout.

When Terry Hale came in, Jayce let go of the bag and Ace took his place. Kellen kept punching until Jayce called him over. Kellen sized Terry up, knowing he'd dated Zoey a little over a year ago. He was a good looking guy, a couple years older than Kellen and Jayce.

Kellen still hadn't figured out that Jayce had invited him here to talk. It wasn't until he handed them bottles of water in his office and they all sat down that Kellen finally caught on. "What, is this a support group for victims of hurricane Zoey?"

Jayce's expression remained neutral as usual. "Thought we should hear Terry's story."

Kellen shook his head. "I already know Terry's story."

"What did she say about me?" Terry asked, a pained expression on his face.

"Nothing, man. She just said I should talk to you. But now I've been through it, I already know how it went for you."

Terry shook his head sadly. "I was pretty crazy about her. She's so—fiery. Lots of passion."

Okay, now Kellen wanted to hit the guy, but he reined in the impulse.

"But I just couldn't be what she needed."

"What did she need?" Jayce asked.

"Everything. She needed me to jump up at a moment's notice to help her. She needed me to not get offended when she bitched me out. She needed me to support her but not make her feel like she was weak."

"That's fucking unreasonable," Kellen said. "She's gotta meet you halfway. It's ridiculous to beat yourself up because you're not Superman."

"I tried so hard to give her everything she needed and wanted, but eventually I just couldn't and I snapped. I said some awful things to her. And—and you just can't do that because as much as she seems like this hard-ass, strong woman, she's actually really fragile. She doesn't get hurt, she…shatters. And then, in that moment, you've lost any chance you had of being with her." Terry's voice was numb. He shook his head, dumbfounded.

Kellen leaned back in his chair. "Sounds like I'm lucky to be out."

"You're not, though. I was happier with her than I am without her."

"I don't think I was in that deep," Kellen rebutted.

Jayce snorted.

"What?" Kellen asked. "You got something to say?"

Jayce's eyebrows went up. "You're getting awfully mouthy after only three days of boxing lessons. No, I don't have anything to say."

"Good. Because the reason I'm so together today, as much as breaking up with Zoey hurt, is because I didn't let myself get too close. I was careful. After all the warnings I got, I should never have started seeing her. But, at least, I was careful."

Jayce frowned and nodded. "Good. Thanks for coming in, Terry."

"Sure, Jayce. I'll come by the bar tonight for that beer you promised me."

After Terry left, Kellen just sat there, staring at Jayce's desk. "Wanna go work out some more?" Jayce asked.

Kellen exhaled. "Nah, I think I'm done."

"You wanna—like—talk or something?"

Kellen laughed. "That's big of you, but I wouldn't want you to overextend yourself."

Jayce shrugged. "I can talk. Just works better with the bar between us."

"It does, doesn't it?"

"Yeah. So…let's go over there."

Kellen started to laugh at him and tell him it was completely unnecessary, but then he realized he wanted his friend's company this morning. He showered in the gym locker room and dressed and then drove to Jayce's bar, which wasn't open yet. But Jayce led him in through the back and then stood behind the counter while Kellen sat on a stool.

"Whiskey?" Jayce asked.

"It's nine in the morning."

"Mimosa?"

Kellen laughed. The great thing about Jayce the bartender was he always knew the right drink to serve. He was mixing something even as he was joking about Mimosas. He poured two Tom Collins and handed one to Kellen, who took a drink and then sighed. "I cried actual tears the night we ended it."

Jayce didn't say anything.

"I don't know how I got so hooked so fast. It's like all or nothing with her."

"Some chicks are like that."

"She just…needs you so intensely, but then at the same time she's shoving you away. I can't live like that. I don't want to."

"Then don't."

Kellen nodded and drank. "Wish I didn't miss her, is

248

all. Wish we hadn't had those few insanely memorable moments together."

"Sex good?"

Kellen looked at him and shook his head. "There are no words."

Jayce pressed his lips together in a semblance of a smile. "Well you can throw darts at her face if you want."

"I thought she took that picture down."

"Someone put it up again."

Kellen chuckled. "I'm not angry with her. I'm just—confused…and hurt."

Jayce took another drink. "You ever call Rick's sister? Beverly, right?"

"Yeah, Beverly. No, I never called her." Now hardly seemed the time to be thinking about another woman.

"Faster you fuck someone else, the faster you'll be past the pain."

Kellen narrowed his eyes at Jayce. "You're not even over your high school crush and you've been with dozens of women."

Jayce shrugged. "It's just standard advice, man."

"Yeah, well, what do you think I should do? I don't want standard advice, I want you to tell me what you think of me and Zoey."

He shrugged again. "I think it doesn't make a lot of sense."

"That's all? Me and Zoey don't make sense?"

"I don't know, man. What do you want me to say? You've been seeing each other less than a month, you fell hard and fast—it's surprising is all. Doesn't mean it can't work. It's just—unexpected."

"Well, would it be ridiculous of me to try and make it work? Or would I just be prolonging the pain?"

"Oh, there'll definitely be pain."

Kellen laughed and shook his head. "Yeah, all right. But, like you said, this has been less than a month. Is there enough there to try and salvage?"

"One fight and it's over—sounds pretty weak."

Kellen took a drink and thought about it. "Yeah. I mean, if it falls apart that easily, there's probably just not enough there to fix."

"No, I mean you. You sound pretty weak if you clock out after one fight. I've never actually witnessed this for myself, but I hear tell there's such of a thing as a healthy, long-term relationship, and that those couples actually work through their problems."

"So you think I should work at this?"

Jayce shrugged. "Depends on the nature of the problem. There's some things that can't be fixed, and you have to decide whether you can live with that. Like, maybe Zoey will grow up a little and quit throwing public temper tantrums—but she's always gonna have a temper. Can you live with that?"

Kellen frowned.

"And, she's always gonna have a mother she loves and wants to take care of. Maybe she'll change on that, but you have to be prepared to live with it. Can you?"

"Hmm."

"She'll learn to think before she reacts, but she's always going to say things that are hurtful and then have to apologize for them. Can you live with that?"

Kellen blew out a breath. "I've met Beverly. She

doesn't seem like the kind to lose her temper."

Jayce drained his drink. "Yeah, Beverly probably doesn't have any intolerable flaws. Best call her."

"What's with the tone?"

Jayce just gave him an inscrutable look.

Kellen finished his drink. As usual, not a lot of help from Jayce. He was a good listener and supporter but definitely hit-and-miss in the advice department.

CHAPTER THIRTY

Zoey had only been to Kellen's cabin that once, but she had no trouble finding it again.

She parked and slammed her car door shut, hoping to announce her presence. She made it halfway up the brick path toward the door before Sophie came flying out. "Aunt Zoey!"

"Yay! Sophie, girl, I've missed you!" She lifted the five-year-old into her arms and spun her around.

Matthew came out a second later and gave her a side hug. "Hey, Aunt Zoey."

"Hey, stud."

She looked up and saw Maya standing in the doorway, smiling sweetly. Her bruises were barely visible, just faint discolorations. Zoey put Sophie down and went into Maya's open arms. "I'm so sorry," Zoey apologized.

"You didn't do anything to me. We just wanted you to have some space."

"And you wanted to get your kids away from the crazy Odell women."

Maya laughed. "That too. Come in. Kellen went to the gym. And I think the grocery store, too. We don't have much food at the moment."

Kellen's being gone was both a relief and a disappointment. Zoey followed Maya and the kids inside. The place was gorgeous. Her last time there she'd been hurried upstairs to his bed. Now she got a chance to look around. The floor plan was open. They walked past the living room on their right and a set of stairs on their left that led to a loft.

"That's where Kellen sleeps," Maya said.

Zoey's eyes drifted upwards and she couldn't help imagining him up there, sprawled out naked on his big bed.

The living room was sunken with two steps, making it feel separated even without walls. Beyond it was the dining room and to the left, the kitchen. To the right of the dining room and living room was a hallway. "The guest rooms are that way," Maya said. "On the other side of the stairs is a den-slash-office. You wanna see?"

"Sure."

She followed Maya into the den. It was a large room with lots of windows. Off to the back were some leather couches, a television, and a game console. Toward the front was Kellen's desk and next to that, a drafting table. There were photos everywhere, but there, on top of his desk, were the photos he'd taken at her house. The children with their snowmen.

"Isn't that precious?" Maya asked. "He's going to

frame it for me."

Zoey smiled down at it. She laid it down and picked up the ones he'd printed of her. She let out a laugh as she passed the one of her in the kitchen giving him 'the look.' The ones of her in the snow were gorgeous. He'd experimented with black and white and some other filters.

Suddenly she put them back on the desk and stepped away. "I shouldn't see these. It seems so intimate. He didn't invite me here."

"I wouldn't have brought you in here if I thought he wanted to keep them from you."

Zoey gazed at the photos from a distance.

"Isn't it funny," Maya said, "how photos tell as much about the photographer as they do the subject? I mean, you can really tell how the photographer is feeling in the moment that he takes that picture."

Zoey had been thinking something similar, she just hadn't put words to it. "They're just pictures. Everybody takes pictures." She turned and left the den. She found her way to a sofa in the living room and sat. Maya joined her a moment later.

"How's your mom doing?" she asked.

Zoey sighed. "When's school start?"

"Um, January fourth. Why?"

"I'll have her out by then. So you guys can come back."

"Oh, sweetie, you do what you need to do. She's your mom."

"I want you guys to come back. My place is closer to town, closer to school and jobs. There's kids next door. It just makes sense. Plus, I really like having you and the kids, there. I feel like I finally connected with them and I don't want to lose that."

Maya surprised her with a hug. "Ow," she muttered, but kept hugging.

Zoey laughed. "Don't hurt yourself, crazy." But she hugged her back.

"You know, if you'd said anything else, I wouldn't come back. But just knowing you like my kids—we'll be there. With or without your mom. There's enough room for all of us. It really is more practical for me. And as I get moving around better, I'll be able to help out around the house. You're really the best friend anyone could ever hope to have, Zoey."

"Oh, crap, why do you gotta go and say shit like that?" The tears sprang up again and the two of them laughed over their crying.

They were still laughing when Kellen walked in the door. His arms were full of paper bags full of groceries. He froze when he saw Zoey. He didn't smile, but he didn't frown either. He looked more like a caged animal, scoping out the situation, trying to decide whether to be afraid or not.

"Uh, hey, Zoey," he said.

"Hey," she replied. "Did you want some help with those?"

"Sure," he said.

She nodded and said, "Okay. Well you're gonna wanna walk forward about six yards and then hang a left and set them on the kitchen counter."

He snorted and nearly dropped one of the bags. "Should have figured," he muttered, as he started walking.

Zoey jumped up and caught the bag in the middle that he was about to drop.

"Thanks," he said.

"No problem."

They deposited the bags on the counter. When Zoey turned around, Maya was nowhere to be seen. Discreetly skittering away, quiet as a mouse. Zoey retreated to the bar side of the counter while Kellen started putting groceries away.

"I think Maya's gonna move back in with me soon," Zoey said.

"Oh?"

"Yeah. It's more practical for her than living all the way out here."

"All the way out here? It's seven miles."

"Seven miles of bad roads. A fifteen minute drive to you is an extra hour on the school bus to the kids."

His back was to her as he slid tubs of yogurt into the fridge haphazardly. "Well, she's welcome here as long as she wants. But if she prefers your place, that's cool, too." He turned suddenly and lowered his voice. "I wanna help, too. Financially. And Maya's real sensitive about that sort of thing, so maybe you could let me give you some grocery money once a week or something? For Maya and the kids?"

This was actually a relief to Zoey. She made a good enough living, but she could already see where the food and personal hygiene needs of three additional people was going to wear on her budget. Even after Maya found a job, she was going to need time to save up money. "That would be great, Kellen, thank you."

He drew back just a hint. "You're welcome. Thanks for accepting the offer." Then he turned around and went back to unloading groceries. "So how are you doing?" he asked.

"Well," she said. "Tired." She slipped past him to the fridge, opened it, and lined up his yogurt containers in rows according to flavor.

He nodded and reached up to put some cans on the upper shelf of his pantry. His shirt lifted as he stretched and his jeans hung low, exposing the top edge of his boxers and a strip of well-toned flesh. Zoey broke into a sweat. "How have you been?" she asked, her eyes glued to his abdomen.

When he turned to face her, her eyes snapped back up. He grinned, clearly aware that she was looking. "I've been good," he said. "How's your mom?"

"She's a compassionless whore." She closed the refrigerator and retreated to the other side of the counter.

His eyebrows shot up. "Wow."

"Yeah. So anyway, hopefully she'll leave soon."

He nodded and looked away.

Zoey really didn't want to be the first one to broach the subject, but it was looking like he wasn't going to. Her nerves couldn't take any more waiting. "I want to apologize. You were right about the things you said. My fears and insecurities. I mean, my mom doesn't love me. I'm furious with her. I might even hate her. And yet I give her all my love and take my anger out on the people who truly care about me. So…I wanted you to know that I'm aware of it. I'm working on it."

He nodded. "That's real good, Zoey. I think you'll find

yourself a lot happier the more you do."

She smiled hesitantly. "I was wondering if you and I—
"

"I've been thinking a lot about what you said to me," he said.

She shut up, stunned that he'd interrupted her.

"I mean about me being a coward and a people-pleaser. You weren't completely off track. I don't think I'm necessarily afraid of taking risks or being hurt or whatever. It's just, growing up, Damon was an unstable mess. My parents did everything in their power just to protect him from the consequences of his own behavior. They made excuses for him. They turned blind eyes. He beat the shit out of me, growing up, and they chalked it up to sibling rivalry. So I did, too."

He moved to the counter and hopped up, sitting on the edge. He faced her across the kitchen. "I do that now. I try to protect people from the consequences of their own behavior. I try not to let them know they've hurt me because I don't want them to feel bad. I try to make sure they're never embarrassed or hurt or lonely. It's not always a bad thing. I think it just keeps people from really seeing me and my needs."

Zoey nodded. It made sense. He'd really thought it through.

"That was what was so great about being with you, Zoey. You rained so much hell down on me that I had to bite back once in a while. It felt good. So I'm grateful to you for that."

She laughed. "You're welcome, I guess. It's a sad testament to our relationship that that's the thing you walked away with."

He shrugged. "Even so, I still spent a lot of energy trying to take care of you. There's just a balance I need to find somehow."

He was staring off into the middle distance. Zoey watched him for a while, taking in his beauty from head-to-toe. And then, "Kellen?"

"Mm?"

"Do you think you and I could, I don't know, try again?"

The way he looked at her broke her heart. Broke it the rest of the way, because it had already been fractured when she'd sent him away. Her eyes filled with tears and she looked away, having cried enough for a lifetime in just that one day.

"Zoey, let me tell you what I like about you."

She folded her arms over her chest and arched a brow.

"You're the hardest working person I know. I admired that even back in school. You worked, what, thirty hours a week and still got straight A's? Professionally, you have a good reputation. I talk to people who know you as their accountant and they've got nothing but positive things to say. You're an extremely loyal friend. Generous without limit. Loving. Caring. You're doing great with my niece and nephew. You're beautiful and strong and smart."

She stood there blushing more than she'd ever blushed in her life.

"But the rest of it, Zoey—it's bullshit. This attitude of yours, the tirades, the bullying—it's bullshit. You're a grown woman. You've succeeded in so many important areas in life. Now it's time to stop being afraid. Stop being angry. And stop pushing people away."

"I know," she said, grateful for this chance to talk to him. "I know, Kellen. I'm going to work so much harder, I swear. I feel like I've come out of a haze and I see it all so clearly now. I'm thinking of doing some counseling. I wanna be a better person."

He smiled. "I'm really glad to hear that."

She stared up at him, fidgeting with the hem of her shirt. "So—"

"Zoey, before you and I started doing whatever the hell it was we were doing," he said, "I had a conversation with Jayce. I told him I wanted someone sweet. Just a nice, sweet girl to cozy up to at night. Someone not crazy." He winced. "I mean, not that you're crazy—"

"No, it's okay," she said. "I know what you mean."

He sighed. "Anyway, I think after all of this…that's what I want."

"Someone sweet," Zoey said faintly.

He nodded.

Zoey took in a breath and blew it out slowly. Then she stood and smiled up at him through her blurred vision. He hopped off the counter and leaned on the bar, facing her. "I'm sorry, Zoey."

She shook her head. "No, it's okay. You're right. You just can't handle all of this." She gestured to herself, trying to make light of the moment, but it didn't work because the smile he gave her was sad. She'd expected pity, but behind that, there was genuine sadness.

"I wish I could. It was good, Zoey. Really good."

"I thought so, too." She stepped around the end of the bar, getting closer to him. "Kiss goodbye?" she asked.

His eyes honed in on her lips and he moved toward her. He slipped his arm around her waist and pulled her up against him. Then he kissed her, and she melted into him. That kiss was so righteous, so true, so earth-shattering. Surely this was meant to happen. Surely they should fight for each other.

As he pulled back and stepped away, she realized that he didn't want to fight. He was done. She touched her lips with her fingertips, trying to hold on to the sensation of him. She turned and calmly walked out of the cabin.

CHAPTER THIRTY-ONE

Kellen sat across the table from Beverly, whose number he'd gotten from her brother, Rick. The new year had begun, the old one sloughed off like a bad hangover. He rested his chin on his fist and frowned in concentration. She was adorable. From her blond curls to her chirpy voice, she was absolutely sweet. But he wasn't connecting with a thing she said, and it was taking all his brain power to keep focused on her conversation.

"So you're a photographer?" she asked.

It took him a moment to process that he'd just been asked a question. He sat up and relaxed the tension in his face. "Yeah. Freelance photojournalist."

"So, not like taking pictures of people's babies in a studio?"

"No, not like that."

"Is it fun?"

"Yeah. I travel a lot. Do you like to travel?"

"Definitely. I mean, when I can afford it."

The server approached. They were at a steak house in St. Louis, halfway through their meals. "Is everything to your liking?" the server asked.

Kellen looked at Beverly for an answer, but Beverly was looking to him for an answer. So they both laughed and said, "Yes."

After the server left, Beverly took a sip of her wine. "So, a week, huh?"

"Huh?"

"Since you broke up with Zoey, the devil woman."

"Hey, I never called her that," Kellen said, though he couldn't help but laugh.

"Rick does. So…a week. That's not too soon to be dating?"

He shrugged. "It really wasn't a full-blown relationship. I mean, the feelings went deep, but the whole thing was a flash in the pan. I felt like I'd been picked up by a tornado, spun around violently for a couple weeks, and then dropped off in the middle of nowhere."

This time, she was the one with her chin on her fist, listening. "Sounds intense."

"It was awful. And wonderful. And then awful. But no, a week is plenty. I'm over her."

"It wasn't love, then?"

He took a sip of his beer to give himself a moment. He forced out the words, "No. Not love."

She laughed. "That's convincing."

He didn't want to be a bad date to this girl, but her questions were making him very uncomfortable. "You know, maybe we could change the subject. What about you? Ever been in love?"

She blinked a moment. "Um, okay. Yeah, I think I was in love back in high school. But, you know, I'm sure it's different as an adult—"

She kept talking, and he found his mind wandering to those kisses he'd shared with Zoey, to the silent communication, the kind of communication that worked between them. On a physical and spiritual level, their relationship had actually been functional. "You know, if it weren't for her goddamn mouth, we might have been able to work something out."

Silence.

He looked up and realized he'd interrupted her. She stared at him in shock.

"I'm so sorry," he said. "You'd asked about love, and I got to thinking about all the things we didn't say to each other."

Her smile was wry. "That can be a challenge in a relationship. Reading between the words."

"Yeah, no shit." He leaned back in the booth and frowned down at his half-eaten steak. "She could just be such an out-of-control bitch, but the moment I kissed her, she gave up. She just gave herself up to me. Let me have control. It was—I gotta say, it was one of the most incredible experiences of my life. Just holding her in my arms and looking into her eyes, knowing I put that satisfied smile on her face." He shook his head, wondering what it all meant.

"Could you talk to her at all? Or was it only the physical stuff that worked?"

"No, we talked. We had some good conversations.

She's actually really funny and fun. And, I mean, I could cut loose with her. I could snap back a little and she wouldn't get offended. I could be myself and not worry about hurting her. God knows if I did something she didn't like, she'd just flip me off or something. It's nice to be with someone who can deal with her own emotions. You don't have to worry about making sure you didn't offend her or whatever because she'll let you know. No guessing games."

"What went wrong, then?"

"It was that. The flipping me off thing. She'd get angry about other things and take them out on me and then tell me I should be strong enough to put up with it."

"She wasn't holding up her end of the relationship."

He snapped his fingers and met her eyes. "Exactly. See? You get it." And then it hit him. He gaped at her and leaned forward. "Bev, I am so sorry. I am being a horrible date. Let's go back to talking about you. What did you say you did for a living?"

She laughed and folded her napkin. "You're a great person, but I think we both know this date is over."

He was shaking his head before she finished. "Beverly, you are exactly the kind of woman I need. Listen to yourself. You're calm, reasonable, thoughtful. You're a damn fine woman, and I wanna get to know you. You gotta give me another chance."

She reached across the table and took his hand. Her eyes sparkled with humor and kindness. "I think if we'd gotten together a month ago, we'd have hit it off great, but you're in love with Zoey. And for that reason, I've lost all respect for you."

He grinned, then he dropped his head and laughed. "Shit," he said. He leaned back in his seat and signaled the server for their bill. "You know, Bev, I've got about a dozen funny bad-date stories, but as far as I know, I've never been the subject of one."

"Until tonight," she said.

He nodded and handed over his credit card.

"Yes, sir, I'm going to be telling this bad-date story to a lot of people. A lot of people we both know."

"I feel that's your right as a victim of the bad date. And I'm deeply sorry. If I'd seen all this about myself, I would never have called you."

"Well, it was a free meal, for me, and a good one."

"At least there's that. I've always had to pay for my bad dates."

The server returned and Kellen signed the receipt. He stood and held out his hand to Beverly, taking her elbow and leading her toward the exit.

He drove her home and apologized once more. He didn't want to go to his empty house, so he drove out to Jayce's bar. Rick, thankfully, wasn't there. It was crowded, so he'd likely be drinking in peace. He ordered a shot and a beer. Jayce gave him a funny look, since whiskey was rare with Kellen.

The bar noise was composed of pool balls cracking together, women laughing too loudly, men shouting and telling dirty jokes…typical sounds. Kellen let himself zone out on the noise. He didn't want to do much thinking. He kept a buzz going until around midnight and then switched to water.

The crowds died down and Jayce made his way to the

end of the bar. "Date didn't go well?"

Kellen glared at him. "I'm in love with Zoey."

Jayce showed no reaction.

Kellen took a drink of water. "My life as a bachelor is over. She's it for me. I just gotta figure out how to deal with all her crazy."

"Something wrong with Beverly?"

"No. She was perfect. But Zoey's my girl. I love her. I don't even have any interest in the perfect woman. Guess that makes Zoey better than perfect."

"You got it pretty good, Kel. All you gotta do is go get her. You love her. You want her. You go get her. Pretty easy indeed."

"Best of all, she remembers making out with me."

Jayce grabbed a handful of peanuts and flung them at him. "Asshole."

Kellen laughed. "I'm sorry. I can't stop thinking of how you looked. And Maya sitting there trying to remember."

"Glad you got a laugh out of it. Never mention it again."

"Wounded your ego, did she?"

"Ya think? How the fuck would you feel?"

"Pretty crappy, I guess." He thought about it some more. "God, that would kill me. It was hard enough when I wasn't sure I could get her to go out with me. Now—shit, I don't know what I'd do if this was more important to me than to her."

Jayce had gone expressionless, again and Kellen realized he was being insensitive. "Hey, I'm sorry," he said.

Jayce waved him off. "Don't worry about me. I've got

Janice. Shake that hot ass, Jan!" he shouted.

The blond waitress across the bar flashed him a smile and did a little shimmy move for him. Jayce nodded in appreciation.

"Nice," Kellen said sarcastically. "You are aware she's sleeping with Don down at the bank."

"No problem. That woman needs more than one lover."

The door to the bar opened and Addy came in, looking way too classy for Jayce's bar. Expensive clothes, expensive haircut, and already she was learning to wear that air of condescension that her mother had spent so many years drilling into her. She perched next to Kellen, but it was Jayce she spoke to. "That scotch you bought me? I need to know something about it so I can sound smart when I talk to Grey—I mean, Dr. McDaniel."

"Hmm," Jayce murmured. "I'm not a scotch man. I've got a book back in my office."

"Perfect," Addy said.

"Man the bar?" he asked Kellen.

Kellen nodded and Jayce slipped down the hall toward his office. After he was gone, Kellen turned back to Addy. "How's she doing?"

"Zoey? She's fine. She's an independent, modern woman. She doesn't need a man to be happy."

Kellen chuckled. "That what she said?"

"Says. Pretty much every time I see her. Between you and me, though, I think she's been happier."

Kellen nodded. "I've been happier, too."

"Easy problem to solve."

"Yeah. That's what I was thinking."

Jayce came back and handed a book to Addy. "Here you go," he said. "You'll either get really educated on scotch or else discover the cure to insomnia."

"Thanks, Jayce. You're the best."

She stood and kissed Kellen on the cheek. "Good luck. I'm really hoping it works out. Honest-to-God, she's never been as happy as she was with you."

After she left, Kellen sat in silence for a while, deciding how he was going to go about getting back into Zoey's life.

CHAPTER THIRTY-TWO

Kellen went shopping for groceries the next day. He got a bunch of pantry stock items, such as macaroni 'n cheese and instant oatmeal...stuff Maya and the kids would need. Then he took it all to Zoey's house. When he knocked on the door, it was Tracy who answered. Her smile turned lascivious when she saw him.

Here we go. "Zoey home?" he asked.

"No, she's at court."

Ah, the angry Christmas shopper. He did the mental math and realized it was, indeed, her court date.

"Come on in anyway, if you want," Tracy said, stepping aside.

"Thank you. I told her I'd help with groceries while Maya and the kids are here." He walked past her into the kitchen. Maya was there making peanut butter and jelly sandwiches. He set the bags down and took her in his arms. "Maya, there's not enough of you to hug. You been eating?"

"I have, but stress sucks the calories right away."

Kellen unpacked the groceries into Zoey's pantry. Then he took a breath and turned to the bar where Tracy was sitting. He had no idea how his stomach was going to handle this, but his plan was to flirt with her to get her to do what he wanted. He leaned against the bar on his palms and smiled. "How are you doing, beautiful?"

She sat up taller and beamed at him. "Just dandy. It's been quite a restful vacation."

He nodded. "Good. I'm sure you needed that. I noticed your car wasn't in the driveway. Is there anything I can do to help you get it back?"

Tracy stuck out her bottom lip and twirled her hair. She could have spared herself the victim act, Kellen had already resolved in his mind to do whatever Tracy needed just to relieve Zoey of some of her burden. "It got impounded," she said. "We can't afford the fee, and they charge twenty-five bucks a day on top of it."

Kellen bit back his irritation. They were racking up an even bigger fee by not getting it out to begin with. "Does Zoey know?"

"Nah, I didn't want to bother her."

Kellen nodded, as though he could possibly understand. "What's the fee?"

"Total, today, it's five hundred."

"What? Are you serious?" He couldn't disguise his surprise. But then, it made sense. The vehicle had probably been towed a week ago. Their fee doubled because they wouldn't take the time to deal with the problem right from the beginning.

Tracy just shrugged as though there was nothing she could do.

"Alright," Kellen said. "Well where's Mark?"

"Sleeping."

It was nearly noon. "Okay, well you go wake him up, and me and him will go get your car back. Sound good?"

He was glad when Tracy went to get Mark. He was afraid she'd want to go with him herself, but he really didn't want to be alone in a vehicle with her, even for the short drive to the car lot.

Mark finally came around and they retrieved the car fairly easily, aside from the hit to Kellen's bank account. He took Mark to a gas station and filled up the tank for him, because apparently they didn't have enough money for even that. Kellen's goal was to get them into a position where they could leave if they got the itch. He'd give them just enough money to get them far enough down the road that they forgot all about Zoey for a while. Then he'd make sure that they never stepped foot in her house again.

Back at Zoey's house, he found Maya in the basement watching television while the kids played. "Any word from Zoey?" he asked.

"Yeah. She paid a fine and has, like, two weeks of probation or something. She's on her way home. Should be here in about thirty minutes."

He nodded. "Great. Let me see what I can do about getting Tracy and Mark out of her bedroom."

He turned to leave, but Maya halted him. "Hey. How do you propose to do that?"

He shrugged. "I'll use my never-ending supply of charm."

Maya smiled. "Next question—why?"

He looked into her. "You know why."

"Say it anyway."

"Because, I love Zoey."

Maya folded her hands over her heart and squealed. Kellen rolled his eyes and went upstairs. He found Tracy in the kitchen, digging through Zoey's secret candy drawer. He steeled himself for the disgusting task, swallowing down the nausea that crept up his chest.

He went up behind her and braced his hand on the counter next to her, leaning over her. "What is that scent?" he asked, smelling her hair. God, he hated himself.

Tracy leaned back against the counter and used her arms to press her breasts together. Her shirt was two sizes too small already, he didn't need any assistance in viewing her cleavage. "Herbal Essences shampoo. You like it?"

"I do. You'll have to let Zoey use some."

"I thought you two broke up."

"We did. I'm getting her back, though. I wonder if you could help me out with that?"

"Sure, baby. What can I do for you?" She trailed her fingertips up the side of his neck and along his hairline.

"It's kind of a big favor." He dropped his eyes to her chest and let his gaze meander its way back up to her eyes. She was fully blushing, now.

"Anything for you, Kellen."

He grinned. "See, I've got this old back injury from football in high school. Last time I slept on that hide-a-bed downstairs, I could barely walk the next day. I'd really like to show Zoey a good time. You think we could have the master bed? Just for tonight?"

He wanted so badly to just kick her and Mark out of the room, but he reminded himself that he was focusing on making Zoey's life easier. Since it was important to her that she not hurt her mom's feelings, he was having to act like a slut to get what he wanted.

Tracy, still touching him, smiled lustfully. "I'll bet that flimsy hide-a-bed would completely give out with what you're planning to do tonight."

"You know it. So—can we have the bed?"

She laid her hand along his cheek and gave him a pat. "Sure, baby. Just for tonight."

"Thanks, Tracy. You're an angel." He kissed her on the cheek and then got the hell away from her.

Just for tonight? No, it would be for much longer than that. Tracy and her stripper boyfriend wouldn't be stepping into that room ever again. He helped her move her things to the basement so he could get the sheets changed and ready for his 'wild night' with Zoey.

In actuality, he was planning on tucking her into her own bed and sleeping on the couch. He didn't have a back injury. He'd flat out lied. He felt no remorse whatsoever.

CHAPTER THIRTY-THREE

Zoey drove home, drained of all energy. She hadn't put up a fight. In fact, she'd even apologized to the man she'd kneed in the balls. She felt defeated but also better. She wasn't angry that the man had pulled her hair before she'd taken action against him. She could have been, but she wasn't. Instead, she was relieved. And tired.

When she pulled into her driveway, there were two vehicles that shouldn't be there. One was her mom's car. The other was Kellen's truck. He'd parked on the street so that she was able to get to her garage. Her heart rate kicked up as she stepped inside her house. He was lounging in a recliner, reading a book and sipping coffee. Maya was in the other recliner sleeping. She could hear the kids in their room.

Kellen looked up at her and smiled. He stood and dropped his book in the chair. "Come here, I've got a surprise for you."

She frowned and kept just standing there. So he came toward her, took her hand, and pulled her back to her bedroom. He closed the door behind them. "What kind of surprise is this?" she asked skeptically.

"I got you your room back. Nice, isn't it?"

It looked exactly the same, except that Tracy and Mark's crap wasn't spread out everywhere. He jogged to the bed and pulled back the covers. "Clean sheets. See?"

She stared at the bed. Then she stared at him.

He pulled the covers all the way back and ran his hand over the sheets. "Mmm. Nice and cool. Don't you just wanna get naked and climb in there."

She still couldn't work up a reaction. "Yes," she numbly. "Yes, I do."

"Well, go ahead. It's all yours." He came behind her and pushed her toward the bed. He helped her out of her coat and draped it over the footboard.

She stared down at the bed, feeling like she should be asking him something. But she couldn't quite think of it, and that bed did look amazingly inviting. She reached down and touched it. Then she bent over and pressed her cheek to the sheet. "Hello, old friend."

Kellen laughed and patted her back. "I'll be here when you wake up. Have a good nap."

She heard the door click shut. Then she stripped out of her clothes, shed her underwear, and climbed into her bed. She piled the blankets on top of herself and fell steadily into sleep.

Her eyes popped open a second later. Only it wasn't a second; it was three hours. And she smelled something. Something good.

She rose and dressed. She followed her nose down the hall and into the kitchen. Kellen and Maya were at the counter. He was cooking burgers on the griddle, and she was slicing carrots and celery into sticks.

"Hey, baby doll!" Tracy said. "Did you have a good nap?"

Zoey didn't understand what was going on. She went to Kellen and tapped him on the shoulder. "What are you doing here?"

He set down his spatula, cupped her jaw, and leaned down. He pressed his cheek to hers and spoke softly in her ear. "I realized that I belong by your side." He held her there for a moment. She gripped his shirt and pressed her legs together as excitement surged through her.

He slid back, his cheek brushing hers, and smiled down at her. She let go of his shirt, filled her hands with his hair, and pulled him into a rough, desperate kiss.

Tracy cheered in the background. The people in the room were the only things keeping her from doing him right there. When they both managed to pull away, she looked up into a face stripped of its cocky self-certainty. His expression was all naked fear and wonder. "I love you, Zoey," he said.

She gasped and scrambled up his body for another kiss. She wrapped her legs around his waist and clawed at his shoulders. This time when he pulled back, he was laughing. "Now, or later?"

She could barely think or breathe or speak, but she realized the children were at the table glancing her direction. "Later," she squeaked and stared into his eyes with desperate regret.

He laughed again and brought her into a hug. "Later, and for a long time."

She nodded.

He moved away from her but held her hand as he picked up his spatula and flipped the burgers.

They sat around the table and ate. She forced the food down, but her stomach wasn't remotely interested. She didn't know how Kellen had managed to get Tracy and Mark to move downstairs, but whatever he had done had caused very little upheaval. Tracy was just as happy as if nothing had changed.

That night, Zoey helped Maya tuck the kids into bed. They liked to get a story from each of them. The next day they would start back to school. Zoey had already started back to work. Her schedule had been interrupted that day to go pay her debt to society.

Right after the kids went to bed, Maya disappeared into her room. Mark was drinking the last of Zoey's beer, again, and Tracy was on the internet doing God only knew what. So Zoey grabbed Kellen by the waist of his jeans and dragged him back to her bedroom. He closed the door and said, "I wasn't going to do this, Zoey."

She started unbuttoning her blouse. "Well, you're gonna now, right?"

"Don't you think we should slow things down a little? Give us time to get to know each other?"

She whipped off her shirt and kicked off her shoes. "I am having sex in this bed. Right now. Are you with me or not?"

He grinned and peeled off his shirt. Zoey took a moment to sigh in appreciation. He stalked toward her, took her in his arms, and kissed her. When his lips moved to her neck, she said, "Kellen, before we go any further, I just wanted to tell you…I love you, too."

He pulled back and studied her eyes.

"I love you," she repeated.

He was breathing heavily, already. He nodded. "I love you, too, Zoey. And you just say those words as often as you want, okay?"

He kissed her again and reached behind her to unclasp her bra. It slid down her arms and to the floor. He filled his hands and moaned. He trailed long, languorous kisses down her neck and between her breasts. He was being so gentle. So loving. Tears stung her eyes and she felt her heart opening to him. Where was she to go with this overwhelming passion struggling to burst out of her?

"Rough, Kellen. I want it rough."

He stood and the two of them unfastened their jeans and shoved them down. "I don't want to be rough with you," he said. "Not tonight."

"I want it rough. I need it, Kellen."

"Not tonight. I'll kiss you and you'll be mine and I'll do whatever I want with you."

His words lit her up. She leapt at him. He caught her and slammed her down onto the bed, falling on top of her. She wrapped her legs around him, urging him forward. Once his lips were on hers, she felt all her will dissipate. He was right. He could do whatever he wanted with her.

While he kissed her long and deep, he took first one of her hands, then the other, and guided them up to the headboard. She gripped, understanding that he meant for her to hold on. Time slowed. His lips left hers and made their way down her body. Her heart thundered in her chest, but she stayed relaxed, sucking in deep breaths and letting her body just feel.

When he went down between her legs, she held her breath. As his tongue stroked her, her body arched off the bed and she sobbed in pleasure. He plied her relentlessly with his mouth until she came hard.

As the waves of pleasure subsided, she felt more awake and alive than she had in weeks. As though he was slowly, systematically purging her of all the toxic emotions she'd been harboring. He rolled her onto her stomach and stretched out on top of her. He pulled her hair back and over her shoulder. Then he kissed her cheek and neck and behind her ear. His hand moved down her side, grazing the sides of her breasts.

She felt his hard length between her legs. He slid into her smoothly, filling her. He laced his fingers with hers and pressed her hands into the bed. His kisses across her upper back and shoulders managed to ignite her passion while blanketing her in a sense of peace. He thrust in and out of her languorously as though he had all the time in the world.

He moved his legs to the outside of hers, so that she was entirely wrapped in him, bracketed in this world and transported to her own, private realm of pleasure. His thrusts became more insistent, and his groans more desperate. When he slipped his hand beneath her and began massaging her, she broke with loud, low sobs.

He continued, harder and faster. He shifted, wrapping his arms around her hips and lifting them, bringing his knees up to support his weight. "Oh, God," he gasped.

She clutched at the sheets, struggling for something stable to cling to. Her world was shattered, and when he came with a sharp cry, she knew his was, too. She felt his forehead against her back, the tension in his muscles slowly draining.

He eased out of her and rolled her to her back. He put his mouth on hers, again, and kissed her until the world made sense.

CHAPTER THIRTY-FOUR

Kellen awoke with the dawn. With his eyes still closed, he smiled and stretched. Zoey stretched next to him, the length of her body alongside his. She moved her head to his chest, and he wrapped his arms around her. "You are amazing," he croaked, his throat dry and parched.

"How did you get my bed back without upsetting anyone?"

"Used my charm."

She let out a little snort. "Whatever you did, thank you. Now maybe you can talk her into going away altogether."

"Zoey, I will physically carry them both out of this house if you ask me to. I'll also cook them breakfast and babysit them if that's what you want. She's your mom, and I understand how important she is to you."

She sat up on her elbow and looked down on him, her hair spilling around her face. "She doesn't love me."

He stared at her and wondered if she was asking him a question.

"My mom doesn't love me." She looked like she was about to choke on the words. "But you do, and you show it by coming into my home and standing by my side, helping me hold up my self-inflicted responsibilities."

He still wasn't sure if she wanted him to respond. He reached up and played with her hair.

"I've always wanted, for as long as I can remember, a mother like Claire Huxtable. Someone I could depend on as a child and respect as an adult. Tracy has been none of that to me. So fuck her. Right?"

He leaned up and kissed her. "She's your mom. It's okay to love her. Just don't lose track of yourself."

She patted him on the cheek. Her expression turned resigned. "All right. Get dressed. Project get-my-mom-the-fuck-out-of-my-house is on." She swung out of bed and Kellen watched her dress.

She either didn't notice him watching or didn't care. She was on a mission. He clambered out of bed and into his clothes, following her around the house. She headed straight for the basement stairs. He followed about halfway down and then crouched to watch. Mark was sleeping on a blanket on the floor and Tracy had fallen into the middle of the bed.

"Hey, Mom!" Zoey said, louder than was strictly necessary. She shook her mom by the shoulder.

Tracy rolled to her back and squinted up at her. "What the hell?"

"Hey, I gotta go to work, so I need your help."

"What are you talking about?"

"I have a job so I can earn money to feed the people who stay at my house. I need you to get up because somebody has to take Maya's kids to school."

"What? I ain't takin' no little kids to school."

"Mom, with school starting back and Maya still injured, me with work, and Kellen, well, he's just plain undependable—so we all have to pitch in. Come on, I've got coffee made."

Kellen grinned at the undependable remark and watched as Zoey pulled Tracy to a sitting position and then waited until she was pulling on her jeans. He went upstairs. Zoey came up a moment later. She grabbed him round the waist and tip-toed up for a kiss.

Tracy stumbled up the stairs. "It's too early. I don't like to get up before eight."

"Well, no one likes to get up before eight, but that's life," Zoey said. "I'm gonna go wake up the kids."

Kellen didn't know what she told them when she went into their room, but Sophie and Matthew came running out screaming, "Yay! School's back in session!"

Sophie charged into Tracy, hugging her hips and causing some coffee to slosh out of Tracy's cup onto her hand. "Shit, be careful, kid," she said.

"Are you gonna take us to school, Aunt Tracy?" Sophie shrieked.

Tracy winced. "I'm not your aunt, sweetie."

Matthew ran up to Tracy. "Can you fix us some breakfast? Mom says we need to have eggs before school, not cereal."

"I don't cook. Kellen?" Tracy batted her eyelashes at him.

284

He sipped his coffee. "I wish I could," he said, "but I don't feel like it." He sat behind the bar. Tracy's smile vanished.

"Zoey!" she shouted.

Maya came in, then. "She's in the bathroom." Maya folded one arm over her ribs. "Ow, my side hurts so badly. Can you go ask Mark to give me back my pain meds?"

Tracy gaped at her.

Maya leaned on the counter and squeezed her eyes shut, even managing to pop out a couple of tears. Kellen moved to the edge of the seat, prepared to help her if it turned out she wasn't faking.

"Please, hurry," Maya pleaded, sobbing a little.

Tracy ran downstairs. Maya blew out a breath and sat at the bar next to Kellen.

"He took your pain meds?" Kellen asked.

Maya nodded. "They were on top of the medicine cabinet, where the kids couldn't get them. I only use them if I've overdone it and am just really hurting. They disappeared, and I didn't feel like picking a fight."

"Son-of-a-bitch," Kellen fisted his hands, angry that anyone could be that selfish.

Tracy reappeared and handed Maya the bottle. "There's a few pills left," she said. "I didn't know he took them."

"Sure," Maya said curtly. She left and went back to her room.

Matthew and Sophie, after a whispered agreement, started jumping up and down shouting, "Eggs and toast! Eggs and toast! Eggs and toast!"

"Jesus Christ, okay, okay!" Tracy shouted back. She

started bumbling around the kitchen, scrambling eggs and toasting bread. The kids grabbed forks, sat at the table, and started pounding the bottoms of the forks on the table.

After Tracy served them breakfast, they started shouting, "Milk! Milk! Milk!"

"God, be quiet already!" She ran back to the kitchen for milk.

Zoey came in, dressed in her work clothes, which was a pencil skirt, blouse, and jacket, her hair pulled into a low, loose bun—looking thoroughly hot. Kellen felt the blood leave his brain. "Oh, good," Zoey said. She pinned some earrings in while moving toward the kitchen. She grabbed a plate and some of the scrambled eggs Tracy had made. "Thanks, Mom," she said.

Tracy glared at her.

Zoey fixed a second plate and handed it to Kellen. "Eat up," she said. "You need to replenish your strength." She patted his face and moved to the table with the kids. Once they'd eaten, Matthew and Sophie went to brush their teeth and hair and gather their book bags. Tracy was still in her pajamas and robe.

"Mom, never mind about the kids. I'll take them to school, since you're not dressed yet, but I need you and Mark to go grocery shopping. And, if Mark's gonna keep drinking my beer, tell him to pitch in, okay? Here's the grocery money." Zoey laid a stack of bills on the counter. "Oh, and if you could have a snack ready for the kids at three-thirty? Peanut butter and jelly will do, unless you want to get more creative."

"Sure," Tracy said dryly, clearly having no intention of fixing food for anyone else that day.

Zoey hustled Sophie and Matthew out the door and then gestured for Kellen to follow. He did and after she got Sophie buckled into her booster seat, she turned to him. In a low voice she said, "Maya's got a doctor appointment this morning at ten. Can you take her?"

"Yeah, I'm free. Are you sure you want me to leave Tracy and Mark alone in your house?"

"That's exactly what I want. In fact, stay out as long as you can. Tracy will take the money and be gone by the time you get back."

"Your mom would steal from you?"

She gave him a look that said he'd asked a stupid question.

He swallowed and nodded. Then shook his head, sorrier for Zoey than angry at Tracy.

The day went exactly as she'd said it would. He took Maya to her appointment, and when they returned, Tracy, Mark, and Zoey's money were gone. Maya breathed relief as she settled onto the sofa. "You know she'll be back, don't you?" she said.

"Yeah. I know. Hopefully I'll be able to help Zoey prevent another invasion, though."

"You really love her, huh?"

"I really do." He reclined in a chair and replayed the last night. It had been like he couldn't get enough of her. Couldn't get in her deep enough, couldn't taste her or touch her enough.

"That smile, Kellen," Maya said.

He laughed. "Yeah. I'm sorry. I'm so happy right now."

Maya's eyes welled with tears. "I'm real glad. You

deserve to be happy and so does Zoey. I hope it all works out for you."

"It will. Everything's gonna work out for you, too, Maya."

The tears spilled over and she lowered her head. "I'm so ashamed."

He moved to her side and slipped his arm around her shoulders. "That's enough of that."

"I can't help it. I'm so ashamed. I think back to how I met Damon and everything was right there. If I'd just had my eyes open, I would have seen him for the monster that he is. I hate this. I hate what this will do to my kids."

"You need to stop blaming yourself and focus on the future. You're doing the right thing, right now. You're strong, Maya, and you're going to give those kids the life they deserve."

"How? I've got nothing. No money, no job skills."

"Your kids don't care about that. They care that you love them enough to walk away from a dangerous situation into a terrifying world to make things better for them. You don't have nothing. You've got me and Zoey and Addy. You're going to make it. I swear. We wouldn't let you fail."

She leaned into him. They held each other for a long time. Then they leaned back and talked about their futures.

CHAPTER THIRTY-FIVE

Zoey stayed in her work clothes. Kellen said they made her look approachable, like one of those orchids that beckoned to the insects with its beauty and then destroyed them. She liked the comparison.

Kellen was going away on a two week trip to Japan the next day, so she needed to get this out of the way tonight. He was already inside. She clutched the bouquet of flowers in one hand and rang the doorbell with the other.

Kellen's mom, Lois, answered, not even bothering to smile. Zoey smiled, though. She smiled until her face hurt. She handed Lois the flowers. "Thank you for inviting me to dinner," she said.

"I didn't," Lois replied, but she stepped aside anyway. "Come in. It's time to eat."

Zoey went in and followed Lois into the dining room, smiling the whole time. Kellen flinched when he saw her, so she turned the wattage down a couple notches. She sat in the chair Lois directed her to. "Dinner smells wonderful," Zoey said.

"It's just pot roast," Lois said, as she rather violently began slapping servings of meat and vegetables onto the plates. The plate was deposited unceremoniously in front of each person at the table.

Kellen was clearly trying not to laugh. He and his dad exchanged looks, but Zoey was too focused on trying to be nice that she barely noticed.

Once everyone was served, Kellen sighed. "Okay, let's clear the air. Zoey, Mom and Dad are going to support Maya. They recognize that she was a victim to Damon's brutality."

"Oh?" Zoey said, trying to sound disinterested. "Why the change of heart?"

"Damon paid us a visit," Bryan said. "Shortly before you shot him in the foot. He was drunk." He looked at Lois.

It was then that Zoey noticed the fading bruise along Lois's cheekbone. Zoey gasped. "Did he hit you?"

Nobody said anything.

Zoey slammed her hands on the table. "That psycho motherfucker! I'm gonna kill him myself. I hope to God he gets out of jail and breaks into my house again so I can shoot him for real this time. I'm so going to the range tomorrow to practice. What kind of sick bastard hits his own mother?"

Kellen just sat back and rode it out. His eyes never left hers, but he gently shook his head in resignation, knowing the tidal wave of rage would subside on its own or not at all.

"Really," Lois said, sounding offended. "You are the most coarse, vulgar young woman I have ever met."

"I'm on your side! What the fuck is your problem?"

"You're my problem. You're insane, and now you're trying to steal my baby, my only son to speak of. I can't fathom what he sees in you."

Zoey opened her mouth to tell her off, but Kellen sat up and cleared his throat. "Remember what we talked about?" he asked.

Zoey immediately switched off. "Oh, yeah. Just a sec." She pulled up what she'd rehearsed in her mind and then took a breath. "I just wanted to apologize to you, Lois and Bryan, for coming to your house and cussing you out a few weeks ago. I overreacted and should have approached the situation in a more calm and reasonable manner. I hope you can accept my apology." She smiled at Kellen, proud of herself. The bastard still looked like he was trying not to laugh.

"Thank you, Zoey, for that…heartfelt…apology," Bryan. "We gladly accept."

"We most certainly do not," Lois said. "Nothing has changed. She's still the brash, rude young woman she was back then. I will not forgive her."

"That's okay," Zoey said calmly. "I can't control you. I can only control myself." She winked at Kellen. "Anger management," she whispered to him with a nod.

He gave her a wry thumbs-up.

Lois simply gaped at her as though completely baffled at what she was seeing.

"Mom, if you haven't lost your appetite yet, this may finish you off," Kellen said. "Zoey and I have decided to move in together."

Lois flung herself back in her chair, a hand flying to her heart. "My God, why?"

"Because we're in love. We were together last night just talking about how much we didn't want to be apart, and it just clicked. There's no sense keeping separate residences when we both already know we want to start building a life together."

Lois burst into tears. "First we lose Damon, and now our sweet Kellen. Why, God? Why?"

Bryan sat forward. "Lois, sweetheart, you're overreacting. We aren't losing Kellen. We're gaining Zoey."

Her sobs increased in volume and flow. Zoey was beginning to feel a little insulted. She looked to Kellen with her eyebrows raised. He just offered her a sympathetic shrug.

Zoey tried to wait for Lois to stop crying, but the woman was not letting up. So she took a bite of her roast. "This is delicious, Lois. Or should I start calling you Mom?"

Lois sobbed louder.

Kellen gave her a warning shake of his head.

They left just as soon as they politely could. Kellen followed her back to her house and they settled into bed together. After some vigorous lovemaking, they were able to laugh about his poor mother.

"She'll come around, she really will. But you saw how long it took her to see the light with Damon."

Zoey nuzzled into his shoulder. "I'm not worried. She'll have to like me eventually, or at least be in my presence without crying."

He stretched and then squeezed her closer to him. "God, I'm gonna miss you while I'm gone. You're going to have to come on some trips with me. I'm gone a lot, and it'll be too painful if you don't."

"After tax season, I'll take some time off."

"Will you move in while I'm away? If you want to wait until I can help, that's fine."

Zoey frowned while the words sank in. "You mean, will I move your stuff here? I'd thought you'd want to pack yourself."

He laughed. "That's funny, Zoey. No, I mean when will you move your stuff to my place? I mean, there's no hurry. It takes a long time to sell a house, but I'm anxious to have you with me, so the sooner the better for me."

She pulled away and sat up on her elbow. "Kellen?"

His smile faded. "I restored that cabin myself."

"I restored this house myself."

"My cabin's bigger."

"My house is closer to town."

"Zoey."

"Kellen."

They both fell back against the pillows. "Shit," they said.

ABOUT THE AUTHOR

Carter Ashby is a hardworking housewife and homeschool mother by day, and a romance reader and writer by night. She lives in rural Missouri with her husband, three children, and two dogs.

Visit her at: http://www.carterashby.com

MAYA AND THE TOUGH GUY

COMING JANUARY 2015

8 years ago

She sat next to him in the back seat of his car trembling and hugging herself. "I'm sorry," she whispered. "I thought I was ready."

The woods surrounding them at the end of the abandoned dirt road resonated with night noises. The windows were down. She wondered if he'd even heard her. Surely he hated her. The hottest guy in school and a senior, at that—she should have known better than to think she could handle him. It was like choosing a Lamborghini for your first car.

His arm lay stretched along the seat behind her. She could feel his eyes on her and she wished he would say something. "I'm really sorry," she said again.

"Stop."

She felt her face flush, her heart pound, and bile rise in her throat. "If you could just take me home."

"If that's what you want, Maya."

She shrugged and waited as he slid out of the car and held the door open for her. She stepped out and he pushed the seat back for her so she could sit in front. He closed the door and she watched him stroll around the front of the car, his white shirt untucked from his black slacks and his tie hanging open around his neck.

He slid in the driver's seat, but didn't immediately turn the key. "I hope you don't think I'm mad," he said.

She gulped and still couldn't bring herself to look at

him. "You aren't?"

"Of course not. I'd like to see you again."

"You would?"

"Of course I would. Can I call you?"

She nibbled at her bottom lip, anxiety creeping up her spine. "Um, my dad…."

He nodded. "Yeah. Well, maybe you call me. How 'bout that?"

She shrugged. "Sure. I could do that."

"Good." He dug around the garbage littering his car and found an old fast food receipt in the cup holder. She handed him a pen from her purse and he wrote his number down. "Here," he said. "Soon, okay?"

"Okay." She folded the number and clutched it in her fist, excited to be holding something that, if made public, would make her the envy of every teenage girl in the tri-county area.

He drove her home and walked her to her door. She lived in a two bedroom house in a run-down part of town.

She started to go inside, but he took her elbow and then touched her cheek. He tilted her face up and kissed her gently on the lips. For the first time since she'd asked him to stop, she met his eyes. He hadn't lied. He wasn't mad. He was something else. Something she couldn't identify.

"Call me," he repeated.

"I will. Thanks, Jayce."

He nodded and then backed away, pulling her screen door open for her.

As soon as she stepped in, her heart constricted. She'd hoped her father would have gone to bed. But he was in his recliner, a pile of crushed beer cans littering his general vicinity. She would have to walk around him to get to her room. She made it halfway.

"Did you fuck him?" he growled, his eyes glued to the television.

She hesitated and then kept walking.

He laughed bitterly. "A whore just like your momma was. Can't say as I'm surprised."

She ignored him and went back to her bedroom. There was no lock on her door. She might have installed one herself if she'd thought it would do any good. God, how she longed for a driver's license and freedom.

She changed out of her dress and into her pajamas. She wanted a shower, but she didn't want to draw any attention to herself. So she climbed into her twin-sized bed and turned off her lamp. She pulled a blanket up to her chin and took the crumpled receipt from her nightstand. She clutched it in her fist and dozed off while dreaming about Jayce's kisses. Maybe she hadn't been brave enough to go all the way, but the making out had been hot.

A sharp pain. Her head jerked back and she hit the floor. Her father's hand untangled from her hair. He stood over her, straddling her. "How long you been fucking around, girl?" he asked, his slurred words mixed with spittle.

She knew better than to answer. There never a safe or right answer when he was like this. Quicker than a drunk man should move, he reached down, grabbed her hair again, and pulled her to her feet. Her eyes stung with tears, but she kept silent.

"Hard to look at ya," he snarled. "I still see a little girl.

But you ain't a little girl anymore, are ya?"

When she didn't answer, he yanked her hair. "Answer me, bitch!"

She squeaked, tears now streaming down her cheeks. "No," she said.

The slap first caused her ears to ring, and then gradually began to sting and throb. Then he slapped her again. His anger swelled and he shook her. "Look at you!" he yelled. "Look at yourself!" He spun her around to the mirror on her door and then flipped the light switch on.

She was facing herself, her cheeks bright red and swelling. She stood only five-foot-two and completely swallowed by her baggy pajamas.

"What do you see?" he asked.

When she didn't answer, he pinched her arm so hard that she cried out. "What do you see?" he shouted again.

"A whore," she answered.

"That's right. A worthless whore." He spun her around to face him, but when he did, her body collided with his and for one horrible moment, time stood still. He had an erection. She could feel it digging into her stomach. She tried to keep her shock off her face, but he saw it anyway. His face morphed from horrified, to enraged. He shoved her. Her back slammed into the doorknob.

"Get out!" he screamed. "Get the fuck out of my house, you goddamn whore!"

She reached behind her, turned the doorknob, and then ran. She ran out the door and down the block. Then she slowed to a walk and sobbed more with each step. She didn't know where she was going or what she would do. Her bare feet were sustaining small injuries from sharp pebbles and occasional bits of glass.

She just walked. Cars drove past her, but no one stopped. She made her way towards town, but then:

"Maya?"

She stopped and turned. She dragged her sleeve across her eyes so she could see better. It was Damon Bradley. She was friends with his brother, Kellen, who was a senior. Damon was twenty-two. His elbow hung out the window of his pickup truck. There was a lawn mower in the back. He earned money doing odd jobs around town. "What are you doing out here?" he asked.

She burst into tears, burying her face in her hands. That's when she realized she was still holding the piece of paper with Jayce's number on it. She sobbed even harder.

Damon climbed out of his truck, took her by the shoulders, and helped her in. "I'm gonna take you home."

"No!" she shrieked. "Please. I can't go back there."

He studied her and then understanding gradually dawned in his gray eyes. He nodded. "I'll take you back to my place, then. Get you cleaned up and a good night's sleep. We'll deal with your troubles tomorrow."

"I can go to my friend, Zoey's."

"That the redhead who flipped off the mayor last week?"

Maya laughed. "Yeah, that's her."

"It's late. She's likely asleep. If you want, I'll take you in the morning."

Maya wiped a stray tear from under her eye with her knuckle. "Thanks."

"No problem." He drove back to his apartment. It wasn't much. In fact, it was rather run-down. Not much better than her home. Except that there wasn't a drunken father trying to attack her.

Then again, how much did she know about Damon? He'd always been around. A friendly face in the community. She vaguely recalled hearing about a bar fight a few weeks ago. But the one thing she knew for sure was that he wasn't her father.

He showed her to the bathroom and offered her one of his t-shirts to sleep in. She set her paper on the counter and showered, grateful to be clean and to wash away the feeling of filth her father had put on her. She dried off and put on the t-shirt and picked up the paper again. The shirt hung mid-thigh on her. She didn't have underwear unless she wanted to wear the ones she'd come in. She didn't.

She gathered her clothes and walked out of the bathroom. Damon was laying blankets and pillows out on the couch.

"Do you have a washing machine?" she asked.

"Yeah," he said. "Help yourself." He nodded back towards the kitchen. She found a small machine in a utility closet and loaded her clothes into it.

"You get the bed," Damon said. "I'll sleep out here."

"Oh, no, I couldn't. You don't have to do that for me."

He shot her a wicked, half-grin. "'Course I do. I'm a gentleman."

She blushed and shuffled her feet. "In that case, thanks."

She made her way into his bedroom. It was cluttered. She got a sinking feeling when she saw two, crumpled beer cans on the nightstand, next to an ashtray and lighter. She grabbed the cans and slipped them under the bed, the better to pretend they weren't there. Then she crawled under the covers and turned off the lamp. She tucked Jayce's number beneath her pillow.

Sleep evaded her. Every time she thought she might doze, she snapped back awake, fear clutching at her chest. At last, she wept. Only the sounds of her sniffles disturbed the night, but her face was screwed up tight in an effort to remain quiet.

Damon must have heard her. He came in, a silhouette in the doorway. "You alright, Maya?" he asked.

She opened her mouth to answer, but a sob escaped. He came toward her and sat on the edge of the bed. He stroked her hair and thumbed away the tears. "Shhh. You're safe tonight. Everything's gonna be okay."

Gradually she calmed as his fingers gently touched her face and hair.

And then his movements changed. She couldn't see his face in the dark, but she could feel the intent in his hands. He cupped the back of her head and his breath was warm on her forehead before he kissed her.

She trembled, suddenly aware that she was in a new kind of danger. He lowered his lips to hers and kissed her gently. Her body responded. She didn't understand the sensations, but he seemed to. His touch heightened everything. Her mind screamed at her to make him stop, but her body was weary and aroused.

He pushed the blanket off of her and dragged his fingertips up her legs and to the hem of her t-shirt. They hovered there for a moment as he continued kissing her lips. And then he slipped his hand beneath the shirt and between her legs. She gasped and felt him smile against her neck.

She could only inhale, her breath a rattling sound in the room.

He stroked her while he took her hand and pressed it to the front of his boxers. He guided her hand in the open front and wrapped her fingers around his length. She'd never felt a man like that before. She'd wondered, but never felt.

"You're shaking," he whispered. "Want me to stop?"

Yes. "N-no," she said.

He stood, removing his hand from her and her's from him. There was enough light that she could see his movements as he peeled off his t-shirt and shoved down his boxers. Then he pulled her upright and removed her t-shirt. She thanked God for the darkness. She could stand having his hands on her, but his eyes—that would have been unbearable.

He lay on top of her and kissed her again, this time parting her thighs with his knee. "I…I don't think I'm ready," she whispered.

"Shh. It's okay, Maya. I'm gonna take care of you, I swear. You don't have to be afraid anymore."

They were the right words at the right time. A voice, way, way back in her mind told her they were a lie, but in that moment, she wanted to believe them so badly. She wrapped her arms around his neck and her legs around his waist. He slid slowly inside of her. It only stung for a moment and then it felt…good. Wrong and right at the same time. Invasive, but intimate.

She clung to him, excited by his pants and moans, thrilled to be the source of his pleasure. When he pulsed inside of her, he whispered a curse in her ear, and she felt chills ripple through her body. She felt powerful and vulnerable all at once.

He collapsed on top of her and she listened to a clock ticking and the crickets outside. When he rolled off of her, he brought her into his arms and kissed her tenderly. At last she fell asleep, feeling safe for the first time in her memory.

The next morning, while Damon was in the shower, she found Jayce's phone number, crumpled on the floor. She used Damon's lighter and burned it in the ashtray.

CARTER ASHBY

Printed in Great Britain
by Amazon